TOW AWAY ZONE

THE SUNRISE TRILOGY BOOK 1

CHRIS TOWNDROW

VALERICAIN PRESS

Praise for Tow Away Zone

"A gripping yarn - quirky characters, a pacy plot and a setting like you've never read before. A fun ol' read."
Paul Kerensa, Comedian & British Comedy Award-winning TV co-writer - BBC's Miranda, Not Going Out, Top Gear

"This is a brilliant story. Clever, laugh-out-loud funny, and mysterious all at the same time. Heartily recommended."

"Really good fun to read with more than a touch of darkness, so much neon, a very odd pet, and the best breakdown service on the planet. Very enjoyable and highly recommended!"

"An original, inventive storyline and a variety of three-dimensional characters that you will genuinely care about. Dialogue sharp enough to shave with, well paced and bubbling with humour."

"This is such an incredibly interesting story. I couldn't put it down. And I could never decide if the town was real or not. But the characters could have lived next door!"

"This is one of those books that will leave you with a smile on your face. Funny, relatable perfect characters, a story that kept me turning the pages and an ending that did not disappoint. This is a great book to take on holiday because it is light-hearted and fun."

"I struggle to compare this book with others. The words 'unique' and 'inventive' come to mind. The dialogue is well-crafted and funny, the characters are wonderfully individual, and the narrative is a kaleidoscope of colourful drama. This book will stick with you."

"The narrative of the story keeps you gripped and there is drama and comedic moments a-plenty! An easy and pleasant read from start to finish."

"I did have a good chuckle while reading this book, the characters are likeable, the twists and turns in the story are unpredictable and the plot itself is quite unusual."

"First of all, Towndrow has an amazing grasp of his prose. It's funny, it's witty, it's hilarious in places and it's also quite serious if need be. I have to say I'm blown away by it."

Valericain
Press

Valericain Press
Richmond, London, UK
www.valericainpress.co.uk

Tow Away Zone / Chris Towndrow. – 2023 ed.
Amazon paperback: 978-1-6962554-0-0
eBook: 978-1-9168916-1-6

To Zoë

For rescuing an average man from an average life.

PROLOGUE

Beckman sighed, took a last look at the double-page spread of the '65 Mustang, and tossed the well-thumbed magazine onto the uneven wooden floor beside the old chair.

He rose and grouched over to the doorway of the treehouse.

'Coming!'

Below on the back porch, Mom stood without hands on hips, which meant he hadn't explicitly done anything wrong. She'd also not used his full name, so he was relaxed about the upcoming encounter. Still, it wasn't dinner time, so he was somewhat bemused. Shielding her eyes from the late afternoon sun, she looked across the scrubby and scorched garden to where he gazed down from the gnarled cedar.

Ever keen to impress she who doted on him, he reached for the rope that dangled nearby, gave it a quick yank, then sprung outward, a teenage Tarzan, swinging forward and careering down the acutely angled makeshift zip-wire until his sneakers grazed yellowed turf and he stumbled to a halt.

He gave himself a 5.2 for that landing, knowing it was rushed by circumstance.

He wanted to flash Mom an innocent smile, but now he could see her expression clearly, he sensed jollity would not be well-received.

From somewhere inside the house, Bruce reminded them they were born in the USA. Beckman was already apprised of that fact. The immediate uncertainty was of more concern. He mentally double-checked that he'd no specific reason to feel guilty or expect admonishment. He didn't—what goes on inside a young man's treehouse is his own private matter.

Besides, cars were cars. Dreaming was not a crime. In treehouses, bedrooms, or dens across the land, other young men were up to far worse. Far worse was not tolerated in the Spiers household.

'What's up, Mom?'

She gave him a look bordering on apologetic. 'We're moving.'

'Again?!' he asked with disbelief.

'I thought you'd rather hear it from me than your father.'

'I don't want to damn well hear it at all!'

'Language, Beckman!'

'But …' he began, realised he didn't know what he'd started, then figured his tone gave pretty much all the information she needed. Besides, his reaction was always the same, and never altered the situation.

'I know.' She laid a hand on his shoulder. 'It's not ideal.'

He sighed as heavily as it was possible for a person to sigh without actually blowing their lungs across a backyard.

How could it be worse?

A noise rang from inside the house.

This is how it could be worse.

Dad appeared, tugged his wife towards him, and kissed her on the cheek. Mom's thick-rimmed glasses, jammed up above her fringe, nearly toppled off their perch but tangled in her thick frizz long enough for her to reach up and rescue them.

Dad slipped off his Aviators, an addendum he sported which never failed to make him look incredibly uncool.

'You tell him?'

'I did,' she replied.

'Better pack, Son. You know the drill.'

'Why?' Beckman gambled.

'Pardon me?' came the unequivocal reply.

'Why do we have to leave?'

'This place isn't working out.'

Beckman had heard those words before, and they implied the same old story. He also knew that saying so would be the passport to his last days here being unpleasant, in addition to unwelcome.

'Okay,' he grumbled, turning back towards his lofty wooden sanctuary.

'Where are you going?'

'To reflect on this … news,' he said daringly.

'You need to pack.'

'I'll do it tomorrow.'

'We're leaving tomorrow.'

'But I'm seeing Janelle tonight,' he protested.

'No, you're not. Might as well cancel your date. In fact, cancel the whole Janelle episode.'

'But she's—'

'Here. And we're not. We're on the road at oh-eight-hundred.'

Beckman hated the way Dad always stated the time like a military order. Notwithstanding circumstances.

His head fell. 'Yes, sir.'

'Good.'

After a respectful moment's pause, he headed for the rope ladder.

'I'll clear out up here first,' he offered as an excuse.

It passed muster, as further words weren't forthcoming.

His feet were heavy on the saggy rungs of the ladder, his heart leaden.

Janelle liked Mustangs nearly as much as he did. She was cool like that. Her dad had a friend who once owned one. A '66 in blue.

Things had been going well with Janelle. Tonight was supposed to be Second Base Night.

Looks like you've more chance of owning a '65 Mustang, sunshine.

CHAPTER 1

Scarlet? Probably.
   Imperial? Likely.
   Crimson? Possibly.
   Spanish? Could be.
   Cardinal? Doubtful.
Beckman sighed. He was bored of this game.

The color was red, which was the important thing. Except it wasn't important, not in the slightest. He'd never even seen red—it was merely a word, a concept.

It was a light, a flickering light. *That* was the important thing—because it was pissing him off. Keeping him awake. Riling him. Mocking him.

He rolled over. The portable alarm clock on the nightstand read 22:11.

The motel was full; no point in trudging down to the grunting oaf on the check-in desk to request a change of room. There'd only be an argument, he'd grow even more awake and still wind up back in Room 12.

There lay a quantum of solace—he'd wangled Room 12.

Yet, now, it didn't feel like such a good peg to hang anything on. Tight as he pulled the curtains to the window edges, the material was much too thin to block out the light entirely. A static wash of red—of any shade—he could cope with. This damn irregular flickering, though? Torture.

He debated the merit of asking Grunting Oaf for the neon frontage sign to be switched off, but knew he'd come across like a petty jerk.

Instead, he reluctantly threw back the covers, flicked on the ineffectual bedside lamp, padded across the thin carpet, and rooted through his open suitcase. Tucked into a side pocket was an eye mask, a freebie relic he'd kept from a TWA flight back aways—a cross-country trip to see Mom, if he remembered right.

Rarely had he found it necessary to sink so low.

The last time was, what, two years ago?

He'd run out of gas in the middle of nowhere and spent a night in the back seat of the car. The moonlit hours and incessant cicadas turned out to be a minor inconvenience compared to the litany of aches he woke with.

It had been even worse than the nights in the treehouse twenty years earlier—though those sleep-outs were more about independence than comfort.

At least tonight he had a bed.

He avoided thinking about what adventures it might have experienced. The long years of a motel-heavy existence had warned him off such seeping imaginations and revulsions.

Instead, he slid under the starchy covers, adjusted the eye mask until his view became blissful darkness, and buried his head as best as he could in the unhelpfully spongey pillow.

The air conditioning unit hummed and, now that the visual distraction had gone, his ears became more attuned to the surroundings. But was the flickering light now making an intermittent buzzing?

'Oh, snap,' he breathed in the darkness.

Could this night suck even more?

He pulled the edges of the pillow up around his ears and hoped sleep would arrive before cramp set into his arms.

Oh, for the ability to count sheep, he mused. He'd have to count his blessings instead.

He got as far as three and lolled his head over. How much time had passed? Would the unpredictable gods of night and slumber grant him morning?

22:21.

He found a fourth blessing; nobody was listening to the TV or playing music at an unsocial volume in the adjoining rooms. No yelling. No we-know-what-you're-up-to grunting.

Nevertheless, on such nights, dormant thoughts resurfaced about trading his Buick for a station wagon or an RV. At least that way, he could make room for a sleeping bag and be sure the courtesy light didn't have a mind of its own or harbour dreams of a career in a nightclub.

Maybe a different vehicle would give him a new lease of life? Something needed to change.

Or did it?

Blessing One: a steady job.

If it ain't broke, don't fix it.

Not every stop-over on the road turned out like this. Tonight's issue was an annoyance, a mosquito. Ironically, it was as likely to keep him awake as hearing such a tiny buzzing in the room, even if he couldn't see the insect. The difference being, he wouldn't wake up tomorrow with a red welt on his arm.

So, another blessing, surely. By that logic, he could come up with a million more.

Maybe he *could* count them:

(1) Steady job.
(2) Travel. Lots of travel.
(3) Meet interesting people. Sometimes.
(4) Health.
(5) Loving family. Well, a semblance of.
(6) No noisy neighbors. Tonight, at any rate.
(7) No mosquito.
(8) A place to call home.
(9) Only four more stamps to go on the loyalty card before the next free coffee.

See—things could be worse. Now, go to sleep Beckman.

Miraculously, the fog descended. The world outside slipped into redundancy.

His breathing shallowed.

Sunday crept towards its end.

His cell phone rang. It could have been an air raid siren.

He mentally hauled himself back up the ladder to reality as quickly as he could muster, pushed aside the eye mask, stumbled out of bed with an 'Oh, snap', and scooped up the chirruping device from the desk. The off-brand charging cable halted his movement, so he rudely yanked it out and hit the Answer key.

Amidst the bleary chaos, he'd noted that the caller was "Office", and his mood nosedived.

Office? On a Sunday? Have I woken in a parallel universe?

'Spiers,' he mumbled.

'Is that you, Beckman?'

He recognised the terse voice. Otherwise, given the time of night and his general humour, he'd have taken pains to point out that (1) this was his personal cell, so who did the caller think would answer? and (2) the caller had addressed him by name, thereby proving he already understood item (1).

However, Beckman kept it zipped, knowing the caller wasn't someone who took kindly to such logic or admonishments.

'Yes, sir, this is me.'

'Malvolio here.'

Beckman took a calming breath; the words were hardly a revelation.

A Sunday? What fresh hell is this?

A flourish of downdraft from the meshed duct in the stained false ceiling wafted cool air down his back and raised goosebumps. The room flickered intermittently scarlet or imperial. Or possibly crimson.

'Yes, Mr Malvolio?' he enquired.

'I've some good news for you.'

Good? Good!

Suddenly, Sunday could go hang.

Beckman waited to hear. And waited. And realised Mr Malvolio was waiting for him to indicate that he was waiting, because what else could possibly be more exciting than to be woken (kind of) in the middle (barely) of the night by a random phone call from your godawful boss, bearing news which doubtless could wait until the first—or ideally second—coffee of the following day had passed your lips?

'I'm all ears, sir.' He scratched his balls.

'Belcher is dead.'

Beckman waited for more detail. And waited. And realised Mr Malvolio was expecting him to say something to indicate a reaction to the apparent Good News of someone's death. Because what could be more sensible than prolonging a phone call in the not middle of a Sunday night when you're standing with itchy balls in a cold breeze in a godawful motel room in the ass end of nowhere?

He really wanted to say, "Get bent and call me in the morning, you atrocious slave-driving freak".

But he liked his job. Well, he *did* his job. It was the only one he had, and he didn't want to lose it.

So, he said, 'Really? How?'

'He got struck by lightning this afternoon.' Malvolio said it with the same level of intrigue or sadness as one might when ordering pizza toppings.

'Wow.' Beckman was stupefied. 'That's a bad break.'

'Not for you, Spiers. That moves you up to Number Two.'

Malvolio had evidently had enough of this heartfelt wallowing in the untimely demise of one of his workforce and was, predictably, getting down to brass tacks. Or, more likely in his case, gold tacks.

'Sheesh. I guess it does. Poor Belcher.'

'Sad to see anyone die while they're still in the race.'

'Or any time,' Beckman suggested. His mind was barely half on the call now.

Belcher's sales volumes are apparently deemed irrelevant to the race, his slate cleaned. One of the riders has dropped out.

'I suppose so. So, get your hiney moving, Spiers. Number Two position—pretty good going for a man like you.'

Such praise.

Beckman gave the illuminated screen a hard stare. Not that Malvolio judged him wrongly—Number Two *was* pretty good going—but for Beckman to verbally concede such a fact would have been a weakness. So, he said nothing.

Would Malvolio take the opportunity to crack the whip further? Beckman mentally wagered his worldly possessions on it.

'Only five days left,' the harsh old voice continued. 'It's not impossible. You can make Number One. Shoulder to the wheel, Spiers, nose to the grindstone.'

'Absolutely, sir,' he lied. 'I'll get started tomorrow morning, first light.'

'That's what I like to hear.' Then the phone *boop-booped* to indicate that the line had been hung up.

Beckman stared at the screen in a casserole of a stupor made up of tiredness, disbelief, revulsion, hope, and itchiness.

Esmond Belcher is dead. I just got promoted to Number Two on the Salesman of the Year chart.

One week to go.

Could I? Could I really make Number One? Finally?

In a pig's eye.

He gave his balls a good long scratch and went to bed.

CHAPTER 2

Beckman tendered a handful of notes to the check-in clerk.

'You might want to get someone to fix up your sign.'

The neanderthal looked like he'd been asked to explain recent developments in quantum theory. Beckman listened for brain activity. Finally, large metal rods engaged with vast cogs and the whole Victorian construction eased into life.

'Harg'll do it.'

'Good.'

'Harg's who fixes the sign.'

A few things were clear. (1) the illuminated sign freaking out was far from an unusual occurrence, (2) Harg wasn't the guy's real name—there was almost certainly a story behind it, and (3) if Beckman weren't careful, he'd be on the receiving end of that story.

'Have a nice day,' Beckman offered emptily, and made himself scarce.

He popped the trunk of his white '09 Buick, checked what he already knew—that the sea of small, plain cardboard boxes left no space for a travel case—smacked the lid closed, pulled open the rear door, and set his valise on the bench seat.

Sinking into the well-worn driver's perch, he flicked the visor down against the morning sun. There wasn't a cloud in the sky, and he foresaw another roasting June Monday of interminable disappointments.

After a beat, the engine caught, and he swung onto the blacktop.

It was the top of the hour, the hour was nine, and the radio announced there were news headlines. They all washed over him unheard. One topic already commanded his mind: Belcher was dead.

It wasn't great news, especially for Belcher. He'd been a decent enough guy, had never given Beckman a bad word—which couldn't be said for everyone else on the Pegasus salesforce—and had been far from shabby when it came to peddling their product. That un-shabbiness had boosted him up the rankings to Number Two.

But struck by lightning? What a way to go. At least it's quick.

Shocking.

Beckman checked both ways at the intersection and prodded the gas, taking the ramp which climbed onto the freeway. In the sparse traffic, he merged in, settled at sixty-seven, and flicked on the cruise.

Dead man's shoes.

Until now, it had been an expression. Today it chimed a reality.

To what end? Last time he'd seen the sales ranks, both he and Belcher had been so far adrift of the top spot as to be irrelevant. Essentially, Mr Malvolio had called to say, "Hey, Beckman, good news in your shot at reaching the Moon—I got you a stepladder."

True, second spot for Beckman represented two places higher than he'd ever achieved, but it made a scant difference. Who was the second person to summit Everest? Who was the runner-up for circumnavigation of the globe? Who's the second-fastest hundred-metre sprinter?

Exactly.

The individual who really needed to get struck by lightning was Tyler Quittle. But how would Beckman feel to win by default rather than honest effort? Hollow? Guilty? Fraudulent? If the Elysian fields of Number One Salesman were even half as bountiful as rumoured, Beckman's moral compass could stand a knock or two. After all, he wasn't exactly a shoddy practitioner of his role—more that he faced… unfair competition.

Forty minutes into the journey, he saw a Rest Area signposted, noted the Coffee Planet logo, and took the opportunity to caffeinate himself and get his loyalty card stamped. Only three more until the freebie.

He checked the fuel gauge, baulked at the advertised rates, and pressed on. All the towns in the neighbourhood had repeatedly proven to be sales washouts—he needed to get further West. If only there weren't so much damn nothing out here in the Arizona wilds. But it had been his sales patch for five days a week, fifty weeks a year, eleven interminable years.

It's a job, Beckman. Pays the bills. Keeps you in steak and coffee.

Keeps you moving.

After another twenty minutes at a steady schlep, traffic thickened, then slowed, then crawled. He cranked the air up a notch, sighed, and curled his lip in despair. Malvolio's apparent stepladder was creaking already.

After ten minutes between zero and five m.p.h., the gas-guzzling metal snake crested a rise in the freeway and stretched into the middle distance.

'Oh, snap!'

He noted an exit ahead and, judging unpredictability to be preferable to the Chinese water torture of stop-start, he manoeuvred across to the nearside lane, then, checking his mirror for law enforcement, took a rare brave pill and eased onto the shoulder.

The car thack-thacked over the expansion joints, his heart thudding, until the exit lane speared off and he fell clear of the melee, if 'melee' was an accurate word to describe a plethora of almost stationary objects, which it wasn't.

At the intersection, he checked his lawlessness hadn't been noticed, then scanned for a sign as to what to do next, ideally in the shape of a sign.

He recognised the name of the town posted off to the right. From memory, he'd made a laughable six sales there last year and, as a bonus, suffered food poisoning from a dodgy burger joint.

So, he threw the wheel to the left and powered away.

Signs of civilisation disappeared after a couple of minutes, and after about ten more, Beckman found himself alone on a road which took all day to go nowhere and whose asphalt dated from the time George Washington wore short trousers.

He laughingly expected a tumbleweed to appear in his wing mirror at any moment.

But it didn't.

Instead, one crossed the road diagonally, causing him to jump on the brake too aggressively. The tires chirped.

'Son of a gun!' he yelled.

Calming, he wound the speed up to fifty and drank in the landscape: great for photographs; pitiful for selling.

A dashboard light flicked on.

He surveyed the world again.

Great for photographs. Pitiful for gas stations.

Easing down to forty to preserve precious hydrocarbons, he scooped up his phone and thumbed through to the map. It was official: he'd reached Nowhere.

He resolved to give it five minutes, then, if Lady Luck remained on her coffee break, pull a one-eighty and return to the freeway cataclysm via a gas station he hoped existed and prayed wouldn't give the Buick fuel poisoning.

Mercifully, before long, a shape rose from the heat haze. A stationary shape. A building-shaped shape. A gas station-shaped building shape.

He exhaled theatrically and slowed the car. Deliverance.

He hoped there would be no banjos.

Out front, a tall pole reached for the clear sky. At its summit, a sign bore the legend, "REGULAR $2.00".

Two bucks a gallon?

The situation was suddenly less pitiful.

He coasted up to the single pump and killed the engine. The guy who emerged from the lone wooden hut looked like he'd stepped straight out of a movie.

'Bet his name's Earl,' Beckman mumbled to himself, as he clambered out into the shrouding heat.

'Morning,' he offered.

'Morning.' Possibly-Earl scratched his stubbled chin.

'Sign says two bucks a gallon.'

'Sure does.'

'Then fill her up, I guess.'

"Earl" thumbed a dungaree strap further onto his shoulder, unhooked the pre-Springsteen pump, and proceeded to give the Buick a drink. He locked off the handle, happy that his part in the process was done (and he couldn't have been making more than a wafer thin a margin to live off at two bucks a gallon, Beckman considered).

Possibly-Earl surveyed the customer and his steed and clocked the license plate. 'Guessing you're a technical guy, musician maybe?'

'Nope.'

'Sound engineer, Mr Beck?'

Beckman shook his head. The guy stared at "12 BECK" again, then the penny dropped.

'It's not one-two, it's twelve. And it's Beckman.'

'Ah. Ah.' Possibly-Earl nodded. 'Where you from, Mr Beckman?'

He let the misunderstanding slide. Hell—everybody assumed it was a surname.

'Ohio,' he replied.

'Uh-huh.'

'Denver.'

'Uh-huh.'

'Washington.'

'Mm-hmm.'

'Baton Rouge.'

Possibly-Earl's eyes narrowed, mistaking Beckman's honesty for chain-yanking.

'Like Frankenstein,' he said.

Beckman gave a faint smile. 'From all over.'

The pump handle clicked. The ageing attendant holstered it, checked the counter, and flicked his eyes to heaven for a ready-reckon.

'Forty-seven bucks.'

'What?'

'Forty-seven twenty. Keep the dimes.'

Beckman checked the towering sign. It still said $2.00 a gallon. 'Sign says two bucks a gallon.'

'Yeah.'

'In black and white.' Even Beckman knew it was black and white. Not maroon and cream, or navy and beige, or any other pair of well-contrasted colors.

'Yeah.'

'So why forty-seven bucks for—,' Beckman looked at the weather-beaten analogue pump display, '—sixteen gallons? You said it was two bucks a gallon.'

'Nope. The *sign* says it's two bucks a gallon. Sign ain't been changed in years.'

Beckman opened his mouth to vent but instead sighed and fished out some bills. 'False advertising, that's what it is,' he grouched to himself.

Possibly-Earl eyed him up and down. 'Salesman, then, are you, Mr Beckman?'

They have irony out here.

'Uh-huh,' he replied warily.

'Reckon you know some about false promises.'

'Not me.'

'Saint in a world of sinners, huh?'

He shrugged. 'Something like that.'

'You want me to take the gas back out?'

'No, thank you.' He handed over fifty bucks.

The attendant brightened a little. 'Want me to wash the windshield for you?'

'Water's three bucks?'

Their eyes met. Would Possibly-Earl be cordial or go postal?

'Water's free. Labour's a buck,' he said with a glint in his eye.

Beckman smiled. 'Labour's a buck or *sign* says labour's a buck?'

The man turned, located a nearby pail of post-Springsteen water, and began the task. 'Back aways, some suits stopped by. Said they were looking at getting the road blacktopped. I said, that's great. They said they knew it was. I said, great. They left.'

'How long ago?'

'Five, six years.'

Possibly-Earl squeaked the rubber squeegee across the glass. A myriad of dead wet flies left their graves.

Beckman looked down the line of the road. The surface, as he'd found, mimicked a teen's face.

'So, what happened?'

'Like I say, they said they were looking at getting it fixed. Looking. Not getting.' He dumped the squeegee in the bucket with a sploshing flourish, jammed hands on hips, and proclaimed, 'Selling dreams. Bringing nightmares.'

'More sinners, huh? You a saint in all this?'

'Something like that.' A full glint appeared this time.

Beckman scanned the windshield. 'Thanks.'

'No problem.'

He slid into his seat and fired up. 'Have a good day.'

'Back at you.'

'Thanks.'

'Earl. Name's Earl.'

Beckman flashed a smile. 'Full service next time, Earl.'

He eased in the gas and re-joined the road, checking the rear-view mirror as the antiquity merged back into the anonymous landscape.

'I'll be a son of a gun.'

CHAPTER 3

It took about five minutes for the smile to fade, realising he should have asked Definitely-Earl whether he sold candy. The breakfast at Busted Sign Motel had been little more than a necessity. He hoped there'd be another rest stop before long and mused on what an appropriate name for the owner might be.

Harlan? Or Sherry if they were of the fairer sex.

He also wondered why he hadn't plied Earl with his product. It would at least have stopped the day from being a guaranteed wash-out.

Fifteen minutes and little else passed.

He checked the phone's map app: still nowhere. Zoomed out. Still nowhere.

He accelerated up to fifty-seven, judging that, out here, he had more chance of being hit by an asteroid than a speeding fine, and fiddled with the radio, painstakingly searching the spectrum for a distraction, keeping one eye on the road now and again. No other vehicles passed.

The frequency roulette offered nothing to his tastes: there were only two stations with zero interference anyhow.

Out of the corner of his eye, he spotted a small shape in the road.

He jammed both feet on the brake pedal, to no avail. The left front tire thudded over something. He winced, hoping it wasn't a sharp something.

The car slewed to a stand across the lane.

Heart thudding in alarm, he cracked open the door, and stuffy air swamped the cabin. Then, after catching his breath, he hauled himself out and walked to the rear of the car, nervous, throat dry from what hadn't been a near-miss.

The armadillo was very dead.

'Aw, shoot. Sorry, little guy.'

He looked at it for a moment, opened the rear door, felt under the front seat, and drew out a sturdy trash bag. Then he walked down the verge, scanning the ground until he found a couple of pieces of dead wood.

With strangely practiced efficiency, he kept the mouth of the bag open and worked the squished corpse inside, pushing it right to the bottom, tied off the bag and eased it into the rear footwell. Then he climbed in the front, opened the glovebox, gave his hands a squirt of barrier disinfectant, rubbed them dry, and slammed the driver's door shut.

The engine fired, the aircon began to return the interior to a comfortable temperature, and Beckman prodded the gas.

First lucky break of the week.

All he needed now was the essence of civilisation, hot black refreshment, and to make a sale or six hundred.

He'd give it another half-hour, or the next turn, then retrace his steps.

There's finding virgin territory, and there's fishing in a barren lake.

The heat of the day continued to build. He racked the air up another notch. The road's anonymity persisted. There were no turns. There were no buildings. There was no candy, coffee, or customers.

This was a rare occurrence—an uncharted part of his sales patch. Clearly there was a reason for it remaining uncharted—it was useless.

He fell into a glazed stupor, accompanied by the whine of rubber on tarmac, the putter of the motor, the grumbling of his stomach.

His phone rang, startling him. The car swerved gently, and he quickly regained control.

He huffed hard. One collision was plenty.

Seeing the caller's name, he hesitated but thumbed Accept.

'Becky!'

Beckman snarled silently and turned the other cheek.

'Tyler,' he said as cordially as possible. Deep down, he too had nicknames for his rival; the type Mom wouldn't thank him for uttering.

'Number Two, huh?'

'Seems so.' He clamped the phone to his ear and steered lazily with his left hand—though minimal effort was needed.

'Good for you, Becky, good for you. Had a successful week?' The sarcasm was barely disguised.

Beckman (1) recalled his still-brimmed trunk and (2) decided not to point out that it was only Monday morning.

'You know, pounding the streets.'

'Pounding here too, Becky.'

That conjured an image, and he wished it hadn't. Then again, knowing Tyler's usual exploits, his mind had every right to be half a step ahead.

'Sucks about Belcher,' he offered, trying to change the topic.

'Not for me.' As gracious and feeling as Mr Malvolio, or at least in the same ballpark.

'I've got a couple of hot leads,' Beckman lied.

'Uh-huh. Closed the first sale already today. Very grateful client. That right, Mrs Jollifer? It's okay, don't speak with your mouth full, Mrs Jollifer. Yep, very grateful client. Very. So, see you on the second step of the podium, I guess, eh Becky?'

'I guess so.'

'Problem with you, is you're a creature of habit.'

'I got my ways, yeah. They work.'

'Not from where I stand—but lucky me. Easy pickings. Thanks for taking part, anyway,' Tyler scoffed.

'I'm doing my damn best—but what do you care?'

'Hey, hey—lighten up, okay? It's not the end of the world. There's always next year. Or the year after.'

Beckman seethed but held things together. 'It'll happen.'

'Sure, sure. Gotta go now before things get… weird. Weirder.'

'Have an amazing week, Tyler,' Beckman offered through teeth as gritted as he could communicate.

The line went dead.

He grabbed the handset awkwardly, reached a thumb round to hit the red button, but butterfingered, and the phone danced in his hands. He tore his grip from the wheel, fielded the device like a leg slip, heart beating, and laid it on the passenger seat.

The Buick eased onto the verge. He snatched at the wheel, tugged it left as the tail kicked onto the even worse surface of the roadside, bumping, rattling stones, before regaining the pockmarked roadway proper.

A loud pop rang out. The rear of the car crabbed.

'Oh, snap!'

He eased on the brake and rolled to the shoulder, coming to rest.

The dust settled around the Buick much more quickly than his ire.

This had to be a much sharper object than potential roadkill. He had a good idea what would be waiting when he walked round to the right rear tire.

He thumped the steering wheel.

First flat in seven years. Here, of all places. Wherever here is.

He looked at his phone. Zero bars.

For some reason, he shook it.

Still zero bars.

He tossed it uselessly onto the passenger seat.

Reluctantly, he clambered out, confirmed his suspicions, and gave the wheel a kick for good measure.

He winced at the self-inflicted pain, then bent down to ascertain the cause of the enforced hiatus in what had been, up until then, a perfect bitch of a morning.

Jammed into the sidewall was a piece of glass. Peering closer, he swore it was a fragment of a light bulb.

He shook his head.

A scarlet one, I'll be bound. Or crimson.

He stood, checked out the infinite road. The sight was rocks and cacti; the sound was insects. He didn't speak insect, but felt it was probably laughter.

Under his right hand was the scorching trunk. Under the lid sat a layer of boxes. Underneath it, another layer. And another. Then the lining. Then the false trunk floor. Then the jack. Then the spare.

The sun seared off the harsh white of the dimpled, dusty, painted metalwork.

He rechecked the road. Listened for approaching assistance.

Unrewarded, he returned to the driver's seat to seek emergency nourishment for the ball-ache ahead. He fumbled around the glove box and under the seats for anything edible that might have found its way into a corner.

Not so much as a boiled sweet.

With a sigh of desperation, he tapped his forehead against the steering wheel, feeling the warm plastic gently adhere as he rested there momentarily.

There was a knock at the window.

CHAPTER 4

He nearly whacked his head on the headrest, sitting up so quickly. He'd expected in that split second of realisation to see a face at the side window. There duly was one—male, tanned, middle-aged, chunky, eye-patch.

Beckman looked out through the windshield, expecting a Harley, a horse, or a helicopter.

There was a tow truck.

'I'll be a son of a gun.'

He blinked, expecting the circus to disappear. It didn't.

Eye Patch stepped back, allowing Beckman room to exit. As he got out of the car, the sun crested his sunglasses, making him wince. Without knowing why, he checked the roadway again in both directions.

Nothing else had changed, apart from what had changed. He had company.

'Flat, huh?' Eye Patch said.

'Yeah,' Beckman replied, still lost for words, thoughts, and pretty much everything except inhaling and exhaling the hot midday air.

'Need a tow?'

Technically, he didn't. As a grown man, he was capable of using a spare tire and a jack. Yes, it would be a pain in the ass, but he was no snowflake.

Still, gift horse and all that.

Shame to drag the guy (which he technically hadn't) all the way from wherever he'd come (a parallel dimension?) only to then blow him off.

'Yeah, thanks,' he replied.

Eye Patch walked around to check the offending vehicular injury. He knelt down and merrily yanked out the shard of glass. He held it to his good eye, nice and close.

'R45, maybe R56,' he said to nobody, with an eerie recall of something Beckman didn't know.

Looking down, Beckman noticed the man sported snakeskin boots, because the day wasn't fully off the chart weird already.

Eye Patch stood. He reached a half-head above Beckman's height, middle-aged spread, thick hair. Maybe if Dr Hook had met late-model Elvis in a cowboy store…

'Tow charge is twenty bucks.'

Beckman was about to ask if that was the actual charge or merely what the sign said, but thought better of it. This was no time, or place, to make an enemy.

'Take thirty.'

'Couldn't do that. Dishonest. Taking advantage.'

Beckman wondered how anyone around here made a living. 'The garage—is it far?'

'It's as far as it is.'

He wouldn't have wanted it to be any farther than that. 'Okay.'

'Get your belongings, sir. I'll hook you up.'

Each did as agreed.

The tow truck was twenty-five years old if it was a day. The winch grumbled, the paint peeled, and the remaining decals read, "Paul's Recovery".

So, this had to be Paul.

Almost-Certainly-Paul nodded towards the passenger side of the cab and climbed in from his own door.

Beckman didn't expect aircon. Instead, he *expected* rattles, litter, grease, and either Country or Western, or more likely both.

He stepped up into the cab and clanged the heavy door shut.

The air felt cool. The seats were clean. There were no tacky ornaments. The surfaces were pristine. Classical music wafted from the radio.

"Stupefied" would have been a word Beckman could have used if he'd been able to come up with anything more loquacious than a soft, 'I'll be a son of a gun.'

Paul lit the V8 and eased them away.

Silence held for a minute, punctuated solely by the occasional crescendo of violins, as the two men exchanged glances. Beckman didn't know where to start. Evidently, Almost-Certainly-Paul did.

'Is it Beck or Mr Beck?'

'Beckman, first name.'

The response was mild curiosity—something familiar to the name's owner. 'Shall I call you "Beckman", sir?'

'Sure, Paul.'

Eye Patch/Almost-Certainly-Paul looked over. 'Saul.'

Beckman's brow furrowed. He must have misread.

'No, you didn't misread. Saul Paul. And yeah, I have forgiven them. Whole other story.' Saul/Not-Paul/Eye Patch gave a half-smile.

'Mine too.'

'Where you headed to?'

'Wherever.'

Saul Paul's eyes narrowed (or Beckman assumed both had). 'Sitting a little low on the rear axle. Heavy trunk. Grey on grey.' He took in his guest's attire. 'Solo. White-collar hands. What d'you sell, Beckman?'

'Miracles,' he offered, without knowing why, other than the truth was in the ballpark.

'Don't we all.'

Beckman couldn't argue that Saul's sudden arrival was certainly in the ballpark. He looked lazily around the cab. On the headlining above the windshield was affixed a foot-long sticker bearing the motto, "Where there is great love, there are always miracles".

Heck, Saul, I'd expected maybe "Honk if you're horny" on the rear fender. Hard to disagree with the infinitely sager words on display. Great love? Miracles? Either one would do just fine at this point in life. Unless…

'How d'you find me?' he wondered aloud.

'Sixth sense.'

'Uh-huh.'

'There are more things in Heaven and Earth, Horatio, than are dreamt of in your philosophy.' Saul shrugged huge shoulders.

Any minute, Beckman expected he'd wake up to a buzzing, flickering crimson light. Or scarlet.

Because this has to be a dream, right?

'You ever see anyone on this road?' he asked, as an icebreaker to the litany of questions he had about, well, pretty much everything from the last hour.

In response, Saul sharply raised his left hand as if craving silence. He reached for the radio and dialled up the volume. Soaring strings and plaintive notes bloomed through the cabin. He remained rapt for two long minutes. Had they not been driving, he'd probably have closed his eyes.

This was an ideal time for enforced quiet because Beckman had mentally run out of gas. His sense of reality felt as deflated as his rear tire.

Saul nudged the music into the background. 'Most of an atom is empty space. Most of the universe is empty space. The life is in the other parts.'

Beckman took a mental note for a journal entry about this: a tow-truck ride with Socrates. Granted, he didn't actually have a journal, but if there was ever a time to start one…

'The other part—does it have coffee?'

He reckoned the answer would go one of two ways: "No", and the day would officially suck, or "Yes, served by unicorns", and he wouldn't be the least surprised.

'It's Arizona, not the Dark Ages,' Saul replied.

'Whereabouts in Arizona?'

In response, Saul tapped the indicator stalk (to warn zero other motorists) and swung off the main road at an intersection. Nothing was signposted. In fact, the intersection seemed to appear from nowhere, like his rescuer had.

'You could understand a guy thinking "serial killer" at this point,' Beckman ventured.

'Because it was too crowded to kill you before?' Saul raised his brow.

Beckman couldn't argue with that—be it logic or opinion, truth or lie—so he pulled out his phone.

No signal. Empty map.

He resolved to stay calm. It would be either coffee and a new tire, or death. Probably a strange one.

Well, at least you made it to Number Two.

CHAPTER 5

After an unfeasibly short time, the road bisected a low ridge, and a roadside sign swept past:

SUNRISE
Population 4274

Except someone had peeled off the first "P" and stencilled on a "C".

Saul had understandably taken it in his stride. After all, he was probably out rescuing stranded motorists on a regular basis, wasn't he? When not busy revising light bulbs, maybe learning Cantonese, or breeding unicorn baristas.

The road dipped.

The hitherto unseen settlement of Sunrise lay in a vast crater in the landscape, but otherwise, at this distance, it appeared to be a regular town. What were the chances of total normality under today's far-from-normal circumstances? Evens at best.

'Not on the map?' Beckman asked.

'Admin snafu.'

That remark left him none the wiser, but, on the other hand, it felt less like the hand of the Reaper was on his shoulder.

The conurbation didn't sprawl, nor was it a one-horse town. As they drew closer, he picked out the main urban district, a few outlying factories and the housing areas. No dragons were circling overhead.

What became apparent was the abundance of neon lights scattered around. No, not scattered around, packed in. No, not packed in, jammed in. The spectacle was amazing and, almost certainly, incredibly colorful.

Saul saw the wonder in his passenger's eyes. 'Pretty, huh?'

'You don't sound convinced.'

'Yeah, but I live here.'

'Power companies must love the place. Bet you're popular with Big Coal.'

'No sir, that's the way to kill the kids. But Big Solar love us.'

'It'd be ironic if I said the town was even brighter than a real sunrise.'

'Yeah, and not original.' Saul shrugged. 'Sorry, Beckman.'

'I'll try not to say anything else you've heard a million times.'

'You're bright. Guess you'll fit in just fine.' Saul smiled at his wordplay.

'Fit in? New tire, coffee, out of here. Or have I joined a cult?'

'We rarely kill or indoctrinate anyone who comes into town. It's not Hotel California.' Saul put a hand on his chest. 'I promise.'

'I still don't, you know, get the whole lack-of-signposts, million-neons vibe? But I guess, the "Horatio" thing, huh?'

'You know, I've been here my whole life, and I'm not sure I fully get it either.'

'That supposed to make me feel better?' Beckman wondered.

'No. But a new tire, coffee, maybe a bite—start with that.'

They swung onto what was signposted Main Street.

'You have a Coffee Planet?'

'We have Buck. And don't mention the other place to him.'

That sounded like more than a mere suggestion.

'He sensitive about comparison?' Beckman asked.

'No, because there is none. In Sunrise, we do lights, we do coffee, and we do friendly.'

'Then I'll try for two out of three.'

The tow truck rolled onto the garage forecourt. The art deco building, low and set back from the road, proclaimed "Paul's Recovery" in tall neon capitals on the facade. To Beckman, it jarred, like the deep sense of wrong you might get if someone in a Hollywood pitch meeting piped up, "Let's remake Casablanca".

Of course, he kept it zipped. Besides, that artificial lighting (in a smart blue hue, he reckoned) wasn't the only example bedecking the building. There were arrows, banners, and flashing zigzags, all somewhat weak in the direct sun and all wholly unnecessary, yet at the same time somehow charming. He decided to roll with it—having not looked the gift horse in the mouth earlier, docking its tail now would have been cruel.

They climbed out into the gentle noise of mechanics doing what mechanics do.

'How long do you need?' Beckman asked.

'Couple hours. I'll give it a once over too, okay?'

He was about to ask whether it would be gratis but didn't want to appear ungrateful. 'Sure. Guess I do a lot of miles.'

'Anything you need to take with you?'

'Yeah.'

Beckman went to the Buick's hoisted front end, grabbed his soft shoulder case from the footwell, plucked a couple of small boxes from the trunk (judging that Sunrise was as likely to yield a sale as any town on this barren allocated territory), stuffed them in the bag, and tossed Saul the keys.

Saul pointed up the road. 'Four blocks, right-hand side. Can't miss it.'

'Buck?' he asked in confirmation.

'Say I sent you. And say hi.'

'Thanks.' He nodded and set off.

As he strolled up the wide street, the concentration of buildings thickened, and the prevalence of neon rocketed. He reasoned that pretty much every factory must be a manufacturing plant and wondered if any of the output ever left the city boundary. Competition must have been fierce to the point of cutthroat, not just for rival bulb brands but for business owners trying to attract custom.

Maybe that's what I need? Some sweet lights on the car: "Get It Here".

That'd show Tyler. Pip him at the post. Worth the outlay just for the look on his face.

The place wasn't chocolate-box pretty, but it had charm. Wooden-sided shops mingled with glass-fronted establishments, all set back from the wide-paved sidewalks, from which sprung ornate street lamps. Between the opposite sides of the street were strung cables holding a myriad of unlit bulbs—Christmas lights, he guessed. At what felt like the midpoint of Main Street, something more intricate crossed at the second-floor level. It appeared to be the town's version of a matrix display; bulbs arranged in an approximation of an 80s-style LCD pattern.

At regular intervals, roadside flower tubs blossomed in probable tones of red and orange.

The faces of those he passed were painted with curiosity but not unfriendliness. Warmth, even.

Soon, he reached the appointed establishment. Ordinarily, it would have been hard to miss, but then everything in Sunrise was hard to miss.

The wide, deep front window held an illuminated outline of a coffee cup in what Beckman reckoned was a mid-brown color. The word "coffee" was spelt out both vertically and horizontally in a bluish shade. Every letter on the facia above glowed a different color. Mercifully, the words didn't flash. The script was even pretty classy. The letters read "Our Buck's".

That tickled Beckman, which clearly was the point of the name. How would the beverage-serving competition take it—the shark to this minnow? He scanned the street and recognised not a single frontage. In fact, he didn't remember seeing one chain store or branded outlet. Was that why Saul had said everyone here was so friendly? No "corporate America"?

He entered the café.

The room housed a long wooden bar, at which stood several stools and on which rested a gargantuan coffee machine of seemingly Victorian design. It jogged a faint memory, and he smiled inside.

In the remaining space, which would hold about fifty people, were sturdy wooden tables and chairs. About five were occupied. On all three walls glowed various neon constructions, most of which were low-key. Huge bowl lamps with intricate filaments hung from the high ceiling. Interspersed with these were lazily rotating propeller fans.

The place smelled delicious.

Beckman debated where to sit. The bar felt like the kind of place a regular would occupy, chewing the fat and watching the probably legendary Buck craft another in an endless chain of world-leading coffees. Yet, as merely a visitor, he didn't want to risk perching on a stool only to discover an unwritten rule that it belonged to a ruthless biker gang, or the Mayor, or the Mayor of a biker gang. Or a biker gang of Mayors.

So, he stood and scanned the carefully wrought legends on the blackboard hanging behind the counter.

A bear of a man approached.

'Hi. Ham and pickle on rye. Root beer. Please.'

Notwithstanding the temptation of likely stellar coffee, his steadfast loyalty to Coffee Planet held him back. Also, he'd not had a root beer for he couldn't remember how long, and felt sure this would be an artisanal effort that would do wonders to slake his considerable thirst.

'Take a seat, sir. I'll bring it over.' The voice was local, warm, but matter-of-fact.

He found a pew, and as he waited, he mulled the likelihood of this being the aforementioned Buck. He was one-for-two on name guessing today and had a pretty good shot at two-for-three.

The order arrived.

Beckman went with, 'Thanks, Buck,' in a slightly questioning intonation.

Probably-Buck held station. He eyed Beckman, towering over him. 'I know you?'

'No. But Saul says "Hi".'

There came a raised eyebrow and a look that hovered between suspicion and acceptance.

'"Hi" or "Howdy"?'

Beckman wanted to dismiss it but sensed it wasn't a matter to be taken lightly.

'Hi. Pretty sure. No, definitely sure. Hi. Yeah, hi.'

But is that the correct answer?

Probably-Buck gave him another visual once-over, then lightened up. His massive paw came out.

'Buck Travis. Good to know you.'

The temporarily stationary travelling salesman sighed with relief.

'Spiers, Beckman Spiers,' he replied and had his hand swallowed up.

'Sorry about that. Saul has a code. "Howdy" means the new arrival's an ass. "Hi" means he's okay. He pick you up on the road?'

'Yeah. A flat.'

'Passing through?'

'I wasn't but guess I am now.'

'Thanks for your custom.'

'No problem.'

Buck nodded and left Beckman to his meal, which he devoured with relish.

In the meantime, a few customers came and went, exchanging words with Buck. In a lull, Beckman went to the bar, ordered another class-leading root beer, and passed the wait time with a bathroom break.

Bee-lining back to his table, his long thirst of the morning still not quenched, he switched seats so that he no longer had his back to the room. Friendly as Sunrise appeared, he'd still felt like an interloper when he arrived but was now less overawed by the place and, besides, had already received the official "Okay Guy" stamp from a veritable gatekeeper.

So, he'd sit there, savour the drink, and watch this charming world go by until the time came to amble back and collect the Buick.

And that was when he saw her.

CHAPTER 6

She sat perched on a stool at the coffee bar, chatting to Buck. Even with his eyesight deficiency, Beckman knew she wasn't dressed like anyone else he'd seen that day. Week. Month. Fiscal. No doubt the ensemble was colorful, although that was hardly news in Sunrise; it was the style.

She could have stepped right out of the Fifties, except, somehow, too much so. It was as if she had a rose-tinted version of the bygone decade. She embodied less 1955 and more what Marty McFly saw in 1955.

Yet, it did her an injustice. She seemed, in his head, like a kook. It was an easy conclusion to jump to: she dressed that way to get noticed, or she was an airhead. More kindly, perhaps she simply enjoyed life or wore that ensemble because it suited her, which it did.

He took a good long look.

Then she noticed him taking a good long look. But she had him wrong, or at least half-wrong—although she didn't know that.

Still, her smile faded. Yet, it wasn't a genuine smile; it had been a forced smile.

She didn't know he'd seen that, too. She swung her legs down and walked over.

It wasn't just the smile he'd been admiring. It was the face and the tumbling brown curls and the figure and the dress and the individuality of it all, but more so, it had been the gestures, the body language.

She was exactly what he was looking for in his life.

A customer.

She stood with hands on her hips. At a near certainty, her swing dress was mustard and cherry, her hair had bangs, and the rounded glasses sported a slight tint. The pose naturally tightened her arms, which betrayed that she could easily manage a minute's chin-ups.

He got his rebuttal in first. 'Sorry. I was just concerned because of your headache.'

Her sails visibly sagged as he sucked the wind from them in one easy move. He shirked from considering it "suave", in the same way he'd refrain from referring to himself as "toned" or "an astrobiologist".

Her (probably) ruby painted lips opened for a comment that never materialised, then closed while she adjusted her angle of attack/defence.

He went all-in. 'I have something that could help.'

She cocked her head.

I hope you've called this right, idiot.

He'd either close a sale or wear his root beer.

'Uh-huh,' she said, unconvinced.

'That's it. No line. No, "That's an outlaw dress". No, "Can I buy you a drink?". You look like you're trying to shake a headache. A few hours, I'd guess. Sorry for staring, but....' He trailed off, shrugged.

This amounted to about as much schtick as he'd ever spouted for either a customer or a girl. How? Maybe it represented desperation—for either. Or he was merely attempting to fit in. If, as Saul suggested, Sunrise was a friendly spot.

Would she prove him wrong?

He cocked his head, mirroring hers, awaiting an answer.

'Some kind of travelling salesman, are you?'

She'd hit the nail on the head. And the tone? Nowhere near "friendly", but he still had a dry shirt, so he remained hopeful.

He pulled over his shoulder bag, took out a box, and laid it on the table.

'Mmm-hmm,' she said.

'Buck says Saul says I'm an okay guy.'

'Mmm-hmm.' She glanced over at Buck.

Beckman wondered (1) if the barista had been within earshot and (2) if he'd side with the quirky citizen or the lone ranger.

Beckman couldn't see a response forthcoming from Buck, though Fifties Girl had one prepped. She took hands from hips and laid one, curiously, on the box.

'So, some kind of travelling witch doctor, huh?'

The fact that her eyes weren't visible vexed him. They were allegedly the window to the soul, although he wasn't trying to look quite that deep yet. Instead, he merely wanted to know what she was thinking—pretty important when you're a salesman.

'My customers have headaches.' He gestured at the box. 'This cures them.'

'Uh-huh.'

'Or you can pop pills every time,' he suggested, taking a slug of root beer to appear nonchalant about whether she believed him.

She examined the plain brown box—a cuboid about eight centimetres each way—seeking clues. She found none because there were exactly that many.

'Not pills?'

'No.'

'What?'

'Instructions are inside.'

'Uh-huh.'

He played the waiting game. Would she ask about provenance or price? She was on the hook, his hand on the reel.

'How much?' she continued.

'Ten bucks, but yours for five.'

She eyed him directly, a hint of a sneer plying her lips. 'Bet you say that to all the girls.'

'Nope.'

'Says you.'

He shrugged. 'Then pay me ten bucks.'

'I bet it's not worth ten,' she harrumphed.

'Pay five then.'

She looked at him again. He wanted to stand but hoped she'd sit. The physical dynamic wasn't great—she held the upper hand. Situations like this were why he'd only hit Number Two. Well, that and the bonus of a large atmospheric electrical discharge.

'Can I get any guarantees?'

Over a measly five bucks? This is like pulling teeth.

'The money-back form is in the box.' Which it wasn't, because nobody asked for their money back. So, yes, he was technically lying, but not denying her anything she'd need. People like Tyler's spur-of-the-sales-moment conquest Mrs Jollifer proved that gratitude, not recriminations, followed the purchase, as sure as night follows day (which he assumed it did, even in Sunrise).

In response, she located an Abraham Lincoln from a hidden pocket in the folds of her skirt, slid it across the table to him, and scooped up the box.

Technically, that concluded offer and acceptance.

He'd closed a sale!

'Have a nice day,' he beamed.

'Yeah.' She half-smiled, still unconvinced, turned and left.

The water around Beckman fell calm again. Inside, he did a little dance.

The clock on the wall was fashioned with ancient metal, a full metre across, and read past two-thirty.

He sipped his drink and wondered how well word of mouth worked in Sunrise. One gets cured: one tells two. Two tell four. Then eight. Then more math. Thus stood the theory. It seldom happened like that, at least to Beckman.

The area around him darkened. Buck stood there.

'I'm out on my ear for harassing your customers?' Beckman asked, worried.

The big man shook his head. 'Lolita gives as good as she gets. And I would have stepped in earlier anyway, especially for her.'

Lolita, huh?

'Regular customer? Favourite customer? Favourite niece?'

He regretted the last one. Buck was maybe fifty, and Fifties Girl—Lolita now—was shading thirty-five on either side. The math didn't work. Would Buck take offence? Would a sodden shirt have been a better result than this paw through his face? Laundromat versus Emergency Room?

'I left her alone to talk on account of you're an Okay Guy, despite not being her kind.'

'An outsider?' he wondered.

'A salesman.'

'I get it—we're on the rung above lawyers, two above roaches.'

Buck looked out the window at where Lolita had gone. 'It's a whole other story.'

Beckman nodded, without understanding. 'Like the outfit?'

'No. That's called individuality. Expression.' He scanned Beckman up and down, taking in his black shoes, charcoal pants, grey jacket, and white shirt.

Beckman didn't mind. He'd had such withering looks before.

He gently tugged a lapel in acknowledgement. 'This—whole other story.'

Buck glanced at Beckman's bag. 'Will it work? The box?'

'Absolutely.'

'Because if you'd conned my Lolita, you wouldn't need Saul to ride you out of town. I'd kick you out myself.'

'Don't doubt it.'

'Where you headed?'

'Wherever I can help people like her.'

Buck's expression proved the words fell on fertile ground. He held silence for a moment, then said, 'You're an Okay Guy, Beckman.'

'You're not a bad judge of character yourself, Buck.'

The proprietor's face cracked into a full smile—the first Beckman had seen since arriving.

A metallic splashing sound broke mutual bonhomie. Buck turned, and Beckman followed his eye-line towards the counter. There, a tall, thin man had emptied a jar of coins onto the bar.

Buck raised his gaze to the ceiling, offered Beckman a barely-explanatory 'Gulliver', jabbed his thumb in that direction, and returned to his duties.

Beckman watched from across the room as the man—Gulliver, he assumed—painstakingly sifted through the mound of what appeared to be quarters, inspecting each, dropping most back into the jar, and pushing the occasional one towards where Buck stood, tending one side of the coffee bar, and accepting the drip-fed payment with admirable patience.

After a couple of minutes, with a finger of root beer left, Beckman got bored of this sideshow and turned his attention to the world outside.

Diagonally across the street, a guy stood propped against a wall, baseball cap jammed down over his head, apparently engrossed in his phone, but every few seconds throwing a glance across to Beckman's position. This was quirkiness was getting irksome. Three minutes later, the activity hadn't changed.

Inside Our Buck's, the door thudded closed as a woman set out onto the sidewalk, cut in front of the window where Beckman gazed and headed out to his left. Instantly, Baseball Cap abandoned his routine, checked around, then set off in the same direction, remaining on the other side of the street.

Relieved he wasn't the target but still intrigued, Beckman went to the window and watched the pursuit until it left his view.

Maybe not everyone in Sunrise was so friendly.

CHAPTER 7

'How was the coffee? Good, huh?' Saul's eyes were full of expectation.

Beckman flooded with guilt but decided to come clean. 'I went for a root beer. Trip down memory lane.'

If there was disappointment, Saul hid it. 'Meet Buck?'

'Said hi, too.'

'Oswald there?'

'Not that I know.'

'Gulliver?' Saul asked.

The quarters guy.

'Oh, yeah.'

'Get in line behind him?'

'I waited 'til he'd gone.'

Saul nodded. 'Good call.'

'No joke. What's the deal?'

'He'll only pay with the oldest quarters in the jar.'

'On account of?'

'We all got our thing, Beckman, we all got our thing.'

'Well, all my bills are equal. How many d'you need?'

'Hundred and twelve bucks.'

'Hundred and twelve?' Beckman was taken aback before he reached polite acceptance.

'You ever get towed for twenty bucks?'

'I guess not.'

'All comes out in the wash.'

'I guess....'

'Want the busted tire back on?' Saul asked.

Beckman closed his eyes, calmed his disquiet.

'I ran a leather over it, too. You know, on the house,' Saul continued.

Beckman opened his eyes and turned to where the Buick was reversing out of the garage towards their spot on the forecourt. Before, the car had been white. Now it was WHITE.

His shoulders fell. 'I'm an ass.' He fished out his wallet and counted bills.

'Call it a round hundred. For an Okay Guy.'

The passing lackey tossed Saul the car keys, which he plucked out of the air with alacrity. Saul may not genuinely have had a sixth sense about the breakdown, but he coped pretty well without perfect depth perception.

Beckman pulled the second and last box from his bag. 'Ever crack your head changing a muffler or whatever?'

'Want to crack my head open dealing with a customer, more likely.'

'In friendly old Sunrise?' Beckman jibed.

'Even the sun has dark spots.'

'Lyrical.'

Saul took the box and examined it. 'A stress ball?'

'For headaches.'

'Like a pill?'

'Swallow what's in there, I'll be impressed. And you'll need a doctor, which would defeat the purpose.'

'Then I won't.'

'If you like it, tell your friends. Then call me.' Beckman pulled a card from his top pocket.

Saul looked at it. It was plain white, except for a small logo with the legend "The Pegasus Corporation" and the salesman's name and cell number.

'So, happy trails, Beckman.' Saul offered his hand. 'Where next?'

Beckman hadn't considered that. He checked his watch and wondered how much more wilderness stood between him and the next civilisation. He recalled last night's disturbed sleep. He couldn't face the same again.

He'd made a sale and sowed a seed of word-of-mouth, so why not hang out for a few hours?

Plus, he remembered the date.

'Is there a hotel in town as good as that root beer?'

Saul was pleasantly surprised. 'Further on past Buck's.' He handed back the car keys. 'Junction of First and Tungsten. Tell Kinsey I sent you.'

'And say hi? Or howdy?'

'We both know that one.'

'So, next time you see Buck, tell him I said hi.'

Saul nodded in appreciation.

Beckman slid into his gleaming chariot, carefully turned around on the crowded forecourt, and eased onto Main Street for the short drag to his overnight.

Neon words and shapes in a multitude of greys jostled for his attention as he cruised slowly through town.

His gaze was constantly drawn left and right as hardware stores, clothing outlets, barbers, realtors, grocers, and lighting stores hawked their wares in multi-hued shapes and shimmers.

Distracted, he missed Tungsten.

He'd reached Main Street and Watt Avenue, and what passed for the urban sprawl had thinned, so he sought a spot to pull a U-turn. Ahead lay a gas station, offering its wares at a more realistic per-gallon rate than Earl.

The Buick ambled off the road and turned an arc behind the pumps. The solitary vehicle on the premises was a gorgeous '65 Mustang convertible in red.

It's not a '64 or a '64.5, but hell, it's still damn fine.

Dream on, sunshine.

In the passenger side sat a tall woman with sunglasses perched on her head. Beside her was evidently her beau—a slightly wiry guy with horn-rim spectacles, who handed over a soda he'd bought in the kiosk. She pecked him on the cheek in thanks.

The guy doesn't look cool enough to have a machine like that. Yet he's still got the girl? Probably because of the Mustang, not because he's cool.

This is precisely why you need a Mustang to find a girl, Beckman—because you'll never be that cool without it. Or probably even with it. Even in an industrial freezer.

The gleaming coachwork on the Mustang's prow drew Beckman's attention until his own, much lesser, steed crossed back over the dropped sidewalk and retook the street.

He didn't miss Tungsten this time, crossed First, and dived into a parking spot at the side of the road. Grabbing his overnight case, he walked the short distance to three steps that led up to the lobby of Sunset Hotel.

The place was smart, airy, and surprisingly modest in its neon quotient. The receptionist was "Ardal". No Kinsey in sight.

No matter. Did Ardal have any rooms for the night?

He did.

Did Ardal, by a stroke of fortune, have room 12?

He did.

Beckman sent Saul good vibes.

The (very likely) copper-colored sign behind the counter announced that rooms were fifty bucks a night. So did Ardal.

As quarters-in-a-jar Gulliver wasn't ahead of him, Beckman was able to quickly pay up, go to the first floor and ease the room door closed behind him.

He unpacked methodically.

First, hanging items in the narrow wardrobe. Then folding items in the drawer. Next, ablution items laid out neatly in the bathroom. Shoes off. Jacket hung on the chair back. Curtains two-thirds closed. Air to 21 degrees.

A solitary item remained in the bottom of his case, which he removed before closing the lid.

He grabbed the TV remote, propped two pillows up at the head of the bed, and sat against the soft support.

The envelope read simply, "Beckman".

He fingered it open and drew out the card. The front was typically cheery and cheesy—he'd expected as much. Yet it was the thought that counted, as it always did.

Inside was written, "Happy Birthday, son. Late 30s now, dear. Time to find a lady? All my love, Mom."

For years she'd been willing him to settle down. Now she'd as good as said it.

It didn't make him love her any less. He pensively drummed fingers on the card for a few moments, then laid it down and flicked on the TV.

Home, again. As every day.

CHAPTER 8

The bank account of Beckman's stomach dipped into the red by about eighteen-thirty on the clock, so he set out in search of a hearty dinner.

Based on the day's relative successes—but also in hope as well as judgement—he visited the Buick to stuff four boxes into his shoulder bag and took it along for the walk. Best to be prepared.

Faintly recalling Buck's menu, he'd need to look elsewhere for a good steak. Three blocks down Main Street, he came upon a relatively traditional diner emblazoned with "Jen & Berry's" in unapologetically garish and almost certainly lime green and orange neon.

Inside, the lighting was similarly unrestrained, but he was used to Sunrise style by now and took it in his stride. As long as the steak came thick and juicy, the place could boast a giant glitterball, and he wouldn't care.

He took a seat at a small table. The place was sparsely populated this early, and he was quickly attended to by Berry—one of the two female proprietors, he presumed—who took his drinks order. She was short, blonde, smartly dressed in the same colors as their fascia sign, and sported roller skates. His eyelids remained un-batted.

While waiting, he checked his phone. Still no bars.

He scanned the menu.

Someone appeared beside him. He was about to order, but the color scheme didn't match—the shape of the dress gave the game away.

Lolita's hand emerged from her pocket, clutching a five-buck note.

He tried to meet her eye, but the tinted glasses still held a barrier.

'Same again?'

'No. I owe you the difference. And more than the difference. I don't just feel better, I feel better than I did *before.*'

'Glad to help.'

'Miracle, that's what it is.'

'I only sell. I didn't invent the thing,' he admitted.

'No. I meant you. An honest salesman. We should have you stuffed and mounted.'

'Well, that would be a hell of an end to a birthday.' Then he wished he'd kept his mouth shut. That could have come across as a cry for help. But dare he deny, deep down, there was a fragment of that?

'I guess,' she said with a half-smile, then caught his comment. 'What?'

But before he replied, Berry reappeared. 'Can I take your order, sir?'

'Yeah, eight-ounce sirloin and a local draft.'

He wasn't a big drinker, but (1) it was his birthday, and (2) if the local draft was a patch on Buck's root beer, he was in for a treat.

'Thank you, sir. Hi, Lolita.'

'Hey, Berry.'

'Who's your friend?'

Lolita was about to swat it away, deny he was anything of the sort, but checked herself. 'This is…,' she began, then realised she hadn't a clue about her mystery snake-oil merchant.

To save her blushes, he stood and offered a hand. 'Beckman. Good to meet you, Berry. Fine place you have here.'

'Why, thank you, Beckman.'

He took the chance to kill a second bird with the same stone.

'Charmed, Lolita.'

She took his hand, and he held it for many seconds fewer than he wanted.

'New in town?' Berry jiggled her feet back and forth on the tiny red wheels.

'A travelling salesman,' Lolita replied, 'Although more salesman than travelling, by the look of it.' She gave what he assumed was a pointed glance.

'Figured I'd stay the night. I hear good things.'

'You won't taste a better steak this side of the state,' Berry said.

'Mouth is watering already.'

'Where are you sitting, Lol?' she asked.

'I'm not. I mean, I'm just here to thank Beckman for his help earlier. Besides, I don't want to cramp his evening.'

'You're kidding, right?' he chirped. 'Like I'm having company when I've known three people for six hours here, and one of them is you.'

'But it's your birthday,' Lolita suggested, a hint of piteous insistence in her voice.

'Happens about this time every year, wherever I am.' He shrugged. 'No big deal.'

'Well, now if I walk away, I'm going to feel like I passed by a beetle on its back.'

'Beetle, huh? And I told Buck we're a rung *above* roaches.'

'No, I didn't mean….'

'Really,' he held up a hand in mollification. 'It's fine.'

Berry gave Lolita a pair of raised eyebrows and the merest nod in his direction. Lolita's hand rested on the back of the chair opposite. He held his breath.

'I guess it's the least I can do. You helped me out today. Unless....'

'A second wheel is fine. If I'm not keeping you from anything.'

'I was in town anyway.' She drew the chair back. 'Make it two,' she said to Berry.

The mobile waitress squiggled on her pad, flashed them both a smile, then coasted away, zigzagging between tables with ease.

Lolita sat. 'I would last about an hour on those things.'

'Plus, it would technically make you a travelling salesperson too, and that doesn't sound like your favourite line of work.'

Behind the tints, her eyes shuttered as she took stock of how she'd behaved. 'Okay, I take it back. Too much baggage, I guess. Forgive me?'

'Already done. Skin's pretty thick. Has to be, in this job.'

'Even though your little box is a marvel? I bet you never had a single complaint.'

'Not one.'

'It doesn't have any nasty side effects you want to share? Rashes, addiction, cancer?'

So, she wasn't the unswervingly grateful pushover she'd appeared to transform into during the afternoon.

'No. But it can cause you to repeat the last word in every sentence sentence.'

'What?' Her brow shot up.

'Good. Seems it hasn't affected you like that that.'

She tilted her head and leant forwards to peer into his eyes, searching for an answer. 'You're a bad, bad man, Beckman,' she said with a smile of recognition.

'I think you already said people like us are all rogues.'

'Time out, okay? You're an honest salesman. I paid you the full ten bucks, since you cured me. So, you broke the mould. I wish it happened more often.'

Berry arrived, deposited two tall glasses onto the table, and pushed away.

'I'll bring it up at the Tri-State Con-Merchant's Convention.'

'You want to wear this beer?'

'Really? Squash the beetle while you're at it, huh?'

She raised her glass, and he followed suit. Then, to his surprise, she chinked. 'Happy birthday, Beckman. And thanks.'

'It's nothing. And thanks.'

They drank. It was ambrosia.

'So how d'you like Sunrise?'

'What's not to like? Good people, good food. Customers.'

'Everything a guy like you could ever want, huh?'

'And a good bed,' he added.

'Where are you staying?'

'The Sunset.'

'Then you're four for four.'

'Figures. Maybe good company would be five for five.'

'You must have a pretty low bar on that.'

'Believe me—any company is good company.' Instantly, he wanted to suck the words back into his throat.

'Squash the beetle while you're at it, huh?' she said, her eyebrows raised. His head sank. 'It's fine. I get it,' she continued. 'Call it a draw, okay?'

'Okay.'

The steaks soon arrived, and the conversation turned to his life at Pegasus, the Holy Grail of the Number One Salesman chase, the untimely passing of Belcher, the freeway snarl-up, the flat, and Saul.

Earlier, he'd found her interesting. Now, she was actually interested in him. She was also rather delightful in a don't-mess-with-me kind of way. Out of his league, of course. Yet, on this most individual of days, perhaps there was scope for the unexpected. In fact, he practically expected as much.

They were past the end of the steaks and towards the bottom of their glasses when someone approached the table. Slightly wiry, a good tan. Horn-rim spectacles.

Beckman held in a comment.

Horn-rim gave him a withering glance and turned to Lolita. 'Who's this?' he rapped.

She rose oddly brusquely. Horn-rim gave her a kiss that Beckman felt sure was for his benefit.

'This is Beckman. We just met. He gave me a great cure for my headache.'

'And you're, what, buying him dinner suddenly?' Horn-rim wasn't even trying to mask the jealousy and distaste.

'Carlton, honey, he's at the table, it's his birthday, I needed to eat, he sold me this amazing box, only five bucks—'

'Ten,' Beckman reminded her.

'So, grow up, okay?' she continued.

'Some kind of travelling salesman, huh?' Horn-rim sniped.

She nodded. 'Sure.'

'He leaving tomorrow?' Carlton looked down at him. 'You leaving tomorrow?'

'Absolutely.'

Especially if crap like this is going to happen. Why do people like Lolita get jerks for boyfriends?

'Good. Then I won't see you again, *Beckman*. But I'll see you later, honey, huh?'

'Absolutely.'

She received—almost endured—an over-zealous kiss, then Carlton strode away, and she sunk into her seat.

'Sorry,' Beckman offered, feeling responsible, or at least feeling like he should assume responsibility for the social faux pas.

She shook her head. 'Carlton's a good guy. He's just… protective.'

'I'll take the Fifth. Anyway, good to meet you, Lolita.' He held out his hand, ready to vacate the premises.

'Do you always give in to people like Carlton?' she asked.

'For your protection, absolutely.'

'Very sweet, but I give as good as I get, believe me.' She still hadn't shaken his hand goodbye.

'So, I won't lie awake tonight.'

'Not like last night, huh?'

Holding his hand mid-air was past redundant, so he lowered it to his glass and took a slug.

'Because of a neon light. Better chalk it up to irony,' he suggested.

'Won't be one of ours, then.'

'You want to back up aways?'

'Milan Enterprises. We make the things here in Sunrise. It's my dad's outfit. Second biggest in town.'

Berry hit the brakes and stopped beside them, a querying glance as she scooped up the empty glasses. Lolita looked him the same refills-related question he'd been about to offer her, which provided the answer.

'Two more, please, Berry. And could you run the lights down for me, hon?' Lolita asked.

'Sure.' Berry wheeled away.

In different circumstances, this might be verging on a date. He just about remembered what those felt like. Yet the presence of Carlton confirmed the diamond ring on the third finger of her left hand to be precisely what he'd feared.

CHAPTER 9

A minute or so later, the lights duly dimmed, though the neons continued to cast their various grey hues across different segments of the wall.

Now, Lolita slipped off her glasses and laid them on the table. Her eyes were blue, her lashes impeccable, and Carlton was a lucky man. He wanted to find out more about the reason for her glasses but passed.

'I guess there was a good chance you were in lighting somehow.'

'Me, no. Dad, yes,' she replied with some resignation.

'Not your path?'

She shook her head, lowered it. 'No.'

He'd touched a nerve. 'So, what then?' He expected maybe a designer, artist, even dance coach.

'I buy Egyptian artefacts.'

He pursed his lips, processing. 'Interesting revenue model.'

'I sell them, too.'

'Sell? Surely not. That line of work is for charlatans, says the word on the street.'

'You can go off a person, you know.'

'Sorry. I'll back up. Say, that's an interesting line of work, Lolita.'

'You can still go off a person.'

'Okay. Why the swing dress?'

Might as well go down in flames if I'm going.

'Because I look damn fine. That okay for you?'

Now he saw her eyes, there was a gentle fire there. Good thing this wasn't a date. Plus, he was leaving town in the morning. Mercifully, Berry arrived with their refills, puncturing the atmosphere. They both drank for a minute.

'Listen, I'm sorry,' he began.

'Forget it.' She sighed.

'How's business?' he asked. She looked unsure. 'Seriously,' he continued. 'You know I suck at what I do. There's no way you can live in a town this great, have a fiancé that doting, carry a look that could stop a train, and be a sucky-assed businesswoman.'

She laughed. 'Business is just fine, thank you, Beckman. And anyway, what is it with that name of yours?'

'Believe me, I've had enough nights at enough single tables in enough diners to wonder a million times.'

'You maybe want to ask your parents?'

'Feels… I don't know, disingenuous. If I hated it that much, I'd have it changed. But, hey, it starts conversations. And what does a salesman need? Conversations.'

'Can't deny that.'

'So, why Egyptian artefacts? You major in Egyptology?'

'Do I look like the type?' He held in his response. 'I majored in business studies.'

'The reason why business is "just fine, thank you",' he noted, sipping.

She gathered herself, which he took as a sign that the ice was well and truly broken.

'Here's the thing. A few years back, I bought an Egyptian vase—for the house. Lovely piece. The salesman was smooth as you like. Letters of providence, the works. I got the piece back home, looked a million dollars. Problem is, turns out it's a fake. Mr Smooth? Gone. So that's it—come one, come all—you're all smoke and mirrors.'

'Present company excepted?'

She nodded, drinking. 'I figured the best revenge is to steal his market. So, I set up the business. Now I've got buyers all over. I have great hours. I have a place. I have Carlton.' She shrugged. 'Plus, I get to be Number One Saleswoman every year, so who wants more than that?' She smiled.

'Yeah, but what's there to aim for if you have everything you want?'

She looked down, toyed with the glass.

'Scratch that,' he said, having fired one too many searching questions. The last thing he wanted was to make any enemies in Sunrise, least of all her.

She checked around like there was a secret in the offing.

'My lips are sealed. Especially as I'm never going to see you again,' he said. 'Or anyone in Sunrise.'

That tipped the balance.

'I want the family business,' she said.

'I thought lighting wasn't your—'

'It wasn't,' she interjected. 'At first. Then Jack… Dad made it be.'

'Then how come…?' Beckman sensed thin ice beneath him this time. He clutched his glass. If he were about to wear a beer, it would have to be hers. That way, at least he'd have his own in which to drown his sorrows afterwards.

She took a slug as if for Dutch courage. 'He won't leave the firm to a woman. You believe that? My father's a sexist pig.'

He raised his glass. 'My father's a career failure and doesn't even send me birthday cards.'

They clinked glasses.

'So, I'm marrying Carlton,' she said.

'That sounds like revenge or Plan B. As opposed to love.'

'It's all three. Carlton's the company accountant. He's like... I don't know, the son Jack never had. The one he would have had if Mom hadn't walked out on him. Us.'

'Want me to point out that a son marrying a daughter is frowned on, even in Arizona?'

'Enough with the jokes, okay? You've got five fingers of beer left tonight—don't blow it.'

'Well, my mom walked out too, so let's have a finger for that, huh?'

She hesitated, then they chinked and drank again.

'So,' she said, 'Carlton inherits the company, down the line. If we're still together, I'm close to having my hand on the rudder.'

'Your father's prioritised your fiancé over you in the Will, even though Carlton's not family yet?'

'What can I say? Mom left because Jack stayed glued to his desk and would never consider leaving town. He didn't give her any family time. So suddenly the breakup is her fault, all women are untrustworthy, even his daughter, she's not good enough, never will be, skips around town like a dolled-up throwback, would never be taken seriously as the CEO, here's the glass ceiling Lolita, happy to have you come work for me but the boardroom's off-limits. So, you know what, Beckman?' She locked him in a gaze, her anger not truly directed there. 'Screw him.'

'You'll find a way. Not a way to screw him, I mean. You'll succeed. Get what you want.'

'Damn straight, I will.'

He raised his glass. 'To... scaling peaks.'

She raised hers. 'Defying odds.'

'Lighting up our lives.'

They chinked for the third and last time, draining their glasses. His heart felt heavy, knowing that, in counterpoint, a small but rather wonderful light would soon be going out of his world.

Then, literally, many lights did go out. Not inside the room but out on the street, where dusk had already fallen.

'Power cut?' he asked, which was dumb, given the evidence.

'No, birthday,' Lolita replied. He was about to ask a few Hows, Whats, and Whys when she stood. 'Come on.'

Clueless, he followed her out onto the sidewalk.

All the bulbs strung across the street were lit in what he assumed was a colorful display. A hundred yards away, a makeshift sign was illuminated in letters one metre high: HAPPY BIRTHDAY IOLANTHE.

Chattering voices approached—happy female tones.

A gaggle of twenty-somethings click-clacked down the opposite sidewalk, each girl wearing a different party hat. They were pointing at the sign, laughing, and ribbing the birthday girl, whose exact age the town billboard was keeping dark about.

'Hi, Lolita,' Iolanthe called, waving in their direction.

'Happy birthday, honey! Have a margarita for me!'

After a minute or so, the sideshow ended, the celebrant and her friends disappearing into a bar down the street. The sign remained lit, but the main streetlights resumed their duty, reducing the spectacle.

'Does everybody get that?' he wondered aloud.

'Young or old,' Lolita confirmed.

Hence the reason every guy and gal doesn't get their age literally put up in lights for all to see. In ten years or so, even you won't want to be reminded. Ladies of an even more… singular vintage would undoubtedly take umbrage.

Sunrise seems unfailingly pleasant to its residents. It's like I turned over a rock and found a diamond.

He followed her back into the diner, and they retook their seats.

'If only they'd known about yours truly,' he suggested.

'We know for next year.'

'Except I won't be here then. Haven't spent more than a week anywhere in the last lot of years.'

'Things change.'

'*Most* things change,' he clarified.

She picked up her glass, forgetting it was empty, and extracted only a few drops from the bottom.

He saw someone approach the table. If it was Carlton again, he hoped the guy had brought his beer, as he was out of luck if he expected to lob Beckman's over him.

Instead, an unfamiliar face appeared. A female face. A smiling female face. Looking not at Lolita but him.

'Beckman, is it? The little box guy?'

Without feeling the need for suspicion, he replied, 'Yeah, that's me.'

She tendered a ten-buck note. 'Thank you.'

'For what?'

'The box you gave to Saul—I work for him. I'm his clerk, Pandora. I barely made it to work today, crushing headache. But I pushed through because I don't like to let Saul down, then I guess you turned up, and he got the box, and he thought of me and, well, now I'm right as rain. In fact, right as sunshine.'

She pushed the ten-buck note into his hands. Then she looked at Lolita. 'It's near a miracle, it is.'

'I know. He fixed me too.'

'Thanks, Pandora,' Beckman said. 'Pleased to help.'

'I'm telling all my friends. We're so lucky you stopped by.'

Then, without ceremony, she bent down and gave him a peck on the cheek.

Well, not quite at the level of Mrs Jollifer's gratitude, but I'll take that, thank you very much.

She gave them both a beaming smile and skipped off.

'I guess, maybe if you light up enough other lives, you'll light up your own,' Lolita said.

'Amen to that.'

Berry returned, so he ordered the check and paid, mainly using Lolita and Pandora's tens. Lolita stayed behind to talk to more townsfolk, and he left her with a wave at the door.

Another day, another town, another chapter.

Across the road, unseen, two pairs of eyes peered out from behind a frosted ground floor window. On the adjacent door was stencilled the legend "TAYLOR'S".

Carlton's finger pushed against the glass, pointing in the direction of the man who'd just left the diner.

'That's the guy.'

CHAPTER 10

Room 12 welcomed Beckman into its embrace.

Though it was barely mid-evening, he kicked off everything bar his jockey shorts, and flicked on the TV for company.

Then, realising his upbeat mood had sewn the seed of chaos, he collected his things together, put them in their allotted places, and returned to sit, cross-legged, on the bed.

No light, crimson or otherwise, flickering or steady, doused the room. No fizzing, crackling, beeping or clanging was apparent, either. No grunting neighbours, city sirens or aircraft noise.

He had a good shot at a solid eight hours.

He checked his phone. By a miracle, two bars held steady. He scrolled through the short list of contacts, found the desired number, and hit Dial. Voice call sufficed; he wasn't about to let FaceTime offer an opportunity for comments on his fledgling man boobs.

'Hi, Beckman,' came the female voice after a few seconds.

'Hi, Mom.'

'Happy birthday.'

'Thanks. And thanks for the card.'

'How are you? Where are you?'

'Fine, and no idea. Well, kind of, but… you know, Arizona.'

He saw no point in regurgitating every detail about Sunrise or any recent call-ins or overnights. To do so every time they spoke would blur into a series of meaningless anecdotes, tales of woe about poor sales weeks, bright spots like today, and endless bitching about tailbacks, overcooked diner bacon, or the antics of Tyler Shitbag Quittle. "Fine" was a good catch-all. It let her know he was, well, fine.

'Are you eating well?'

'Mom, I'm thirty-six.'

'Thirty-seven.'

He checked his watch.

In five minutes. Okay, old woman, I'll pass on that.

'How's Dad?'

'I'm sure he's fine.'

Which meant they still hadn't spoken. Not that he'd fared much better.

Well, it takes two not to pick up the phone.

'Are you still dating, Mom?'

'I could ask you the same. Except without "still".'

He let it lie. 'I'll take that as a "Maybe".'

'I'll take that as a "No".'

Change the record, old woman. Besides, I got a kiss today. Share that? Best not. She'll be down to the Pastor before the phone screen's dimmed.

'I'm up to Two in the Salesman list. If I make Number One, who knows, I'll get my picture in the paper, fame and fortune. Girls'll have to take a number.'

'Well, I won't pretend it isn't good news, honey, but you've been chasing that the whole time. So maybe, you know, it's not your thing?'

'Or maybe, Mom, maybe it is.'

'As long as you're happy.'

He weighed up this particular Monday. He'd be going to sleep with a smile on his face, rare as it was. 'Yeah, Mom, I'm happy.'

'Then, good. So, don't....'

'Pick up hitchers, I know. Don't speed. Drink plenty. Always have breakfast.' He rolled his eyes.

'And don't roll your eyes at your mother, Beckman Spiers.'

He made a face, hoping she wouldn't infer that as well. 'It's getting late, Mom, so I'll let you go.'

'Okay, Son. Good luck.'

i.e., "Get successful, get married, or preferably both. I'm a long time dead, and I want to be a grandma."

'Night, Mom.'

He hung up. As the screen dimmed to black, the two bars called it a night as well.

Probably a sign. A rare one, of the non-neon variety.

He plugged the phone into the charger, took a leak, brushed his teeth, and bedded down.

The clock on the nightstand read 21:21: laughably early for some people. Those people could go fish. He turned off the light.

Slumber descended.

He caroused through a world of dancing armadillos, flashing lights, swirling frocks, masked ne'er-do-well boyfriends, a chorus line of tire-gun-wielding mechanics, and a cascading fountain of overflowing goblets of root beer.

And, presently, a rapping noise.

A sound of tapping on wood.

A sound that didn't belong.

He realised it didn't belong in his dream because it *wasn't* in his dream.

He woke.

Two nights now? What's a guy got to do?

He fumbled for the light, winced at the glare.

There came a further knock on the door.

He hauled out of bed, located the free (not that he would ever steal it) towelling gown, pulled it on, and unlatched the door.

Outside he was greeted with, if not a sea of faces, a decent-sized paddling pool of faces. The faces were attached to bodies (basic human anatomy persisted, even in Sunrise), and the bodies had arms. Naturally, the arms terminated in hands.

Each hand clutched a ten-dollar bill.

Beckman's eyes were wide.

This would necessitate a walk down to the Buick, where the apparent Messiah kept his loaves and fishes.

CHAPTER 11

Breakfast was the whole works and damn fine.

It was also interrupted by more calls for his wares. There were a surprising number of headaches in Sunrise. Maybe because of all the lights? Or, logically, joyous bumper sales brought by word of mouth in a friendly town?

Or maybe he still existed in a netherworld of altered consciousness, below the surface of those damn flickering lights, sucked into a sleeping-waking state by the rhythm of the incessant strobing at Busted Sign Motel two nights ago? Indeed, it wasn't beyond the bounds that this whole Sunrise experience represented a cerebral resonance, his mind stuck at the flashing cursor of reboot, the spinning colored wheel, the 404.

He pinched himself hard on the thigh.

It hurt.

As he closed the car's trunk, arm clutching a box of smaller boxes with which to satiate the latest demand, his eye was drawn to a navy Lincoln down the street. It looked occupied.

Wasn't the same Lincoln there last night? Or had that been during an actual half-asleep state, when nothing was guaranteed to be as it appeared?

He dismissed it.

Yet when he returned to the Buick a quarter-hour later—overnight case in tow, room bill settled—it wasn't his imagination. He slid into the driver's seat, angled the rear-view mirror to look down the street, and sat there for a minute. The guy in the Lincoln wasn't taking a phone call, nor checking his watch as if waiting for somebody. He wasn't a potential customer, as he hadn't made an approach, and evidently Beckman's whereabouts were the talk of the town.

Beckman gave himself this much credit: he was a pretty shrewd observer. This was down to many, many hours of people-watching, sat in coffee shops, diners, hotel restaurants, standing in gas station queues, ever in pursuit of the signs of potential custom. A student of behaviour, in fact—and this Lincoln's behaviour smacked of, if not intrigue, at least interest. Maybe even concern. But *his* concern? Should he butt out? Perhaps only when he could confirm it *wasn't* his concern.

Beckman turned the key, moved the gear selector to D, and pulled gingerly away.

The Lincoln nosed out.

He was being tailed. Badly.

Or maybe this defined a Sunrise "friendly" style of surveillance.

Either way, facts were facts. It *was* his concern now. No butting-out would be forthcoming any time soon.

He felt perturbed rather than guilty or panicked. He'd made no legal or moral misstep, at least not in any usual way. Had he broken an unwritten rule? Maybe his seat in the diner last night belonged to the Mayor or the unicorn ranch owner? Except Lolita would have saved his blushes, wouldn't she?

It was nothing more than a case of mistaken identity, he resolved. He forcibly abandoned repeated mirror checks and concentrated on retracing his route towards Saul's garage, not having the first clue how to get back to the main highway, other than it ran beyond that edge of town. The Eastern edge, if his calculations were correct. Sunrise may be quirky, but he was pretty sure the sun took the same path across the sky even here.

Very soon, he rolled past Saul's forecourt, the Lincoln still a careful distance behind.

The suburbs melted away, the choice of routes vanished, and the car climbed towards the low ridge that bordered the town. The tail stayed with him.

This felt familiar; he'd taken the right road.

The landscape merged into sameness, and ahead stood the sign for the town limits. He checked his mirror as it flashed past. The legend remained the same, the eighth-grade humour still there.

Something else happened behind him.

The Lincoln fell back. Further. It vanished to a blob, then a dot. Then it was gone.

Entranced, and buoyed by an end to the episode, his attention was not on the road ahead.

He'd reached the highway intersection.

Both feet hit the brake, and he screeched to a halt.

Naturally, there was nothing to hit on the main desert road.

But how about paying attention, dumb ass. Learn nothing yesterday?

He didn't bother with the turn signal; he simply pulled out left and eased up to a fifty-seven cruise, which would eventually take him back to the freeway. All things being equal.

Sure enough, he soon passed Earl's roadside establishment. Gas still allegedly retailed at two bucks a gallon.

A while later, the freeway intersection arrived. He joined and merged into traffic.

After half an hour, he made the first rest stop, gratefully imbibing one of Coffee Planet's finest and collecting a loyalty stamp.

An hour later, he repeated the routine, adding in an early lunch.

Another half-hour passed before he pulled to a stop outside his building.

The key sliding into the lock of apartment 12 was as good as a sigh of relief.

As welcome as a weekend away from home had been, he could have done without another thousand-mile round trek to Cousin Ichabod's wake. That had made ten days straight on the road, plus neither Mom nor Dad had been there, and the coffee had sucked.

He threw laundry in the washer-drier and switched on the TV as company.

The few remaining things were unpacked methodically. First, hanging items in the wardrobe. Second, folding items in the drawer. Third, ablution items laid out neatly in the bathroom. Shoes off. Jacket hung on the chair back. Curtains two-thirds closed. Air to 21 degrees.

He spied a flicker of movement from a glass-fronted box in the corner of the room, went over to it, and crouched down to look at the inhabitant. The leopard gecko flicked its head this way and that.

'Hey, Bogie. Miss me?'

He took down a tub of writhing soil, slid open the front of the vivarium, and tipped some mealworms into Bogie's dinner bowl. They were devoured mercilessly.

Beckman slid the glass door closed, watched for a moment, curled his lip, and said, 'Here's looking at you, kid.'

He sank onto the tired leatherette sofa and reviewed recent events. After a few minutes, a thought struck, so he went to a neatly organised set of shelves and pulled out a thin sheaf of paper. Clearing a few items from the kitchen table, he spread out the old-school map.

His eye traced the freeway down to the appointed exit and located what he'd named Infinity Highway. He ran his finger down it, passing the mark for Earl's gas station, and carefully traced towards what he knew lay out there.

Except it wasn't.

Not an intersection, not a town, not a speck.

Admin snafu, huh? I'll be a son of a gun.

He gazed aimlessly at the map for a couple of minutes, then folded it along its crease lines and slotted it home on the shelf.

Yet his mind wouldn't rest. The conclusion was inescapable. If he wanted to hit Number One, if he genuinely believed he had a chance to eclipse Tyler, here lay his best shot in the last 12 years. Malvolio was becoming more forthright about redundancy—whether it be a realistic proposition or merely a scare tactic.

The upshot was the same—a light at the end of a very long tunnel.

He'd found a market.

Sunrise could be the meal ticket. Time was short. He'd have to go back.

Or at least, try.

CHAPTER 12

After the washer-drier had done its work, he repacked his suitcase and shoulder bag, patted the door's brass 12 on the way out, and climbed into the still-gleaming white Buick.

Two-thirty had passed before he swung into one of the many empty spots outside the small, low office building, which stood at the end of an otherwise vacant lot in a nondescript part of a generally yawn-inducing town. The only giveaway was the Pegasus logo above the keycode-entry double door, which took him into a poorly lit corridor.

He poked his head into the small office on the left: three desks, all unoccupied. On the right, a closed door led to the warehouse. Faint music played. It was a safe bet that Wilbur was busying himself with dancing in the aisles.

He opened the second door on the left, which was already ajar. His nostrils were caressed by the familiar gentle whiff of musty air overlaid with lavender.

The face at the desk brightened. 'Mr. Spiers.'

PA Amaryllis Broomhead referred to everyone like that. Well, not *exactly* like that—it would be too confusing. If he were James Bond—which would be a significant stretch of the imagination by everyone—she would be Miss Moneypenny. If Miss Moneypenny had a ten-inch beehive and a penchant for garish red bangles.

'Miss Broomhead.'

He always called her "Miss", even though neither he nor anyone else at Pegasus had any clue about whether she was currently married, had ever been married, had been repeatedly married, abhorred marriage, dated the boss, hated the boss, or was married to the job or married to the mob.

He also harboured a notion that she had a soft spot for him. However, she might have been faking it and had a soft spot for everybody, nobody, the job, the mob, the boss, the husband, the non-husband, the ex-husband, the future husband, or long evenings at home with a kilo tub of salted caramel ice cream.

One truism remained: she appeared Of Indeterminate Age and had remained so for the last ten years.

Another odd rumour circulated that she was family to Mr Malvolio. Beckman couldn't see it—but seeing anything in total clarity was far from his strength.

'Congratulations on your recent success,' she offered.

He assumed she meant the completely un-earned promotion to Number Two caused by the voltage-induced demise of Esmond Belcher.

Either that or news of his Sunrise-fuelled upswing in sales had reached these shores, which he sorely hoped wasn't the case. If arch-rival and current leaderboard-topper Tyler Quittle got wind that someone was on his tail, he'd no doubt resort to ever more desperate tactics to secure the prize. Beckman's assault on the summit of the sales chart needed to be SWAT-level in its execution. Surely, Sunrise's apparent isolation and undetectability made that a shoo-in? Still, he needed to tread carefully.

'Thank you, Miss Broomhead.'

She looked at the bag clutched in his hand. 'For Bruno?'

He nodded. 'Is there a condolence card to sign?'

'For who?'

'Belcher?'

'We sent flowers.'

It had surely been her idea. Malvolio would probably have sent the grieving family a tardy slip as a reward for Belcher turning up late for work and as a pile of ash.

'He wants to see you,' she continued.

Beckman gulped. The dark wood-stained walls closed in. 'Okay,' he peeped.

She thumbed the intercom. A buzz sounded in the adjacent room. 'Mr Spiers is here, sir.'

'Send him in,' said the tinny decade-old speaker on the desk.

Miss Broomhead gestured towards the frosted glass door to her right.

'Is he in a good mood?' Beckman asked.

'A what?' He might as well have asked her to outline some peculiar nuances of the legal system in Chad.

Abandoning that conversation, he took a deep breath and breezed through the panelled door as if he hadn't a care in the world, which was far from true.

'Spiers, finally.'

Beckman moved immediately to his right, steering away from Bruno, who would soon sense the contents of the bag he held.

'Morning, sir.'

Mr Malvolio was sixty or so, with a huge mane of unkempt black hair, a black suit, a white shirt, and a black tie. A younger Ronnie Wood, if he were pallbearer.

His desk stood vast and ornate, something Pepys would have used. In the corner towered an old hat stand, which never held anything so much as a beret. All the walls were plain moss-green, apart from one, on which hung a sizeable self-portrait of the CEO, imagined as if he was gunning for Time's Man of the Year. Behind the picture lay a secret—one known only by everyone at Pegasus, including the guy who came in each Friday at 6 pm to empty the wastebaskets: Malvolio's wall safe.

Naturally, nobody brought up the fact, least of all because Bruno guarded the room.

Bruno was a Gila monster. A long chain held him in place to the left of the desk, Mr Malvolio's right-hand side. It wasn't the fastest thing on four legs, but it *was* venomous.

Irking Bruno was likely Not A Good Plan. Neither Beckman nor anyone else at Pegasus felt inclined to test that theory.

Mr Malvolio also possessed a silver-topped cane, which usually rested against the desk but could be snatched up and whacked down for effect.

Beckman wondered if today's visit would pass *sans cane*.

'Twelve years, Spiers. Twelve years you've been here. Finally, a creditable showing this year. Quittle's been here half that time and look where he is. Are you not trying, Spiers?'

"Look, I'm up every day, coasting shitty streets in scattered no-hope towns on the worst sales patch of the whole grid. And still, I make Number Two. How about a little gratitude, you freak?",

was what he wanted to reply.

'Absolutely, sir. Pounding the streets every day,' he said deferentially.

'What were your sales last week?'

He did a ready-reckon. 'Thirty-five, I think.'

'Passable. Barely passable. But a damn sight better than before. What's the matter, Spiers? Don't you want the award?'

'Absolutely, sir. Very much.'

'Vennock's had a good week. And he's only been here two years. You want to watch over your shoulder, Spiers. We don't harbour passengers here at Pegasus. D'you hear?' Mr Malvolio's hand eased towards his cane.

'Totally. I'll redouble my efforts.'

'See that you do. I don't want to have to let you go. But I will. D'you hear?'

'Loud and clear, sir.'

'Good. Now, did you bring the dead armadillo I asked for?'

Beckman eyed Bruno and lifted the bag.

Bruno sensed lunch.

'Excellent,' Mr Malvolio said. His hand moved away from the cane.

Beckman passed over the bag.

Mr Malvolio snatched it away, fluttering his other hand towards the door, and Beckman needed no second bidding.

'Good luck, Beckman,' Miss Broomhead called as he swiftly passed into the corridor, making sure the door was good and shut behind him.

His exhale could have lifted a weather balloon into orbit.

CHAPTER 13

The warehouse at Pegasus HQ was an infinitely less stressful place to be. For one, warehouse supremo Wilbur was a good foil.

Wilbur liked listening to the radio. Wilbur oddly enjoyed counting the stock. Wilbur wore strange hats. Today's gem was a purple baseball cap emblazoned with "Black Holes Suck". Wilbur was the kind of guy who you'd assume didn't get the cap's message on both levels and who would then proceed to prove you wholly incorrect with a treatise on the entire topic.

'Hey, Wilbur,' Beckman called over the strains of REO Speedwagon.

'Hey, Beckman.' He ramped down his dance and sashayed over. 'How's the world?'

Wilbur could have slept here, had Mr Malvolio the decency to spring for overnight HVAC.

'Hot, mostly dishonest, and not suffering enough.'

'Bad times for you, B, bad times.'

He let Wilbur call him "B" because why not. They got on. Plus, Wilbur disliked Tyler Quittle, i.e., the man was a good judge of character.

'Not yesterday, though.'

'Spill, B,' Wilbur said, intrigued, desperate for something to do, or both.

'Found a great new town.' Beckman scanned around for prying eyes and ears. There were none. Except, of course, if Mr Malvolio had had secret cameras and microphones installed.

Was that possible? Possibly possible. Wilbur was partial to some skateboarding in the afternoons, but hadn't yet been fed to Bruno, so surveillance was unlikely.

Wilbur leant in. '"Great" pronounced "Lucrative"?'

'Kinda hoping, yeah.'

'Think you can make Number One? Couldn't happen to a nicer guy.'

'Thanks. Who knows? I might have a shot. So, on that—I need more stock.'

Wilbur's shoulders fell. 'Shoot. Thing is, B, I'm kinda out.'

'Out?' Beckman asked in surprise and obvious disappointment.

'Out.'

'Serious?'

'Serious.'

'Out?'

'Out.'

'Shoot.'

'Yeah.'

'How come?'

'Tyler.'

'Shoot.'

'Yeah.'

'Tyler cleaned you out?'

'Yeah.'

'When?'

'Like five minutes ago.'

'Shoot.'

'Yeah.'

'He gone already?'

'Search me.'

'Next shipment?'

'Monday.'

'Shoot.'

'Yeah.'

The background strains of the radio held sway for a few moments.

'Have a good weekend, Wilbur.' Beckman dashed for the door.

'Good luck,' the now-jigging operative called.

Beckman poked his nose into the office. Mercifully or annoyingly—whichever way he looked at it—Tyler sat there, tapping away at the keyboard.

No doubt validating his latest sales figures.

'Snake,' came Beckman's opening gambit.

Tyler swivelled on the chair. Dramatically, like Blofeld. His face lit up with false cheer. 'Becky!'

'You cleaned me out.'

'*You?*'

Beckman shrugged. 'Wilbur.'

'First come, first served, Becky. Need my stock, got to hit my targets, got to get my prize.' Tyler flashed a smile which said, "And that's an end to it", then returned his attention to the screen.

'You saw my car. You *know* why I came to the office. You stole the last batch.'

'Stole?' Tyler deigned to look up. 'Took out, fair and square. Besides, since when d'you need more stock? Your trunk's been full for two weeks. Why in hell would I ever expect you to be here for *more* stock? There's no conspiracy against you. A man makes his own luck.'

'And I made some luck.'

'Kudos to you, Becky, kudos to you.'

'So? There's no delivery 'til Monday. How in the heck am I supposed to have a shot of catching you?'

Tyler theatrically clutched his hands to his chest. 'You're breaking my heart.'

'I'm onto a good thing!'

'All the more reason for me to put on the running shoes. Finally, I get the dream. Number One Salesman. Vacation. Sandy beaches. Beautiful women. New Camaro.' A dreamy sigh. 'Goodbye Pegasus. Out on a high, like all the rest. Tough shit, Becky. Maybe next year.' He finished with a snigger under his breath.

Beckman didn't usually *hate* Tyler—he didn't know him well enough. Yes, he despised his methods. Yes, he wished the guy wasn't five-eleven with perfect blue eyes and a salesman patter that could kill. No, he wouldn't forgive him for out-wooing Glenda Ramage then doing the damage on Ramage instead of him all those years ago.

No. If anything, he mostly envied Tyler Quittle.

How he'd like to have punctured that smug balloon this year at the last gasp. After all, Tyler would always have next year, wouldn't he? His trajectory was always forty-five degrees on the sales graph, compared to Beckman's maybe ten.

If only it had been Tyler underneath that lightning bolt.

The loathsome man finished typing with a flourish and clicked the screen off.

Jeez. He even looks after the environment. Probably the only thing he won't screw.

'Taking a leak, Becky. Don't come in—wouldn't want you to get jealous.' Tyler flashed a knowing glance and slid out the door.

Beckman sagged like the belly skin of a crash-dieting Sumo.

Outside, contrary to Tyler's expectation, the Buick's trunk lay half-empty. Beckman needed more stock to service Sunrise. Without it, he'd never out-sell Tyler. Yet, nearby in the parking lot, Tyler's trunk was freshly brimmed.

Oh, for that stock.

Then he spied a set of car keys on the desk.

Surely, he couldn't sink so low. Could he?

Time was short, though. Too short even for a swift repatriation.

Unless…?

The black Chevy started first time. Beckman gave the gas pedal a solid prod, and the car leapt across the small Pegasus parking lot and onto the service road.

He didn't look in the mirror.

In two minutes, he reached the highway. In five, he was out of town. In ten, he hit the freeway.

Finally, his pulse returned to normal. Yet, his conscience would never forgive him.

His mother would never forgive him.

Lolita would never forgive him.

But if he made Number One? They would all have to rethink.

Wouldn't they?

His phone rang. The caller was inevitable. If he didn't pick up now, it would descend into an irate barrage of texts and declined calls.

The lesser of two evils, he hit Accept.

'You goddamn shit, Becky!'

'You'll get much better gas mileage on the Buick.'

'You thieving, no-good shit, Becky!'

'I just want a fair fight, Tyler.'

'You scratch that car, I'll tear you a new asshole!'

'Sorry, Tyler, going into a tunnel.' Beckman held out the phone, gargling, whistling, and hissing.

'You shit, Becky. There are no tun—'

He jabbed End, then hit Mute and tossed the phone into the cubby.

His heartbeat had returned to a gallop. A voice inside suggested he'd angered a wasp, disrupted the natural order of the universe, dared to mess with Fate. Worse, he'd done something that, while not illegal, wouldn't go down well with Mom.

Well, Mom would have to suck it up and appreciate that it was for the greater good. *His* greater good. After all, his greater good equalled her greater pride, didn't it? Not as a goal, but certainly as a consequence.

Anyway, the slight feeling of guilt gnawing away in his stomach was a positive sign. It put him many rungs above Tyler, who didn't know the meaning of the G word.

After twenty minutes, he pulled off at a rest stop, brimmed the tank to match the trunk, got his CP loyalty card stamped, inhaled a burger, and hit the road again.

Soon enough—maybe out of good spirits—the appointed freeway exit hove into view. No tailback this time. He dove off, took the left turn, and was again staring down the empty road.

The phone had vibrated on and off most of the journey. Missed Calls would be in double digits.

He didn't care about phone calls, only sales calls.

The road arrowed onwards. Earl's joint flashed by.

Then nothing.

Then more nothing.

He scooped out the phone. No signal.

He pulled up Tyler's sat nav. No signal.

Infinity Highway continued.

Where is the intersection?

He scanned the area for evidence of the low ridge that bordered Sunrise.

There were outcrops, yes. Dips, yes. Cacti galore.

Intersection? No.

Sign? No.

He must be going a touch crazy.

Was it this far? Was it further?

He'd been maintaining a steady sixty-five (because, heck, it was Tyler's car), so logically he'd be there sooner than before. But he'd not had to stop for the delay of an armadillo crisis, making timing and distance confusing.

He pushed onwards. Still no intersection.

He slowly looked a complete one-eighty.

Something caught his eye.

No, just a dust devil. He watched it for a second.

The Chevy drifted right.

He corrected. The shrapnel clatter of the roadside rang out.

'Shoot.'

A bang lit the air.

He hit the middle pedal. The Chevy coasted to a stop, a juddering sound from the rear.

What are the odds? The universe is telling you to give this up as a lost cause, or maybe getting its karmic revenge for your impromptu auto theft.

He thumped the steering wheel. Shook his head. Closed his eyes and held in a few choice words (after all, he'd already done enough wrong by Mom that day). Reached across for the phone.

There was a knock at the window.

CHAPTER 14

'New wheels? Very smart. Didn't take you for a Chevy guy, Beckman.'

The world's most unlikely car thief didn't want to burden this knight in shining metal with his tale of wickedness/justifiable levelling of the playing field.*

(* delete as applicable).

'Thought you'd at least transfer the license plate,' Saul continued.

'Still waiting on that.'

After a few miles of the tow into town, Beckman decided he'd been too circumspect about the whole affair, so he declared the reason for coming back. He explained the Number Two situation and how, with a sliver of a chance, Sunrise might be an absolute gold mine. The whole outsmarting-Tyler and car-swapping part he carefully omitted.

The tow truck rumbled past the town sign and rolled through the modest industrial suburbs. This time, Beckman spectated with interest rather than wonderment.

A large grey (truly grey, not just a Beckman grey) square two-storey building slid past. The sign outside the entrance gate proclaimed, "Milan Enterprises".

So, this is what Lolita is not the heir to.

It was oddly bereft of neon. A missed marketing opportunity? A way to keep the electricity bills down? Or Milan didn't have money to burn?

Perhaps Lolita was better off not being the heir.

There you go again, poking your brain where it isn't wanted. Stick with selling the damn boxes. Happiness will come from making sales, not making waves.

A minute later, a not dissimilar structure was sited. The entrance stood grander, the place a storey higher. The legend read "EVI Lighting". A car lolled through the gate.

An early model Mustang in red.

A little bird whispered in his ear. He silenced it, then after a pause he considered suitable, asked Saul what car Carlton drove.

'Beckman, I tell you, it's the one car in town I crave. The most beautiful Mustang. Not a word of it, okay? The guy is so suspicious he'll have me accused of looking at it the wrong way. Then he'll go somewhere else for its service, on account of I'm itching to take it out for a spin on the QT.' He shook his head.

Beckman held in a response. Day Two, and he didn't want to come across as the Spanish Inquisition, riding into town (okay, being towed, again) to accuse people of misdeeds based on random incidents fleshed out with conspiracy theory.

All the same, why is Carlton visiting the opposition? So late in the working day?

Okay, slow down. Sunrise is quirky. This is a quirk.

They eased to a stop on Saul's forecourt.

'Shutting shop in a half-hour. Guess you're back for a spell, though, huh?'

'Tomorrow's fine. I'll get to the hotel. I walk too, you know. Close on thirty-six years now.'

Beckman hooked out his shoulder bag and night case, stuffed both to the brim with boxes from the trunk, shook Saul's hand, and trekked off down the sidewalk.

Three blocks later, a middle-aged woman hurried across the street to intercept him.

'Mr Beckman?'

Were there Wanted ads out for him? Was it the monochrome attire? Was it his devilish good looks?

Probably not the latter. Definitely not the latter. The middle one. Yes, the middle one.

'Yes?' he asked, a hint of suspicion in his voice.

'You're the man with the magic boxes?'

He pulled one from his bag. 'Like this?'

'Yes! Like that! I have the most crushing head pain.'

'Then you're in luck.'

She unslung a purse from her shoulder, scrabbled around, and pushed a crumpled ten-dollar bill into his top jacket pocket.

He tendered the box. 'Feel better!' he chirped.

She beetled away.

Not a hundred yards later, a similar thing happened with an older man.

Then a young couple.

Then a pregnant woman pushing a stroller.

When he reached the centre of town, it was almost time to return to the car for a tactical satchel refill. But he wasn't going anywhere in a hurry, confident that any more customers would keep until tomorrow.

Plus, it had been a long day already. It was six in the evening, but it felt like nine.

He headed onwards to Sunset Hotel.

Did they still have Room 12?

They did. He mentally punched the air.

'Saul says you're an Okay Guy,' Kinsey added, 'So head right on up.'

He unpacked methodically. First, hanging items in the narrow wardrobe. Then folding items in the drawer. Next, ablution items laid out neatly in the bathroom. Shoes off. Jacket hung on the chair back. Curtains two-thirds closed. Air to 21 degrees.

Settled into his stay, Beckman took a first look at the view from his room. Nothing exciting, just the street from one floor up. He watched absentmindedly for a few minutes.

No sign of the mysterious navy Lincoln.

He didn't know whether to be happy or confused. He went with 'hungry' and perused the Room Service menu.

A night of no interruptions.

Bliss.

News hadn't got around about his return. He hoped it soon would. He was counting on it.

Wednesday. Three days to the deadline. Three days to overhaul Tyler.

He sprang out of bed. Showered. Breakfasted. Repacked the shoulder bag with the product. At the hotel door, he bid Kinsey good morning, then checked the immediate vicinity: no navy Lincoln.

Guess he's out hunting for a white Buick. Well, up your ass.

He looked around. It might be a good idea to get more of a feeling for the place.

Across the road, a guy got out of his parked car. He was maybe forty, thick beard, waistcoat, shoes you could see your face in. He locked up, tried the handle to make sure it was good and locked, walked round to the passenger side, and tested its handle too. Then he did a full circle of the car, bending down to look at each tire. Satisfied, he walked two doors down to a clothing store.

Before he reached the store, though, he stopped, retraced his steps, and proceeded to try both door handles again. Then he checked all four tires. Satisfied, he walked back to the store. Then stopped short, returned, checked both handles, all four tires, and set off.

When he turned back to the car again, Beckman abandoned the spectating and resumed his journey.

On the three-block walk, he was accosted seven times.

Inching closer, Tyler. And without being an ass, too. You should try it sometime.

Ha! Tyler not being an ass? As likely as... a lightning strike?... a teleporting tow-truck driver?... Beckman Spiers stealing cars?

Well, car singular.

He aborted that daydream. Adjacent to Our Buck's was a convenience store whose door stood propped open. He stepped inside.

There was candy. There was a news rack. There were sundries. And a woman at the magazine stand. A woman in a swing dress, bangs, and tinted glasses.

He was about to call out but decided against over-friendliness, in case her beau was nearby, temporarily hidden by a shelving unit, and would waste no time slapping Beckman's cheek with a gauntlet before declaring pistols at... Sunrise.

Instead, he observed the unfolding scene. History had shown that observing in Sunrise was a fruitful pastime.

Lolita thumbed down a stack of magazines and slid the fifth one out. Then she stepped to the News rack, located the required title, counted down five, and pulled out a copy.

Hmm. Some people and their routines, huh?

Attention now lost, unfocussed in the array of wall-mounted neons, he was absorbing this, finding it an added endearment to someone he'd already taken a shine to, lost in his own world, when,

'Beckman! You came back!'

He jolted. His gaze met her face, then her eyes (well, glasses). 'Yeah. You know. I travel. So, I travelled away, and I travelled back. You know us travelling salesman, we love to....'

'Travel?'

'And sell. Especially sell. Not at the same time, though, always a bad idea. I don't do car-to-car transactions on the freeway—I have a rule about that. A passing biker will take your arm off soon as look at you. Whoosh, snap. Bad idea.'

'Beckman, you're funny.'

'And I can do it while travelling. Look, let's walk, and I'll tell you a joke.' He turned for the door. 'Won't sell to you though—not at the same time. I just have a rule about that. Biker will take your punchline soon as look at you.'

She cracked a smile and shook her head in amusement. 'Forget what you came in for?'

'Oh. No. I wondered if there was a local paper. You know, find out some about this crazy place.'

'Crazy, huh? Well, we have this.' She held up one of the two she'd bought. The Sunrise Beacon probably hadn't changed typeface since the Gold Rush.

'Right on point.'

'Here.' She handed it to him. 'I only buy to support the staff. Not much goes on anyway that I don't know about. Or anyone, probably. Guess you're the target readership.'

'What do I owe you?'

'"Thank you", I believe is customary.'

He bowed slightly. 'Thank you.'

Tucking the paper under his arm, he gestured chivalrously to the door. They broke out into the morning sunshine. Her lenses darkened further.

Reaction glasses. But they never go clear? Surely, she has the means to replace such a faulty pair? Or is it part of the "look"?

Across the street, he noted Waistcoat Shiny Shoes checking his door handles again.

'What gives?' he pondered.

'That's Franklin. Has OCD, like off the scale. Takes him forty-five minutes to go anywhere.' Her eyebrows raised above the rim of her glasses. 'Some people and their routines, huh?' she mused.

Twilight Zone music.

Physician heal thyself.

Ahead of them, a woman emerged from Our Buck's and walked up the street. Then Beckman's attention was drawn to the building opposite, where a familiar guy pocketed his phone and headed off in the same direction.

Groundhog Day music.

He gently touched Lolita's arm to draw her to a stand. 'Did you see that?'

'What?' she asked, a little worried.

'I think that guy is following that woman,' he hissed.

She looked across the road. Instantly, her demeanour lightened. 'Oh, yeah, the Gleesons. They do it all the time. It's like a sex game.'

'A what now?'

'Beats me. But it's harmless. Trust me.'

'Okay. Some people and their routines, huh?'

She gave him a friendly shoulder nudge.

They carried on walking, past the coffee shop. All the while, Beckman hadn't a clue where they were heading, and neither had enquired. They were just… walking, plain as day, natural as long-time friends.

And across the street, unseen, a man exited Taylor's and, keeping a low profile, began to follow them.

CHAPTER 15

Moments later, a car eased alongside and rolled to a stop slightly ahead.

Instinctively, Beckman got the frights.

Except it wasn't the Lincoln, but a cab.

Naturally, not a regular cab. A mobile neon display unit festooned with all manner of graphics. It probably made about two horsepower at the wheels, the rest vanishing in a puff of electricity generation.

Was this another Saul-type scenario? A cab arrives out of nowhere precisely when you need it?

Except you didn't need it. So that theory was shot to all heck. Unless...

'You call a cab?' he asked Lolita.

'No. You?'

'No.'

The driver got out, pinching his forehead. Beckman joined the dots and reached inside his shoulder bag but came up empty.

'Saul says you're the guy to see for what I got. Hey, Lolita.'

She gave him a courteous nod.

'I absolutely am,' Beckman confirmed.

The driver fished in his pocket. Beckman held out his palm, but vertically. 'Except I'm out. Price is a ride down to Saul's, and then I'll fix you up.'

'Deal.' The driver opened the rear door for his ride, then retook his seat.

'See you tomorrow?' Beckman asked Lolita.

'If you get a minute's peace.'

'At this rate, I'll be out of stock by dusk.' He climbed into the car and clanged the door shut.

Lolita's face appeared at the open window. She was bent over towards him at almost ninety degrees, hand on the roof. Luckily for him, the collar of the dress lay tight against her skin.

'Come up.'

'Come again?' he asked.

'Come up to the house. For lunch.'

That gave him a touch of the frights, too. 'Are you sure?'

'As a favour. I have a new piece being delivered. I need a strong hand in the stock area.'

'The house?'

'Yeah. Yonder.' She pointed, but he couldn't see. Then she noticed he couldn't see. 'Clint'll give you the way, okay, Clint?'

The driver said he would.

'You sure?' Beckman double-checked.

'Why, you have a medical note against moving stuff?'

'No, I mean, what about Carlton? Won't he—?'

'He's away at a supplier meeting. Couple of days. Besides, what's he going to do?'

Beckman had a pretty good idea what he might do. Equally, if some douche thought Beckman was not an Okay Guy, there were plenty in town who would set Carlton straight on the matter. Probably. Hopefully. Chunky-built, coffee shop-owning, and eye-patched truck-driving types of plenty.

Plus, Beckman would gladly walk into a polygraph test room with head held high if ever accused of having designs on Lolita. She was somebody else's fiancée, and messing with women in that situation was Just Not Done.

Lunch and a bit of heavy lifting? What harm could it do?

Besides, I'll make it a Thank You for being my new advocate around here. The first domino.

'One o'clock?'

'One o'clock.' She nodded in agreement, tapped on the roof, and Clint tickled the gas pedal.

Unseen, the man across the street watched them go, then frantically sought out his Lincoln.

At Saul's, the Chevy was still in the shop, so Beckman pulled a box out of the trunk, paid Clint with it, received Lolita's address in turn, and waved the guy off.

Saul walked out to apologise for the delay. 'Had one of my mechanics roll in late this morning. His car broke down. He couldn't fix it. You know they say, "Can't get the staff"? Exhibit A.'

Beckman brushed it off. 'Don't bother with the wash, it's not my—,' then stopped in time, doubled back, and wrapped up with, '—business to make your day any busier. I'll take a seat in the waiting room.'

Saul hollered for a mechanic to make quick with the tire.

As Beckman disappeared into the bowels of the building, a navy Lincoln slid by at tick-over, the driver scanning the streets.

Fifteen minutes later, Beckman slid the Chevy back onto Main Street and found a parking spot near Buck's.

Inside, he took a window seat and was glad he did.

He was easy to spot, which yielded four more sales.

But he was also easy to be spotted by undesirables: halfway down the lazy root beer slurping, peanut-munching and people-watching, a certain navy Lincoln pulled up opposite.

Luck or judgement? What does it mean? Too much of a coincidence.

The Gleesons were playing a fake espionage game—an odd excuse but certainly an explanation for their antics.

If Beckman was being tailed, what lay behind it? Surely, he'd gained enough acquaintances in Sunrise for one of them to tip him off that something was amiss? Which meant nothing could be amiss. Didn't it?

By the same logic, wasn't it entirely probable that Carlton was also doing nothing wrong? Lolita said if anything important were going on, she'd know about it. So, did she know about these curios?: (1) Carlton at the gas station in a clinch with another woman, and (2) Carlton visiting the offices of his firm's fierce competitor, especially since (3) Lolita had been told he was due elsewhere.

Yet, Sunrise was Sunrise and Beckman was not acquainted with its… uniqueness. Surely, Lolita knew just fine, and everything was roses and chocolates?

He wasn't convinced. He had a tingle, like his headache-spotting Spidey-sense, but worse.

He got an idea.

He checked his watch: Twelve-fifteen. Enough time.

He unfolded the Sunrise Beacon and flicked past the news to the Ad section. He dragged a finger down the page until he found what he wanted. Then, expecting to be unable to walk the streets without being accosted (in the revenue-generating, rankings-climbing, beach-attaining way he liked being accosted), he grabbed the shoulder bag and set out onto the sunny Sunrise streets, feeling duly… sunny.

Taylor's, on the block near Our Buck's, was a detective agency.

Behind the frosted windows and stiff entrance door opened a small room with three desks, behind which lay what looked like the same again.

On the walk up (actually a gentle downhill), he'd imagined dark oak panelling, deerstalkers, microfiche machines, grainy black and white images plastered on the walls, endless filing cabinets, and maybe a lingering whiff of cigar smoke in the overly warm air.

The desks were modern, the walls clean, the computers sleek, and the temperature read a digital 20.5.

Two of the desks were occupied.

Behind one sat a man of indeterminate late middle-age, impeccable hair, open shirt, and suspenders. Plus, a monocle. Above the desk hung a framed black and white photograph, technically a movie still. A famous one.

If Suspenders-and-Monocle wasn't the business owner—Taylor (first or last name)—Beckman was a son of a gun. Possibly two sons. Or two guns. Or both.

At the second desk, and engrossed in mouse-jiggling activity, sat a younger woman, probably early thirties, cropped hair, navy pantsuit.

Surely-Taylor looked up from his paperwork, a fraction bemused. Maybe a tenth. Two ninths at most.

The man rose, offered his hand. 'Welcome to Taylor's P.I., sir. I'm,' Beckman held his breath in anticipation, 'Zebedee Taylor, founder here.'

The accent wasn't local. Texas maybe?

'Beckman Spiers, passing through.'

True enough? As opposed to a resident. Now, how much of a movie fan is this guy? Assuming it is his poster.

'That so?'

'I'm just here for the waters,' Beckman offered.

'The waters? What waters? We're in the desert,' the founder replied after a pause.

'I was misinformed.'

Taylor (last name) flashed a knowing smile and gestured to the chair. 'How can I help, Mr Spiers?'

'I'd like to hire a P.I.'

'Then you've come to the best place in town.'

Because this was the *only* place? Or, given what Beckman had observed to date, perhaps the town was as replete with private investigators as it was with inert gas-filled illuminations?

'Starting immediately, if possible,' he clarified.

'Certainly. That okay, Reba?'

The woman looked over. Beckman stared at her until he'd confirmed he was staring at what he thought he was staring at, which had taken such a duration of confirmatory staring to confirm.

She had a glass eye. Luckily for her, it was the only glass thing in Sunrise that didn't glow red. Or green. Or blue. Or a million other colors.

'Sure,' she said, ignoring his now-completed stare. 'D'you want to scooch over and give me the details, sir?'

Beckman went to rise, but the chair had wheels, and the floor was wooden, so he did what any other self-respecting eternal nine-year-old would do and pushed himself across to her. He refrained from saying "Wheeeee!" because this was a serious matter. Lives were at stake (not really).

'What's the subject's name?' she asked, fingers poised above her keyboard.

'Carlton—' He hit the buffers.

Of course, Carlton would have a surname. Only he couldn't remember it. Because he'd never been told. Unless, of course, it *was* the lanky guy's last name? Possibly? Carlton was fine as a last name. Like… Beckman. Usually.

His mind raced. His gaze flicked between Reba and Zebedee. They were on tenterhooks. There was something else there, too—like they were making efforts to avoid looking at each other. A private joke in the making? Were they trying not to make each other corpse?

Throw me a bone, folks. How many Carltons can there be in Sunrise? Or is that another thing here? The dozen or so people I've met are the only people not *called Carlton?*

'Carlton drives a Mustang. Tall. Glasses,' he offered.

'Carlton Cooper.' Reba made a note. 'And what's the nature of the concern or assignment?'

'Infidelity.' He didn't say it; the word just emerged from his mouth. He wanted it back. He wanted to reach out and stuff the naughty word back down his throat. And yet….

'Twenty-four-hour surveillance?' she asked.

He nodded, assuming this was the way to go. On the flip side, he might as well have been Emperor Caligula, throwing swords into the sea to defeat Neptune.

Onwards they went, through the mercifully brief customer registration rigmarole, to the two-hundred bucks daily fee declaration, handing over two hundred as a deposit, and finally to the receiving of Reba's business card.

With the wall clock indicating 12:55, he exchanged handshakes with both people, outwardly business-like, inwardly wondering what on God's green earth he was doing, and passed out onto the street.

At least Reba would be keeping an eye on Carlton.

He slid inside the Chevy and purred up the hill towards Lolita's place.

The Lincoln pulled out and followed.

CHAPTER 16

1002 Edison Avenue struck him as a cross between the Psycho house and the Disney castle, and its position up a sloping drive on a prominent rocky plateau encompassing five houses did nothing to dim this impression.

He slid the lever into P and checked the parking brake. Of course, it was only Tyler's car, should it roll away, but any collateral damage down the line would be more worrying. Plus, he'd just sprung for a new left rear tire and wanted to at least get decent mileage out of it before Tyler tracked him down and demanded they un-Freaky Friday their vehicles.

Lolita's front garden (and soon jointly Carlton's, he guessed) was beautifully manicured. The lawn flourished the lushest shade of what he believed a lush green to be. Three pine-cone cacti reached to the heavens.

The house was painted his version of New England blue. There were shutters, mostly closed.

It was a very decently sized place. The Egyptian artefacts business treated her well. Or possibly Carlton did, at least financially. But it was unlikely she'd be a kept woman. She didn't seem the type; more likely to be the one who wore the pants (even though she wore swing dresses).

In the drive sat a Miata. He'd expected a pristine decades-old T-bird in peppermint or possibly mauve.

There wasn't a single neon light on the place. This alone equated to Sunrise's definition of "quirky".

As time waited for no man, he terminated the solo show-around tour and approached the entrance. As he reached for the bell pull, the door opened.

Her head was angled to one side and the voice stern. 'You show up this late for all your appointments, Beckman?'

He checked his watch.

13:01.

'Gotcha,' she said, flashing a smirk that instantly calmed his hackles.

'I had business in town,' he said.

Saving your engagement, likely as not. Thanks all the same.

She ushered him in.

Unsurprisingly, the hall was outfitted like downtown Cairo, back aways in history when folks walked funny and the guys wore miniskirts.

Through the lounge, which was mostly ditto. Back in a circle to the kitchen diner.

On the table lay a spread like the Pharaoh was coming. He took a wild guess that the way to Carlton's heart, as it was for many, was through his stomach.

Unless she's had it catered?

Yet, it was a fancy kitchen for a baking kind of person.

'I did eat this year already.'

'You didn't see the artefact you're moving,' she replied.

It stood in the kitchen beyond, against the wall, as tall as himself, and rectangular. It appeared to be made of solid stone.

'Thought it would be delivered outside.'

She followed his gaze and sniggered. Then she went to the vast casket, found a handhold in the front, and swung it open. She pulled out two chilled beers and closed the door.

'Oh, snap,' he chided. 'The box you wanted moving is outside, huh?'

She nodded, holding in her amusement, and tentatively offered him a beer.

'Or do you not drink on the job?'

'Mr Malvolio would kill anyone soon as look at them for breaking any of the rules. But that's not one of the rules.' He prised off the cap and drank. 'Racking up the sales to fill his bank account, though? Definitely a rule. The main one.'

She tore off the cap and drank. 'You're a salesman—you have to make sales. That's kind of 101.'

'If you ever meet the guy, you'd get the picture.'

She led him over to the table and sat opposite. They dug in.

'So why do it?'

He shrugged, tearing the best off a rib. 'It's a job.'

'A life, more like.'

He shrugged again. 'It's a life.'

'You think you'd be more excited about what you do. Faces are lighting up around town. It's a hell of a thing. If that's what witch doctors are selling now, I say bring it on.'

He devoured a handful of sweet potato fries. 'I guess.'

'Hell, Beckman, you're Number Two on the salesman list. You have to be good at it. Doesn't that fire you up?'

'Shooting for Number One fires me up.'

'Good. Most guys will do it for the commission, the chance to travel the country, maybe even the superiority of screwing a customer over, seeing the patter break down defences. Maybe it's a small dick issue.'

She tore into a chicken wing. An eyebrow crept above her left lens.

You were so much easier to talk to with your glasses off. What is it with that?

'But that's most *other* guys, right?' she continued.

'The product sells itself—you know that.' He deliberately dodged the question/inference/innuendo. 'Career success is not the same as peddling out a string of boxes. Rank and promotion—that's the achievement.'

'Gotta please the old man?' She slugged her beer.

Didn't everyone want to make their parents proud?

Best to share. What harm might come of it? She had her head screwed firmly on. Was there even a life lesson here? She'd endured being ripped off. She had motivations for her actions. So did he. Everyone did. The question was whether a person knew them or was willing to admit them, especially to virtual strangers.

He watched her for a second, tried to set her looks apart from her good nature, and resolved that another friend in Sunrise wouldn't be a bad thing to have.

'He never... achieved his potential,' he replied.

'Military man?'

'How'd you guess?'

'A rank and file guy. The way you walk, hold yourself. "Stand up straight, son".' She studied the top of his head. 'Even the haircut.'

'A chip off the old block?'

'You tell me.'

'Each time he didn't make promotion, we moved so he could try a different army base, which happened often. I guess he never got the picture that he just wasn't good enough.'

'So, the million-dollar question is, are *you* good enough?'

'I tried and failed eleven years running. Difference is, I didn't run.'

'Even though you hate the place.'

'"Hate" is a big word. I'm hardly ever at the place. They say Malvolio is worth a hundred million. Every day, we build his stack higher. The payback is you top the league, it's milk and honey baby, and all the graft is worth it. So they say. It better be.'

'Then what would you do?'

'Honestly? Not the first clue.'

'Well, at least you're in control of your destiny. You have a shot at what you want.'

'Here's an idea. Why not marry Carlton, get a great prenup, divorce him, take half the company?'

'Wow, Beckman, I wouldn't take you for someone so scheming.'

Don't mention the Chevy. No, that was circumstance. We are cool with that. Repeat: we are cool with that. Still, best not to mention it.

'I don't like people getting screwed over.'

'How in hell is a nice guy like you not married?'

That took him by surprise. Still, the answer was obvious. 'Because being a ship that passes once a week is not a way of building a life.'

'But if you got Number One?'

He shrugged. 'Ask me when it happens.'

'Which could be three days, three years, or never.'

'Never? So, the pep talk before was just blowing smoke?'

'Who cares what I think? I'm an antiques dealer from a small town. I've known you barely two days. Question is, do *you* think you can do it?'

'Every year.'

'And this is, what, your twelfth year?'

'Call me Mr Tenacity. Or Mr Deluded.'

'How about this. Why did you ask for Room 12 again?'

He wasn't sure which riled him more—the coincidence or the fact she was aware of his every move. Could it be Lolita who was running the Lincoln guy? Really? All lunch and interesting conversation and endless referrals, but really she felt, deep down, he was not only an outsider but a naturally untrustworthy product peddler, too?

It must have shown in his expression.

'It's okay,' she continued, 'It's a small town. Word gets around. Especially when you're a guy people need to find.'

He remained unsure.

'Come on.' She rose. 'This is a meal-for-chores deal. You've got eleven years of moving boxes around. What's one more?'

CHAPTER 17

'Afternoon, Mr Beckman, how are you?'

I feel older than Yoda, and I've got aches in places I didn't know I had.

'Upright, Kinsey, and wondering how. Is there a chiropractor in town?'

'As luck would have it, she's in the building right now.'

'You have a concierge service?' he asked in disbelief.

'No, she's waiting for you in the lounge.'

Beckman's eyes narrowed. 'She's not related to Saul Paul, by any chance?'

'No.'

'Did Lolita call you up?'

'No?' Now Kinsey himself was approaching Beckman's Bemusement Quotient.

Beckman looked towards the doors to the Guest Lounge. Hubbub seeped out.

A penny dropped.

'Do I need to go out to the car first?' he asked tentatively.

Kinsey gave a slight bow from the shoulders. 'I think that would be wise, Mr Beckman.'

Fifty sales in five minutes officially marked a PB. It just shaded his previous record of fifty in a whole day.

Ordinarily, he would have punched the air in delight, but the manoeuvre would probably have snapped his fragile spine.

He'd identified the requisite practitioner early on in the rugby scrum and asked her to stay behind.

Now, he lay flat out on his hotel bed, being tended to by Miss North.

Miss North was very nice. She wore flat shoes, no make-up, had peroxide hair, and proceeded to remove his all-encompassing pain by inflicting more pain.

If he possessed a big brown box equivalent of his little brown box, which removed pain from one's entire being, he would have immediately availed himself of the product. But he didn't, so he couldn't, and he hadn't.

Instead, he put faith in Miss North's assertion that she counted "many happy customers". She didn't explicitly say they were happy *mobile* customers. Still, as he had acquired a similar litany of disciples for his own (well, Pegasus') miracle cure, he felt a kindred spirit with the chiropractor, which continued even as he wailed in pain at her every touch.

The shine of the apparent connection soon faded when he parted with payment: he got rewarded for *removing* pain from his customers; she for *adding* it. Nonetheless, it wouldn't hurt to try the remedy (apart from the hurting aspect), and, on balance, he didn't hold a grudge against Lolita for buttering him up with a feast and then ageing him ten years in ten minutes.

He lay on the bed, mulling The Carlton Issue.

Then promptly fell asleep.

He woke with a start, cursing himself for slacking with so much at stake.

He sprang from the bed, then wished he hadn't. Miss North had only been partially successful in removing the temporary advancement in age.

As he showered, his mind fell to math. Could the Salesman race, in fact, be winnable, or would he be running himself ragged for nothing?

He finished in the cubicle, pulled clothes on, and drew the chair up to the room's small desk. There, on hotel paper and with undoubtedly the most slick complimentary pen he'd ever encountered, he worked the sums: Tyler's and his sales figures, the gap, and what each man held in their current vehicles (given the impromptu swap).

In the end, after a double-check, Beckman's shoulders and spirits fell. On past performance, Tyler would almost certainly sell out his stock. If that happened, the Smooth Operator couldn't be overhauled in the rankings.

It was late Wednesday. The end of the final sales week loomed.

He mulled, chewing on the end of the pen. It was undoubtedly the tastiest complimentary pen he'd ever encountered.

Did the week end at five on Friday? Or only the *working* week? The regular five-day stretch for Joe Schmoe.

Neither he nor anyone else at Pegasus had ever been invested enough to graft on into the weekend. Why would they? Plenty of miles for barely adequate financial recompense during those weekdays anyway—why work for free on rest days?

But for a glimmer of hope? If….

He grabbed his phone and dialled.

Wilbur's voice was expectedly accompanied by a backing track. It sounded like Taylor Swift, but he wasn't sure and wouldn't admit to knowing, anyway.

'Hi B, what gives?'

'Cutting to the chase, Wilbur, any status update on Monday's delivery?'

'Still Monday.'

'Not Sunday?'

'Monday.'

'Shoot.'

'Yeah.'

'Where's it coming from?'

'Great Lakes somewhere.'

'Shoot.'

'Yeah.'

Beckman mused, pensively tapping the pen on the desk. It was undoubtedly the most tappable complimentary pen he'd ever encountered.

There was no time to get that far across the country and back in time, even if the supplier stayed open at the weekend.

'Still there, B?'

'Yeah.'

'I shouldn't say this, but…,' Wilbur said conspiratorially.

'Yeah?'

'Esmond Belcher's car is on the lot.'

'Yeah?'

'No next of kin, so it got recovered here.'

'Okay.'

'He filled up the day before he, you know….'

'Yeah.'

'Flash, bang, crackle.'

'Yeah.' Beckman got the picture. 'So?'

'So, I might know where the keys are.'

It only took a split-second for the penny to drop. 'You think…?'

'Maybe.'

'You reckon Malvolio will catch on?'

'Sure of it. Mercenary like that wouldn't want stock lying idle when it could be going out on the road, making him richer.'

'So, I'm doing him a favour. Kinda,' Beckman suggested hopefully.

'Works for me.'

'Wilbur, anyone goes near that car, call me. Stall them. Shoot them. Whatever. I'm coming back.'

'Sure, B.'

Beckman hung up quickly.

He snatched his (Tyler's) keys and clattered down the hotel stairs to the Chevy. Safety first, he unloaded the remainder of stock from the trunk and carried it, tottering, back to his room.

Then he grabbed his overnight bag, double-locked the room door, and pelted back downstairs.

The falling sun was flirting with the urban skyline as he drew into the Pegasus parking lot.

It was quiet; there were three other cars on site. The owner of one of them exited the building. Not the one he'd hoped.

Mr Malvolio carried Bruno in a cage case. This was the time of day when a person was most safe from its venomous jaws. However, Malvolio's toxic words were more often the nerve-shredder. As he made a beeline for Beckman, there was proof positive the cane was only there for show. Whilst he wasn't a quick man, he had little need for it as an aid—he was more likely to use it for an impromptu tap dance routine.

'Good evening, sir.'

'Spiers, isn't it?'

Beckman often wondered whether this apparent unfamiliarity was a front. They'd known each other eleven years, and there were a mere forty other salesmen. Mr Malvolio appeared far from senile—it was infinitely more likely that he used the mechanism as a modicum of belittlement, mental torture for his charges.

'Yes, sir.'

'Any dead chickens for me?'

'No,' he said dejectedly.

'I don't hold court with slackers, Spiers.'

'No, sir.'

'Sort it out. Plenty of young salesmen have their resumés on my desk. I don't owe you a job, Spiers.'

'Understood.'

'I expect some excellent figures end of Friday.'

'Absolutely.'

'Good.'

With a hard stare, Mr Malvolio terminated the discourse and traipsed over to his vast automobile. It was, unsurprisingly, black. It was also allegedly bulletproof.

'Mr Malvolio?'

With a theatrical sigh, the CEO turned. 'What?' he barked.

'Technically, the thirtieth is Sunday. Can I post sales over the weekend?'

'Do what you damn well like, Spiers. Just don't expect overtime. We banned it in '95.'

'Understood, sir.'

Malvolio waited in case there was more, but there wasn't. He resumed his trudge.

'Goodnight, sir.'

A grunt.

Beckman turned his back on the encounter and went to locate Wilbur.

When they re-emerged from the building a few minutes later, Beckman scanned the lot to check the coast was clear: the mechanical behemoth and its owner had mercifully departed.

'Anyone else call?' he asked.

Wilbur scratched his head and pulled up the rim of today's cap, which proclaimed "As If" in a red-stitched blocky font.

'Hubbard.'

'About the Monday delivery?'

'Yeah.'

'And?'

'He gave up. He's only sixth anyway. Like I'd ever stiff you, Beckman, but no point doing it for a guy who can't scrape fifth.'

'Gotta ask—what do you get from helping me?'

'Honestly?'

'Always.'

'Remember Ramage?' Wilbur asked.

'Do I ever.'

'Thought I had a thing there.'

'She was a good bookkeeper.'

'Great ass, too.'

'Couldn't say I noticed,' Beckman lied. Everybody had noticed her ass. He wasn't the only one who'd chased it. He knew where Wilbur's story was headed. 'Tyler beat you to the punch?'

'The guy has a knack for subversion.'

'Tell me about it. He'd have shot Tuco, not the rope.'

They approached Belcher's Cadillac. As Wilbur's hand went into his pocket, the sound of rubber on tarmac washed across the parking lot from the service road. They turned.

A white Buick, 12 BECK, was being hastily piloted to their position.

'I never breathed a word,' Wilbur said.

Beckman sighed, boiling inside. 'He's like a vulture. A rutting vulture.'

The car slowed, with surprising care, to a halt beside them. Beckman ran his gaze over it. Tyler hadn't hit anything more substantial than a fly during his tenure. Amazingly, the guy did have some level of rectitude. The question was, would that extend to restraint vis-à-vis physical retribution?

Tyler hopped from the car and, without offering either man a word, inspected his steed with interest. Satisfied, he came over.

'That was a dirty trick, Becky.'

'All I want's a fair fight.'

'I'll bet. You keep it under fifty-five?'

'Did you?'

Tyler avoided answering. He held out his palm. Beckman tendered the keys. Tyler snatched them away and returned the favour.

Okay, what gives? This is not the Tyler I know.

The guy popped his trunk, found it empty, went to the Buick, and emptied its modest stack of boxes back into the rightful place. Beckman remained relaxed; it had become Tyler's stock, and the guy was entitled to take it. He felt rightly smug that he'd left his own balance of boxes in a safe place not even Tyler would find. Otherwise, the booty would have been sequestered by a guy who showed a sixth sense Saul would be proud of.

Both trunk lids were slammed closed. Tyler eased into his Chevy, fired it up, blipped the throttle for bullish effect, and then climbed out and left the door open.

He reached inside his jacket.

There was a gun in his hand.

Beckman and Wilbur leapt in the air.

'Relax, Becky. What, you think I'll shoot a guy over that stunt? I'm not stupid, you know.'

Beckman did indeed try to relax. Wilbur, however, inched away from the fray.

'But I will be Number One,' Tyler concluded. Then he took careful aim and shot out both of the Buick's right-side tires. He checked his wristwatch. 'Enjoy your walk to the tire shop. If it's open.'

Then he flashed a smirk, hopped into his Chevy, and burned away towards the low golden skyline.

Silence descended.

'I'm not sure I earn enough for this circus,' Wilbur suggested.

'Yeah. What a douche.'

'I hear he lives at home.'

'Don't we all?'

'With his mother.'

'His mother?'

'Yeah.'

'Tyler?'

'Tyler.'

'Sure?'

Wilbur shrugged. 'A rumour.'

'Wow.'

'Yeah.'

'Think that's why he's an ass?'

'Search me.'

'I guess.'

'Yeah.'

'Any chance he's not an ass? You know. Outside of this…,' Beckman cast his eyes around, 'World.'

'Playground bully?'

'Just a thought.'

'We all got a shtick,' Wilbur said.

Beckman (1) tried not to look at Wilbur's hat, and (2) wondered if he was interesting enough to have a shtick of his own.

Nope, nothing quirky about me. Just a regular guy.

'Maybe I should be real nice to him. Like, kill him with kindness,' he mused.

'One of two ways it'll go.'

'I guess.'

'Yeah.'

Both nodded, little the wiser.

He looked down at his steed's two deflated tires. Too far for Saul, that much was certain.

He held out his hand. A new key was duly deposited there.

Wilbur followed him over as he unlocked the late and crispy Belcher's maroon Caddy and opened the trunk. It was about three-quarters full.

'This isn't stealing, right?'

'I was only going to put it back in stock.'

Then he studied his sorry-looking ride. Weighed up the situation. He cracked open the Caddy's door, plopped into the seat, and fired the engine. He contemplated the litter-scattered interior. The odo read 134,994.

Wilbur appeared at the door, proffering Beckman's overnight bag, which had been left on the tarmac.

'His casket's too short to reach the pedals now, huh?'

'It's not stealing if nobody, technically, owns it,' Wilbur replied.

'Let's hope, huh?'

Beckman took his bag and dumped it on the passenger seat. Then he pulled out his wallet and handed over a fist of notes.

'Malvolio will write you up for littering the place.' Wilbur indicated the Buick.

'Yeah.'

'I'll get it fixed.'

'Thanks.'

'You and Ramage too, huh?'

'Yeah.'

A moment's silence. 'You're an okay guy, Beckman.'

'So I'm told. You too, Wilbur.'

'Take it easy.'

'See you Monday, I guess.'

'As Number One, okay?'

'I'll do my best.'

He tossed Wilbur the keys to the injured Buick, eased the door shut, and trickled out of the parking lot. Sunset was on the way. It had been a long day, and despite the Caddy's plush but creased seats, he still ached. The bed was calling.

Sunrise would be plenty early enough to aim again for Sunrise.

CHAPTER 18

The morning's burning white sun fought to escape past the Caddy's faded grey visor and challenge Beckman's sunglasses, so he angled it down a few more degrees and kept dodging the glare.

Soon enough, he reached the prescribed freeway exit and struck out down the arrowing, undulating blacktop towards his destination. The orb now behind and to the left, he stowed the visor and eventually took to scanning the road for the required turnoff.

Yesterday, he'd had the brainwave to note the interval between the freeway and Sunrise intersection at a steady fifty-seven. Now, the clock was closing in on that marker. He began to search the roadside margin ahead for a glint of light on glass, shards of deliverance, the apparent hotline to Saul Paul.

With the timer on his phone chiming, he slowed and deliberately eased two wheels onto the roadside, trawling for a flat. After two minutes with no luck, he pulled Crispy Belcher's Caddy across to the wrong side of the deserted road and hoped for deflation there.

No luck.

He braked to a stop, jumped out, and traversed the scraggy tarmac's edge, scouring the ground for something sharp. He soon came across a broken bottle, which he took and placed underneath the front tire.

Then he started the car and rolled gently forwards, ear cocked.

Nothing happened.

He reversed slowly and tried again.

No dice either way.

'Oh, snap.'

Sighing, sensing the inexorable rise of the sun sucking precious minutes from his time-limited sales schedule, he walked the roadside again, begging for inspiration. Sadly, today Captain Irony bestrode the state like an overconfident cockerel; not one of the rocks was sharp enough.

Eventually, Beckman found another sturdy shard of glass and went full-on Psycho shower scene on the radial.

God chuckled.

He kicked the tire.

God laughed at his toe pain.

He threw back his head and bellowed at the sky.

God smirked at his plight.

He exhaled through gritted teeth and eyed the car with burning intensity.

Then God had to suck it up because Beckman had a flash of inspiration.

He jumped into the car, span it around, and barrelled back towards the freeway junction at not fifty-seven.

In the Town of Six Sales, he cruised the main retail strips until he found what he'd hoped for. He left the Caddy out front and entered the emporium that was Quinn's Arsenal.

Not knowing precisely what he wanted, beyond (1) effective, (2) inexpensive, and (3) guaranteed not to explode and take his face off, he gave Possibly-Quinn a cockamamie story that alluded to the three (bullet) points and was duly directed towards something that was unarguably a pistol and probably a specific type with a detailed provenance he didn't give a rat's ass about.

As Beckman possessed ID and cash, and Possibly-Quinn didn't get any vibes as to why he shouldn't sell this clearly responsible and sober individual a gun, the transaction was concluded.

Beckman walked out like he was carrying the Ark of the Covenant. It was the first gun he'd owned. It was also the first gun he'd ever held. Dad would be so proud that his son's balls had finally dropped.

Presently, around the correct time and distance down the appalling monotony of Infinity Highway, he pulled over, praying that something wouldn't give him a flat tire and make the whole round trip a waste. Luckily, it transpired that Captain Irony hadn't supped his morning coffee yet and hence wasn't totally with the program.

Beckman hopped out, loaded a single bullet into the box-fresh pistol, estimated the best position to stand to balance (1) hitting the tire and (2) not getting caught in the flashback, and took aim.

Blam.

Wild Beckman Hickok gazed at the sorry squashed rubber mess, checked around (because he was an idiot) to ensure nobody could see, then blew across the barrel of the gun. He would have twirled and holstered it, except he hadn't sprung for a holster and would likely trap a finger in the trigger guard and have some embarrassing explaining to do when he saw Lolita again.

Hmmm. Why do you care what she thinks?

He leant into the car, opened the cubby, and eased the gun into its hiding place.

Then he snuggled the box of ammunition in there too and flapped the plastic door shut.

There was a knock on the roof.

'You change cars like I change underwear.'

'Yeah, but a tire's a tire. Long as it keeps you in neon and snakeskin, huh?'

'May have to start a Customer of the Month program.'

'Or leave me a map to this turnoff,' Beckman proposed, as they speared off down the Sunrise access road.

Saul regarded him like he'd suggested Mother Theresa had been a cocaine smuggler.

The subsequent walk from Saul's garage into town was interrupted, as before, with sufferers needing Beckman's ministry. Seldom had he experienced sales as easy as taking candy from a baby. In Sunrise, the baby lay asleep, and the candy already packed in a carrier bag by the unlocked front door.

All he needed to do was maintain the pace until Sunday evening, hope his math was correct, and pray that Tyler Asswipe Quittle didn't (1) get a flat nearby, (2) have a secret stash of his own to inflate his stock level. Of course, he also prayed—because nothing was off the menu right then—that (3) another one of Mr Malvolio's minions didn't get abducted by aliens whilst standing outside Tyler's house, leaving behind a full trunk and keys in the ignition.

Without that, it looked dangerously like Beckman really did have an outside chance this year.

Life, liberty, and the pursuit of happiness. Pursuit? Well, that had been chiefly a ball-ache. Actual happiness? It was unlikely to suck.

Feeling industrious, he crossed the street and went into Taylor's.

Reba was poring over images on a computer screen. He took a seat. The pictures were of two people he recognised from a specific red Mustang in a certain gas station.

'What's the story?' he asked.

'We're not in the business of conclusions, Mr Spiers. We're in the evidence game. Conclusions equal lawsuits, which equal no more Taylor's, which equals Reba Garrity getting her daughter taken away.' She fixed him a half-glassy look of professional solemnity.

'So, you have any evidence?'

'Sure,' she said brightly.

She scrolled through the photographs. He'd expected they'd be in black and white because movie gumshoes were his only frame of reference, but they were in color… or to almost everyone else on earth, they were.

The photographs she'd snapped showed unarguably incriminating evidence against Lolita's beau, Carlton.

His spirits sank. 'Who's that?'

'Wanda Whack.'

'Who is …?'

'Daughter of Walter Whack, the guy who owns EVI Lighting.'

That didn't sound good. Not good at all.

Not only was Lolita's love life in trouble, but her family business might be compromised too.

Why the hell hadn't he just stayed on the freeway?

CHAPTER 19

As Beckman walked down towards Saul's, his bag was steadily emptied by passers-by, yet it still felt heavy. Everything did. In a daze, he didn't even clock the Lincoln.

Elvis might have walked past, large as life, and he wouldn't have noticed.

The horns of his dilemma were sharp enough to cut paper.

It felt like mere seconds had passed by the time he reached the forecourt.

The third new tire in as many days adorned this latest of 'his' vehicles. He looked through into the garage office, where Saul chatted on the phone. He eased himself onto the Caddy's bonnet and felt its sun-drenched heat soak into his definitely-charcoal slacks. His look was a thousand-yard stare.

Five seconds, five minutes, or five hours later, Saul appeared at his side, cutting a jovial figure Beckman almost wanted to put a fist through. Luckily, the part of his brain that screamed Dumb Idea hadn't gone AWOL.

'All done for you,' Saul said.

Beckman robotically pulled out his wallet, counted the bills, and handed them across.

'Nice doing business with you too,' Saul jibed.

He snapped out of it. 'Sorry, buddy.'

'Death in the family? Tyler call? Get a customer complaint?'

He shook his head.

'Someone in town piss you off?' Saul guessed.

'I got a problem.'

'What shape is it?'

'Huh?'

'What shape is it? Box-shaped? Guy-shaped?' He laid a paternal hand on Beckman's shoulder. 'Gal-shaped?'

Beckman met the proprietor's one eye. Saul understood. He checked the ancient dial high up on the frontage of the certainly-whitewashed garage.

'Buy Uncle Saul a spot of lunch?'

Knowing alternatives were scant, Beckman agreed.

Saul waved at the office, behind whose glass Pandora sat. He gesticulated the international sign for Lunch, and she flashed a thumbs up, so he swung open the Caddy's driver door.

'You've got the look of a guy who'll plough the sidewalk, accident or design.'

Beckman got the message and walked round to the passenger side.

Back home (defined as the place in which he laid his non-existent hat with slightly greater regularity than any other spot), he swore the guy who serviced his Buick put at least ten miles on it every time, some probably in reverse or on two wheels. Conversely, Saul treated the Caddy—even though he didn't know it wasn't his passenger's property—like an injured swan. He could have chauffeured rock stars. Celebrities. Miss Daisy.

The short trip up the street barely cooled the interior, so Our Buck's provided welcome respite from the midday sun.

After mandatory small talk with Buck, they took their beers to a table. Beckman's was not of the root variety.

'Who is she?'

'Jeez, Saul, you sound like my father.'

From memory. Distant memory. And a lot less of an ass than the real thing.

'I thought we were going with "Uncle". I didn't get laid near early enough to be your dad. So, who?'

'It's not like that.'

'You've got a face longer than Seabiscuit.'

Beckman sighed. 'I found something out.'

'Figures. You look like you're carrying the Washington Monument.'

'Something that could hurt someone. Or help someone. Both, maybe. Two people. More than two people.' He took a long draw of his beer and shook his head slowly.

'And this Secretariat look is because you're the stranger round here, it's none of your beeswax, and you'll get run out of town.'

'I figured. Or I'll do the right thing and keep my mouth shut, and who knows what down the line.'

'If you reckon that's the right thing, then there's your answer.'

'That would make this one cheap date.'

The big man shrugged. 'What d'you want me to say?'

'"It's nothing"?'

'Is it?'

'Doesn't look like it.'

'Is it about Buck?' Saul bobbed his head towards the bar.

'No.'

'Me?'

'No.'

'Then, anyone else in town hits you, you got a fighting chance of not eating through a straw the rest of your life.'

'That's comforting.'

Saul shrugged gently. 'Call it as I see it.'

'But you'd both rally round to protect most people from... false allegations.'

'If they're false, why're we here?' Saul took a slug of beer.

'Because I'm the stranger, and maybe it *is* none of my beeswax.'

'So, this table for two is not really about anyone here, it's about Beckman's conscience?'

'That just makes me sound like a needy douche.'

Saul gave a small sigh. 'Okay, here's the thing. There's the kind of boss who pisses on the little guy and counts his stash....'

'Not sure the relevance here, but amen.'

'...and on the flip side, there's the chief who sets a good example, does the job, and, even when he goes to hang with a buddy, still only takes an hour on his lunch break.' Saul made a point of checking the wall clock. 'So, if I throw you a rope, maybe you want to tie up somewhere near the point of this. What's eating you up?'

Beckman needed to stop dancing around the edge of the floor. After all, a problem shared was a problem halved. Someone else needed to know what Carlton was up to... or at least tell Beckman it wasn't what it appeared to be.

He pulled out his phone and, wordlessly, gave his sounding board a look at one image from Reba's collection. Yet, inside, his organs cartwheeled.

Saul drank it in, then reached out a fat finger and swiped. Then again. He considered Beckman, then the phone, then mid-air.

'Taylor's?' he asked. Beckman nodded. 'On account of what?'

'I saw the two of them at a gas station a couple of days back.'

'His car, I see.'

Beckman nodded again, revelling in the fact that he hadn't yet been handed his ass, yet knowing he still wasn't out of the woods.

The lunch plates arrived. They both soundlessly tucked in. Beckman thought it best not to interrupt the jury while it was considering its verdict.

Saul paused about three-quarters of the way through his food.

'Why d'you do it?'

There was no side to the question, merely curiosity. Beckman's motivation didn't alter the facts of the case. Yet, deep down, Beckman knew an element of self-interest had provided the reason. Saul would work it out before long.

Honesty was the best policy. Especially since dishonesty was what he was railing against.

'I don't like cheats. Or what they do to people.'

'Who does?'

'The cheats.'

'And Taylor's crew, I guess. Out of business without them.'

'All part of the food chain.'

'So, what's your move?' Saul wiped his lips on the napkin with surprising decorum.

'If I'd known, I could have saved myself twenty bucks.'

Saul raised his hand, gave Buck the sign for Two More Beers, and casually said, 'Twenty-five.'

'Plus a tip.'

Saul eyed Beckman. 'So?'

'There's more.'

'Like how?'

'He was supposed to be at a supplier yesterday, but he was at EVI.'

'It's not illegal.'

'But it's not odd? Carlton is buddying up to the opposition then lying about it?'

'There's an explanation for everything.'

'Want to give me one?' Beckman asked.

'Takeover negotiations?'

'Discussed with Wanda, not Walter? At the factory, maybe, but the rifle range?' He indicated the picture on the phone. 'On a nice little day out for two?'

'Maybe he's softening her up?'

'Pumping her for information, more like it.'

'I don't think he's that dumb,' Saul suggested, breaking into his second drink.

'How well do you know him?'

'He's a straight enough guy. If he's got a business motivation, it's a down-the-line, financially stable, logical one.'

'Doesn't mean it's not out of self-interest.'

'Beckman, he's marrying the CEO's daughter, meaning he'll get control of Milan Enterprises. It's pretty transparent.'

'Well, there's a thing. The right-thinking guy in me says he's doing it because he loves Lolita. Odd way to go about it. Suspicious, right? But what do I know? Maybe that's not how love works in Sunrise.'

'You should watch your conclusions,' Saul cautioned. 'They were dating before he joined the company.'

'Okay, so I'll suck that up. I'm hardly steeped in local history. Bottom line—would you tell Lolita about this?'

Saul chewed on that for a while.

Beckman let him think—giving the guy a window into his pain—while his gaze roved outside. The Lincoln was on the edge of the shot.

'Saul?'

'I don't know.'

'No, not that. Whose navy Lincoln is that?'

Saul followed Beckman's gaze. 'Delmar.'

'Delmar's line of work?' Beckman asked, fearing the answer he had in mind.

'Gumshoe.'

'Oh, snap.' He shook his head and looked outside again. 'I hope Reba's a damn sight harder to pick out of a crowd.'

'Why d'you ask?'

'I know who one of Delmar's cases is.'

'How come?'

'It's me.'

CHAPTER 20

'So what skeletons is Delmar trying to find?' Saul asked.

'Search me.'

'And I would, too. Will I find anything I shouldn't?'

Beckman sighed, mulled it over. Only one skeleton jumped from the cupboard. 'That's not my car.'

'I know.'

'How——?' he began.

Saul shrugged. 'A guy knows. Well, a guy like me knows.'

'So, no more Okay Guy?'

'You'll have your reasons.'

'The Buick ... suffered some damage.'

'You steal it, the Caddy?'

'It's... a pool car.'

Saul's eyes narrowed a little. Then he gave a gentle nod of acquiescence. 'Okay. So, tell Delmar.'

'Why the hell——?' Beckman had a realisation. 'He's been tailing me since the day I got here. When I had the Buick.'

'Out of curiosity, the Chevy meantime, that a... pool car too?'

'Oh no. I absolutely stole that. Well, borrowed. Exchanged.'

Saul pulled a face. 'You bring me photos of Carlton, a guy I thought I knew, then this? You're walking a dangerous line.'

Without another way out of the cul-de-sac, Beckman ran the Tyler Quittle story. Saul slowly drained his beer and waited for The End.

He gave his verdict. 'Accused pleads self-defence, Your Honour.'

'I'll take the knockdown, honest to God, Saul. If I'm not wanted here, say the word.'

'I'm no sheriff.'

'If I get a flat, would you pick me up?'

'In a second.'

'Literally or metaphorically?'

Saul smiled. 'You wanted my advice?' He pointed at the image on the phone. 'What you have there is as good as C4 if it's what it looks like. I'm not sure you can get far enough away to use it without catching shrapnel yourself. And, much as I still reckon you're an Okay Guy, I won't take the fall planting a bomb for you.'

'That's your advice?'

'For half of twenty-five bucks, yeah.'

'I'll spring for pie?' Beckman suggested.

'I have four minutes left on my break.'

'I'd buy you dinner, but then people would really talk.'

'Even take pictures, it seems.'

'So, thanks anyway.'

Saul rose. 'I'll say this. Show it to Buck. No flannel, no side.'

'For why?'

'Buck kinda carries a flak jacket where Lolita is concerned.' He tipped the brim of an invisible hat and left.

Beckman let out a sigh that lasted about a week. He sipped his beer. His gaze moved between it and the figure in the navy Lincoln outside.

Delmar, huh? Good luck getting evidence, fathead. Reba's the one with the real juicy case. You've got nothing on me.

The environs darkened.

Buck eased himself into the seat opposite.

Beckman's face fell. 'Throw me out for loitering?'

'That'd be counterproductive.'

'Like how?'

'You loiter, you spend. Plus, I get the feeling if somebody spies you in the window, they'll come in, you'll sell them a magic box, maybe they'll stay, could be they'll spend.'

'So, I'm your honey trap.'

'Want a percentage?'

'Hell, all I want right now is a friend.'

'That, I can do.'

Beckman weighed this. 'You're pretty tight with Lolita?'

'We get along.'

'That covers a lot of ground.'

Buck glanced at his own ample John Goodman frame. 'I cover a lot of ground, period.'

Without a suitable response to give, Beckman moved swiftly on. 'Seems like she burns pretty hot, come the need.'

'She doesn't suffer fools, I guess.'

'And you?'

'Why, you hankering to be one?' Buck asked, expression unwavering.

Million-dollar question. Billion. Trillion.

He changed tack. 'When's the wedding?'

Buck shrugged. 'Carlton? No date set, far as I know. Is that what this is about? Planning to go all Benjamin Bratt on the big day?'

The shock of the accusation made him sit back. His mind raced. Then he looked Buck square on. 'I'd be a fool to pull a stunt like that.'

Buck stared directly back. 'Yeah. You would.'

'Because you and Lolita… get along.'

'Yeah.'

'And you want to do right by her.'

'Yeah.'

'And a guy who does wrong by her…?'

'Depends on the guy.'

Beckman took a deep breath. It was fifty-fifty on who would come out the bad guy in the next two minutes. He took a slow draw on his drink. He studied the room. There were a couple of dozen other customers.

This is Buck's place. He'd be crazy to murder anyone in broad daylight in front of so many witnesses.

Wouldn't he?

Heart clattering away, a million butterflies doing a mating dance, he pulled out his phone and located the required image.

'Do me a favour? Count to ten before you say anything.'

The man's brow furrowed in query, then he pulled a Whatever face.

Beckman put the phone on the table between them. Buck peered at the image.

As best as Beckman could tell, the overriding emotion was disappointment. He searched Buck's face and demeanour for anger, watched for flexed arms or balled fists. Either way, he tensed, flight or fight at DefCon 1.

After an eternity, Buck's eyes met his.

Beckman prayed for a quick death.

CHAPTER 21

After only a couple of seconds, Buck pointed at the half-inch in the bottom of Beckman's glass.

'You having another?' he asked, eyebrow raised in an unmistakeable and almost paternal look of disappointment.

Instantly, Beckman had the answer. 'No. Thanks.'

Buck rose. 'I'll see you around.' He walked away.

Beckman's heart continued to flutter. This was a good thing; alternatively, the organ could be sitting in the courtesy bowl in front of him, making the cob nuts pretty inedible while he bled out.

He allowed himself to calm down to DefCon 2.

The most important principle now was to stay in places with plenty of witnesses for, say, the rest of his natural life, and the rest of his natural life would have a good chance of being measured in decades and not minutes.

He sighed, dropped a mollifying horse-has-already-bolted ten buck tip, and took his leave.

The hot Thursday air swamped him as he ventured onto the street. He tried and failed to avoid registering Delmar. Then, quickly, he became distracted by a pony-tailed youth waving a ten-buck note.

So, the Earth keeps spinning, and ol' Beckman's still breathing.

If only this could keep up until Sunday night, then he'd get out of town— calmly or sneakily, whichever circumstance dictated—and wait for Malvolio to call with the good news first thing Monday. Afterwards, it wouldn't matter who in town took murderous umbrage at his daring to set a snoop to upset this most charmingly quirky of apple carts.

The matter was off his chest, a problem shared duly halved, and he walked more lightly along Main Street. The die was cast, and there was no use worrying about what the future held. He'd done what he considered to be a good deed. He'd come clean about it, sought counsel, and even offered hari kiri. If, despite it all, he went down, it would be while giving it his best shot. It would be the height of stupidity to quit a town where sales were strong and hence fall at the final competition hurdle because of misplaced fear.

Sunrise would either mean death or glory, and glory was an infinitely more enticing prospect.

He imbibed everything there was to see and smell, whatever limitless shade of grey. The butcher, the baker and, because why not, the candlestick maker. All with neons. Many, many neons.

He turned corners, block after block.

His shoulder bag emptied.

He traced a path back to the Caddy, restocked again, and resumed the unplanned trek.

The Gleesons made an appearance. Delmar, on foot now, was never far away. Sparse traffic flowed. Milan and EVI both had delivery vans on constant patrol.

A middle-aged woman in thick glasses took four of his boxes, promising to mail three of them to family across the country.

Wow. Next stop International. Mr Malvolio will be pleased.

He had a thought to hop in the Caddy and head over to Milan Enterprises, maybe have a shot at seeing what kind of operation Sexist Papa Jack was running. Except he'd likely shoot his mouth off and wind up making things, assuming they were already bad, worse. He was already attracting enough flies, and his luck couldn't hold forever.

Should he go to EVI and try to snoop first-hand on Wanda, hope to catch Carlton in an illicit visit? Legitimately, he could do either on the premise of seeking customers. Yet, as a lanky guy in full YMCA Construction Worker garb relieved him of another brown box, he reminded himself that in Sunrise, the mountain came to Mohammed, pretty much any time, any place.

Thirst gripped him.

Our Buck's remained off-limits while the silence of unresolved mystery continued to ring in his ears. Across the street stood an ice-cream parlour. He watched as Delmar observed him go inside.

The neon here provided the best show yet; the colors unapologetic—grey candy pink, grey lime green, grey lemon yellow. Plus, it suited the place. At Saul's? One or two gaudy displays would have been in keeping, not a couple of dozen. Buck's? Still overkill. Here? On the money.

He scanned the extensive blackboard menu behind the counter. They did root beer ice cream.

He debated it.

Did it have a chance of holding a frozen candle to Buck's liquid excellence?

He sprang for two scoops in a glass bowl.

Seated, he surveyed the room. He was almost the oldest person there. Nobody had headaches. The dessert just grazed Buck's beverage for taste; the king lived.

Half an hour passed. Still no customers.

He drummed his fingers on the table. Tomorrow, this wouldn't do. The final working day of the week provided an opportunity to be grasped. He must stop expecting success to fall in his lap; there were plenty of businesses outlying, plus the small residential areas. It would be hateful to reach the finish line and still have stock surplus; unforgivable for Tyler to come out on top by a cigarette-paper margin.

He only had to imagine Tyler's glib face, the gloating phone call from the airport, and that spurred him onwards.

Stop slacking, dummy.

He finished up and headed back onto the street.

A light van passed.

"ALWIN'S BLOOMS. HELPING MEN APOLOGISE SINCE 1976."

That's what he needed—mobile advertising.

Was there a signwriter in town? One way to find out. One foot in front of the other.…

He travelled about a hundred steps before he heard his name being called, and not in a Here's Money, Please Help Me way. More in Stop Thief! fashion. The voice rang familiar. He put two and two together, and suddenly four sucked as a number.

He turned.

Lolita strode towards him.

Going to DefCon 1.

He remembered how easily she'd coped with her part in moving the artefact. He foresaw a visit to the ER or at least another call to Miss North. Because a guy doesn't hit a lady, especially one whose engagement you've tried to torpedo.

She stopped more than an arm's reach distant. He hoped it would stay that way.

Her face was a cumulonimbus. 'What in holy hell do you think you're doing?'

'Trying to help.' That came out lame. He wished he'd rehearsed this part because he couldn't deny it had been likely.

'That the best you've got?' she asked.

Course not.

Now, come up with something great. Something convincing. Something honest, logical, non-threatening.

Come on, brain, you can do it.

'I thought you ought to know.'

Wow. Three-point-two for artistic impression. There'll be words later.

'What business is it of yours? You don't even goddamn live here!'

'I know.'

Okay. This isn't going well.

Let's hope she punches your lights out in the next two seconds. At least that way, it'll be over quickly and with marginally less embarrassment.

'Damn right, you do. And that's about all you know. You don't know me, you don't know Carlton, and you've no business fixing up rumours. Hiring a P.I. against us? Really? Jeez, Beckman, I thought you were better than that.'

'So, you don't believe it?'

'What I believe is that some no-good salesman breezes into town, ogles me from across the room with eyes on stalks, and thinks he can poke his nose into my affairs just for curing a damn headache!' She threw up her arms in despair.

'Then I've got it all wrong, and I'm sorry.'

'I'd hope to hell you were sorry. A few photographs and you'll believe anything you want. Life's not like that. It's not black and white.'

It took every fibre of his strength to calm the hackles which sprang to attention like a training ground of recruits.

'If only you knew,' he mustered half-heartedly.

'What I know is I've enough friends in this town who'd speak up if what you're suggesting was going on.'

'I'm not suggesting. Not me. I'm just a no-good salesman. Reba is a professional. It's all there.' He gritted his teeth. 'In black and white.'

'So I hear.'

'And I was looking at you that time because I saw you needed my help. I gave it. To take away the pain. And then I saw what was going on with Carlton. I thought you needed my help there, too. I tried to give it. To take away… future pain. So, pardon me for trying to do the right thing.'

She shook her head. 'Sorry, Beckman. No.'

A deafening silence fell.

The echo of the C4 was dying. The shrapnel so far had only been emotional, yet that was bad enough. Hopefully, he'd dodged a bullet; she had enough leverage over Buck that if she told him to do the punching for her, he would have simply asked whereabouts on the victim's body to deliver the blow.

Except Buck wasn't here. Still, Beckman felt beaten.

'No good deed goes unpunished,' he reflected.

She folded her arms and nodded gently, lips pursed.

'What does Carlton say?' he asked.

'He's out of town.'

In a pig's eye.

'Buck?' he suggested.

'He has no side.'

'That so?'

'Yeah.'

'I guess I'm not used to the different… shades of life here,' he suggested.

'That's true.'

He waited for more from her or inspiration from within. Neither came. He'd had a veritable blow-out, and Saul hadn't attended.

'I have to get to work,' he said for something to say—a get-out. Ironic, then, that work is what had gotten him into this mess. Probably the last thing he wanted was more work, more people in Sunrise to mess with.

'Whatever.'

He tried to look through her damn glasses to glean what she really thought, where she sat on the scale of Anger-Disappointment-Meh. Maybe it wouldn't hurt to appeal to the decency he felt sure ran through her like a seam of gold?

'Please, if not for me, for Buck, ask Carlton about it, okay?'

'To assuage your precious conscience,' she sneered.

'No. So that, if there's the tiniest nagging doubt, the merest hint of curiosity about how I've apparently tried to cause you hurt, you don't leave it there like a burrowing worm that keeps you awake at night. Until it's a dark cloud that won't go away. Or a flickering light you want to turn off, but can't. A pain in your soul. Because not even one of these boxes can fix something like that. And you're a good person Lolita. You already have enough resentment in your life. You deserve better.'

Without waiting for a reply, he turned and disconsolately walked back up the street towards his room for the night.

CHAPTER 22

Getting steaming drunk wouldn't have solved anything, but it wouldn't have hurt either.

As he sat on the hotel bed, he mulled over the last time he'd given in to the temptation. It hadn't helped fifteen years ago. It hadn't prevented or annulled a situation he wasn't in control of.

This time, though, perhaps he should have considered getting smashed *before* he dropped the A-bomb on a woman he hardly knew. Might it have washed away the disappointment he felt at Carlton's (apparent) duplicity? Could it have awakened a realisation that this wasn't his battle to fight? Would he have accepted that some people—too many people—are simply dishonest and hurt the ones they love?

Why did he care so much? He wished he didn't. He wished he'd never walked into Taylor's. He should have left well alone, hung out here until Sunday, emptied his trunk, given Number One his best shot, enjoyed the warm glow of Sunrise's… individuality, then got on with life, either blissfully happy on a desert island, basking in the aura of success, or else racking up the miles for a thirteenth year, scooping the roadkill, enjoying Wilbur's hats, and looking through mental postcards of his time here.

As the TV's early evening ball game wore on, the easy option was to order room service and wallow in pity. His mind drifted onto another plane.

'Struck out again, Beckman?' came a voice.

'Rich, coming from you,' he sneered.

'Snotty little shit, aren't you?'

'Nature, nurture. Hold on, let me explain that second word to you.'

The voice didn't rise to the bait. 'You're thirty-seven.'

'Wow. You remembered. I'll hold the front page.'

'I mean, wise up. Crying never helped. Not then, not now.'

'Like you ever saw me,' Beckman scoffed.

'I dusted down and moved on.'

'And on. And on. And on.'

'Ungrateful asshole.'

'Piss off, Dad.'

He sprang from the bed, brimmed the shoulder bag, and set out in search of a spot for food. Ideally, one that didn't contain Lolita, Buck, Saul, or anyone that might be a recipient of the Chinese whispers he felt sure were creeping their tendrils through town.

The neons bedecking the diner were primarily blues, running that part of the spectrum from aquamarine to navy.

It was called "RAYS".

He assumed this meant Ray's, not rays, for surely a proprietor wanting to riff on the latter would order his neons in shades of yellow and orange, with orbs and beams galore.

No matter; the menu outside the door looked encouraging, and plenty of seats were available.

Inside, he did note a familiar face. Alone, in the corner. He didn't see a reason why they shouldn't be alone together. Especially as he smelled, amongst the mouth-watering scents wafting from the kitchens, an opportunity.

Reba had her head down, pinching the bridge of her nose. He unfastened his bag and laid a box on the table.

She looked up. 'Mr Spiers.'

'Only the boss calls me that. It's Beckman.'

'But you're a customer.'

He laid a finger on the box. 'So are you.'

'What is it with you?'

'How? Specifically?'

'You... feel things.'

'Miss Garrity, I'm just a salesman. If I can't spot a lead, I'd be better off saving a ton of money on gas and new rubber and working a desk job.'

She pulled over her purse and began fumbling through.

'It's on the house,' he continued.

She stopped, eyed him. 'For why?'

'You did a good job.'

'Shouldn't that be its own reward?'

The lightning bolt cracked through his skull. Not the Belcher kind; the Road to Damascus kind. The type that spurs life instead of ending it.

Do I really want to live on a beach? No. Do I want to walk a bit taller? Yeah.

'Buy you a drink, Miss Garrity?'

'If this is hitting on me, Mr Spiers, remember I have a daughter. For some, that's a hell of a red flag.'

'Fourth grade, that right?'

Her face bloomed in surprise since she'd only mentioned it in passing, but he'd remembered. She gestured to the other chair at the table. He sat.

'I only have a half-hour. She's at ballet practice.'

'Unless the service here really sucks, I guess we'll be fine.'

That made her smile. She had a friendly smile.

As if to make a point, a server arrived.

'Local draft,' Reba said.

Having not tried that beverage yet, Beckman added, 'Make it two,' and the server departed.

'Mind if I…?' she asked, taking the box.

'Be my guest.'

While she took a minute in the bathroom, he let his gaze wander. It was still plenty light enough outside, and, as ever, some of those distant sunbeams were falling on a certain dark blue automobile.

He found it funny, as if this was more a warning than a discreet tail. Like, "We're Watching You, Spiers". Either that or Delmar had twice as many glass eyes as Reba.

He supped the beer. It tasted expectedly fine.

She soon returned.

'Can I ask you a question, Miss Garrity?' he asked questioningly.

'Sure, if it's not eyesight related. And it's Reba.'

'Delmar's one of yours?'

'We have that… unique honour.'

'I catch your drift.'

'Who is he working for right now?'

She shook her head. 'Client privilege.'

'Oh, snap.'

'Sorry, Mr… Sorry, Beckman.'

'If he's the same two hundred a day as you, I'm lucky I got second pick.'

'That's very kind.' She took a drink. 'But he's one-fifty anyway.'

'He's about as unobtrusive as a polar bear at a Grizzly Convention.'

'Or maybe not everyone's as observant as you?'

'Comes with the territory.'

'Okay. Can I ask you a question?'

'Sure, if it's not eyesight related.'

Her face flushed incomprehension. She looked at him like she'd missed something.

He waved his hand. 'Forget it. Shoot.'

'Why do you care what Carlton Cooper is up to?'

'Because I'm just passing through, none of my beeswax, yadda yadda?'

'Oh, we'll take anyone's money. I'm curious, is all. On a personal level.'

'Why, do *you* care what Carlton Cooper is up to? On a personal level?' He flashed her an edgy, ass-covering look.

'It's okay—you won't risk… alienating me,' she said, mollifying.

'Like I did with Lolita?'

She shrugged. 'Word gets around.'

'I'm beginning to learn.'

'Comes with my territory. You know, the chance of pissing someone off. Digging into people's lives. Has to.'

'But from doing the right thing. Or trying to,' he suggested.

She drank. 'Sure.'

'How do you stop yourself from taking a personal view on a case? Not purely evidence-based?'

'By switching off when the office door closes. Not letting other people's suspicions cloud what at-home Reba knows or thinks. And vice versa.'

He drank. 'Hypothetically, what if you landed a case where you already knew the answer? Since word gets around so fast?'

'I don't follow.'

'I turn up here, and within six hours, I can't walk the street without everyone knowing who I am. I check-in to the Sunset, and word gets around which room to knock on in the middle of the night. Everything I've heard says people talk to each other.'

'We just do. It's that kind of town.'

'So, hearing that, and, yeah, I know I'm not the detective here—'

'—though you'll give Delmar job insecurities,' she said with a smirk.

'Then what are the chances nobody ever noticed what you and I saw Carlton Cooper playing at? Or did all that coincidentally start on the day I happened to walk—well, get towed—into town?'

Though she tried to hide it, her reaction was as plain as, well, a navy Lincoln with a guy at the wheel staring into the window of a diner across the street. Her shoulders sagged. The glass she was bringing to her lips sank to the table.

He sensed the slightest unease, like the scratch of a mouse behind the skirting in the next room.

'Why does it feel like I'm digging this hole bigger?'

Then she did drink. Pensively. Was it Dutch courage?

'You know I'm on personal time now?' she said.

'Absolutely.'

'I mean, I'll take a meeting outside work hours, no problem for any client.'

'Sure. But you're a citizen waiting to collect her daughter.'

She nodded, one good eye searching for the correct turn in a maze.

'I've seen Carlton Cooper is still sneaking around,' she said conspiratorially into her beer.

Beckman subconsciously leant in. 'Still?'

'Six weeks now.'

His spirits soared. Instantly, he refocussed, tried to channel the inner Gossiping Busybody that he didn't, in any sense, possess.

'That Wanda Whack. She's a handsome woman,' he said.

'I feel for Lolita, really I do.'

He put a finger to his lips. 'Not a word, though. It'll break her heart.'

'Dear God, no. Not even Buck would dare do that.'

Again, his heart leapt.

The guy had known all along. He was too good of a man to crush his friend like that. Not you, huh, Beckman? You've got it all in black and white. Which is what Buck's done; he's been your messenger boy. He's not told her what he knows, only what you've seen or think you've seen.

He's not gone out on a limb. He's hung you out to dry. He didn't soften the blow; he allowed you to be the interfering interloper. That's why Defcon 1. You don't know Sunrise. Not at all. There's no way in hell you belong here. You're a germ. You've tainted the waters, upset the ecosystem. You're the first cane toad in Australia.

Well, that's fine. Three days 'til Sunday. Win or lose, it will be time to skip town and hope the ripples dissipate quickly and easily.

They leant back. The play was over; the curtain down.

'Beckman?'

'Yeah?' He came back to the room.

'How in hell does that thing of yours work?'

'Do I look like a medical genius?'

'You look like a guy with a weight on his mind.'

'Maybe I'll change my name to Atlas.'

'So,' she said with a small sigh. 'Guess I terminated my own case.'

'Not on my account. Ballet lessons cost money, right?'

She smiled. 'You're an Okay Guy.'

'I get that. Well, I got that. Not so much now, I guess.'

'You really want me to carry on with the case?'

'Do you want to be a part of what it will do to Lolita?'

'You're asking this of Reba Garrity, single mom and taxi service. I was asking as Reba Garrity, P.I. *She* doesn't do feelings, emotions, gossip. Just the job.'

'Then, yeah, carry on. At least tomorrow. If I'm blowing smoke up my ass, I may as well totally kipper it.'

'That's a beautiful image.'

He smiled. 'Thanks. What happened to Mr Garrity, by the way? If it's not a personal question.'

She took a slug of beer. 'Take a wild guess.'

'Fooled around,' he guessed.

'Bullseye.'

'No guesses how you found out.'

'Funny thing, it was old Delmar out there who broke the case.'

'So, he doesn't completely suck.'

'He has his uses.' There was a glint in her one eye.

'Then here's the million-dollar question. Would you rather you'd never found out about your ex's antics?'

She shook her head. 'No. And I know people danced around it. And, yeah, I forgave them. People try to do the right thing. They didn't want to hurt me.'

'But then some out-of-towner breezed through and dot dot dot.'

'Actually, I smelled perfume on his shirt and hired Delmar myself. Total cliché, I know. But then, men, huh?'

'We can suck sometimes.'

'Or try to do right by people,' she suggested.

'Comes with the territory.'

'Well, I'll tell you something—you've done right by me. That head pain—on its way out already.'

'I'm pleased.'

'Find me a millionaire with a soft spot for one-eyed single moms, and that'll make two of us.'

He chuckled. 'I'll get right on that.'

She drained her beer. 'So, stop by the office tomorrow, and I'll catch you up on your case.'

'Sure.' He bit his lip. 'Can I ask you a last question? Again?'

'Shoot.'

'Who hired Delmar?'

She shook her head. 'Still client privilege.'

'Thought so.'

'You're a client. You understand. You'd want the same.'

He sighed. 'Sure.'

She rose from the seat, shouldered her bag, then paused. She dug into the bag. 'Actually, I did run off some more photos from your case, Mr Spiers. As agreed, I've continued to track Mr Cooper through all his stops.'

She came out with a sheaf of glossy paper and tendered it across.

'Thanks.'

'I hope you'll find it… useful.' She gave the most individual wink he'd ever received.

'Then, thanks again.'

She looked around the room. 'Skip the steak. Try the house burger. Best in town.'

He rose and offered his hand. She shook it, smiled, then was gone. He sank into the seat and took a long sip of his drink.

The first glossy black-and-white (true monochrome) showed Carlton on his cell phone in a nondescript location. The following few pictures were long shots of Carlton and Wanda, one showing them in an embrace. The next captured his car pulling into the EVI Lighting parking lot. The next showed him talking to Saul outside the garage. The next, him with another guy. In the next, he was entering Taylor's office.

The last image was more grainy. It hadn't been taken with the same equipment. Maybe a phone camera? It was askew, almost as if snapped in an emergency. An interior shot. He recognised the location.

Taylor's office.

Carlton was talking with someone. They were discussing a sheaf of glossies, not unlike the ones Beckman was currently examining.

That someone was Delmar.

CHAPTER 23

He slept like a log. An over-tired Rip Van Log that had nowhere to be the next day.

The well-travelled alarm clock glowed 09:04.

His first thought was regret; precious selling time had been eaten into. His second thought was that it was good to wake at all, given the previous day's rollercoaster.

You're in one piece and still mining in dream territory.

He pulled aside the curtain.

'Morning, Delmar,' he said to the window.

In the white bathroom with white tiles, white ceramics, and white floor, he shaved dark grey stubble from his pale grey face, showered, did his best with the shallow side parting in his off-black hair, brushed his whiteish teeth, and, for not the first time in his life, cursed his mid-grey eyes.

He pulled on a new white shirt, the same charcoal pants, dark grey jacket, black shoes. For good order, he took his shoulder bag down to breakfast and returned twenty minutes and three sales later.

He was neatening the bedclothes when his cell rang.

The Incoming Caller was about as welcome as a prophylactic machine in a nunnery.

'Becky!'

Why d'you have to pick up? Pick up for Malvolio and Mom. That's it. Learn a lesson, dummy.

'Tyler,' he said flatly.

'Guess who I bumped into beside the highway last night?'

'The Grim Reaper?' Beckman hoped.

'Scoot Pippins.'

'Uh-huh.'

'Got a flat, poor guy.'

'Not from you shooting out the tire, I guess.'

'Becky, Becky. You're making me the bad guy here. Besides, Scoot's so far down the table he'd barely make top ten if he had the Millennium Falcon.'

'Fascinating anecdote, Tyler, really, but I have customers to call on.'

'So, thing about Scoot, his heart's not in it this year, and his trunk was so damn full, I'd have hated the tow truck to snap an axle hauling all that extra weight around, so—'

Beckman irately balled a fist. 'You piece of work, Tyler.'

'Hey, I'm not being called black by the pot that stole Belcher's load.'

'That's a world of difference. It was… redundant stock.'

'You're gunning for me, and I know it. Besides, it's almost the weekend, and what's Scoot going to do? Work? Guy's a clock-watcher.'

'Yeah, like *you're* working through.'

''Fraid so. Pushing it to the wire. I'm not letting a journeyman loser like you dip at the tape.'

'Say this gets back to Malvolio, what you did?'

'You ever have all four limbs in traction, Becky?'

'Is that a threat?' he asked, knowing full well it was.

'Have a good weekend, Becky,' Tyler sang. There came a brief laugh, then the line cut.

He threw the phone onto the mattress so hard, it bounced high enough to catch. So he casually tossed it onto the nightstand and sank to the edge of the bed, head in hands.

No need to do the math again.

Facts were facts. Game Over.

Five minutes on, nothing had changed—except he'd reached a conclusion.

He methodically packed the wash bag and clicked the ensuite light off. Then he unloaded the wardrobe and drawers, took the portable alarm from the nightstand, and arranged everything in his roller case.

Then he gave Room 12 one last scan and pulled the door closed behind him.

At the front desk, he thanked Kinsey for the hospitality and settled his bill with a ten-dollar tip.

Outside, he saw Delmar watch him sink into the Caddy's comfortable embrace, pull a one-eighty, and purr back to Main Street.

There, he took a right and climbed the gradient to the rocky outcrop on the fringe of town.

The Lincoln remained a blob the whole way.

Another car stood in the driveway at 1002 Edison Avenue. A Ford-red '65 Mustang.

He puffed out a breath, slid the lever to P, climbed wearily out, and plodded up the inclined drive towards the doorway. And destiny.

The front door burst open long before he reached it. He winced, stopped.

There were raised voices. Well, one raised voice. A woman's, emanating from the hallway.

Then a figure emanated from the door, backwards.

Carlton was in full retreat. Understandably so. In his position, Beckman would be doing the same. Even if little green men from Mars, with no word of the human tongue having ever passed their ears (or whatever they used to hear with), made first contact right here, right now, even they would have surmised that Lolita Milan was, at that precise time, Not Best Pleased.

Pretty Riled About Something.

On The Warpath.

The little green men would have heard, 'You're a cheating, lying, self-serving son of a bitch, Carlton Cooper, and you can shove this engagement up your ass!'

Beckman eyed the poor bastard, who was having his own Game Over incident of the morning and similarly aware that fighting it was a waste of breath.

So, Carlton didn't. He backed off, warmed by the fire in her eyes, waiting for the right moment to turn his back and walk to the Mustang. The right moment being when he was far enough away to be beyond the range of any missiles that might come to her hand.

Sadly, he didn't reach such a distance before she threw something. Luckily for him, it was small. Fortunately for his future bank balance, it was also valuable.

He fumbled the catch. The ring danced in the air and then in his hands before he clutched it gratefully, steadying himself against the slope, and slid it hurriedly into a pocket.

Spectating, Beckman instinctively eased back towards the camouflage of a tall border hedge, felt the prodding caress of myriad stem-ends, and, knowing that worse torture lay before him—should Carlton discover his true nemesis—pushed himself as far into the tangle of the shrub as tolerable.

Payback's a bitch. That goes for you as well as him.

Thankfully, the no-longer-future-Mr Lolita Milan trudged obliviously down to his gleaming machine, collapsed into the seat, fired the pony to life, and reversed down the drive, onto the road, engaged D, then accelerated past a similarly unnoticed navy Lincoln and away.

Probably to a quiet spot to lick his wounds.

Beckman took a breath, then un-greenery-ed himself and stepped onto the drive.

No point in waiting for a quiet moment, a better moment, the right moment. What would be, would be. Not only had the horse bolted, it had gotten over the hills, across the border, and far away. Probably applying for Mexican residency just about now.

Lolita saw him.

He hoped any incoming missiles would be equally as featherweight as previously launched, if not as bejewelled.

She folded her arms. No PhD in Body Language Interpretation was needed here. He walked, outwardly calm, to her. What he would have given to see her eyes. One time, of all times.

It wasn't to be.

'I've come to say goodbye. I'm leaving town.'

One eyebrow crested the tortoiseshell frame. 'Light up a room and leave, huh?'

'I kinda thought, throw in a grenade and leave.'

He couldn't know the gamut of emotions she was cycling through, although the small movements of her lips gave some clues.

'You were right,' she said with neither gratitude nor harshness.

He could only shrug. Bulldozing a person's future is not the place for an I-told-you-so.

Then he said, 'I wish I hadn't been.'

Her arms unfolded. Still, he remained at DefCon 2.

'Nobody else would tell me. People I call my friends.'

'They *are* your friends,' he countered. 'They're just afraid to tell you things you don't want to hear.'

'And you?'

'I've nothing to lose, nothing to gain.'

'But you're leaving town.'

'Like every week, every day, somewhere.'

'Leaving on account of me.'

'I trashed your relationship, your future happiness, and your inheritance. I don't think that makes me an Okay Guy anymore. Certainly not with you. Probably not with anyone here.' He hung his head.

'What about your sales deadline?' Genuine concern rang in her voice.

'There's next year. But not for you. I'm sorry.'

She relaxed a mite. 'Aw, I'll come up with something. I'm not what it looks like.'

'I know that.'

'I might even forgive you. Eventually.'

'Not sure I deserve it.'

Silence fell. She put a hand on a hip. 'So, really leaving, huh?' Now there was an edge of disappointment in her tone.

'You're the last call. Only call, actually.'

'Why?'

'Least I could do.'

Her face softened. 'You know, Beckman, you may be the most decent, honest guy in town.'

'For the next fifteen minutes. And look where it got me. Us. That is, you.'

'Life goes on,' she suggested.

'Sunrise, sunset.'

That triggered a smile. Then she frowned. She leant to one side and peered over his shoulder. 'Is that who I think it is?'

'Oh yeah, Delmar. We've been… hanging, you know, for a few days.'

'You know he's…?'

'Sure. P.I.'

'What did you do, Mister Honest?'

'Not a thing. Well, took dinner with an engaged woman earlier in the week.'

The penny dropped very quickly. 'You mean…?'

'Yeah. Carlton hired him.'

'Because we had a *chat*?' she asked, stunned.

'Another guy on his patch. A torrid affair, I guess he thought.'

'Torrid?'

He shrugged, corrected himself. 'Affair. Well, who knows? I mean, last evening on the street, not going to win Prom King and Queen, are we?'

Again, she smiled. He took a leap of faith—large enough to clear more buses than Evel Knievel would dare—and dropped to DefCon 4. Understandably, she was still processing the situation.

'He's got a camera and everything in there, I guess.' She nodded towards the Lincoln.

'A regular Ansel Adams. Never catches my best side, though.'

'I hope he's billing Carlton good and strong. Possessive, cheating sumbitch.'

'And all for nothing, huh? Money down the drain. Gotta love the irony.'

'Man, that feels good. I hope he keeps on paying. Bankrupt the douchebag,' she sneered.

'Well, not because of me leaving. I think he's straight-up enough to stop the case. And he's got book smarts, your ex. Even if not behaviour smarts.'

She looked towards Delmar again and cocked her head. 'All the same, poor guy must hate to have wasted the whole week on no evidence.'

'My heart bleeds,' he deadpanned.

'Say goodbye, then,' she said out of the blue. Yet there was no malice in it, merely a polite request.

So, being an Okay Guy, he acceded to it.

'Goodbye, Lolita,' he said with a slight nod of courtesy.

'Goodbye, Beckman.'

And then she stepped in and kissed him, full and long on the mouth.

CHAPTER 24

When their lips parted, her gaze immediately turned towards the road.

'There,' she said, 'That'll give him something to chew on.'

If she'd been expecting a response, she was SOL. Beckman was too busy hoping she didn't have a feather to hand that might accidentally poleaxe him.

'Yeah,' he said finally, as the taste of her permeated through his skin.

'So, good luck, I guess, if you're leaving.'

He didn't want to give her chapter and verse or revisit the whole Tyler Does It Again development. The universe had sent its message loud and clear: Sunrise is not the answer.

Yet Lolita didn't appear to be one hundred percent "on message". Still, it had been a much better goodbye than a palm across the cheek. He could rest easy that he'd done the right thing. He wouldn't be leaving under a cloud.

Well, not a black one.

'It's for the best,' he said.

'I suppose.'

'Good to meet you. And thanks for everything. And… sorry.'

She gave an awkward smile, stepped back and gently folded her arms. He took the cue and walked down towards the Caddy.

'Don't get a flat, huh?' she called.

He gave her a thumbs up.

Inside, fifty-one percent of him knew it was indeed for the best. He'd spoiled a fledgling friendship. Carlton would find out the cause of the breakup soon enough, and probably set out for vengeance. Tyler was going to win the Salesman race, so selling in Sunrise was a hiding to nothing.

Beckman simply didn't fit in here.

Time to get on the road again. Back to life as it should be.

He gave Delmar a cheery wave, popped the car door, and climbed in. Without looking back at her, he knocked it into D, arced round in the road, and eased in the gas pedal.

Behind, because the alternative would have been too crazy, the Lincoln fell into tow. Poor guy must have thought Christmas had come early: actual evidence of misdeeds. The problem was, they technically weren't misdeeds.

She was single, and so was he. All Delmar had seen was evidence of two consenting adults kissing.

"Kissing"? Exchanging one very unexpected meeting of lips.

Beckman had half a mind to drag the tail around every street in town, just to rack up the mileage charge on Carlton's bill. Except that would be petty, salt in the wound, not a thing an Okay Guy does. Instead, he piloted the Caddy straight down Main Street.

He kept the speedo at twenty, taking the opportunity to drink in every last neon. At the same time, he couldn't deny he was scanning for customers.

Hell, why not one last hurrah? Maybe failure isn't a certainty. It would only take one slip on the other side, one jealous husband, to put a house-calling Tyler in the hospital for a couple of days, freezing his sales figures, and you've got a chance of overhauling him.

Yeah, or maybe lightning will strike twice, fry the asshole, and the same afternoon I'll win the state lottery and get the Nobel Prize for Chemistry.

Well, you're certainly able to generate explosive reactions—only not when they're wanted.

He passed Candela and Lumen Avenues, Watt and Electron, Bayonet and Globe.

On the sidewalk, he spied the Gleesons, Mrs tailing Mr this time. A block down, Franklin was in the middle of leaving-his-car-but-not-leaving-it. The immaculately coiffured Zebedee Taylor was striding down towards his office.

Beckman smiled. Then something caught the corner of his eye. He braked hard for the crosswalk.

A woman passed in front, waved her thanks.

Was she after a miracle box…? No.

He accelerated up to twenty again.

Something nagged him. Should Lolita *really* be his last call? He'd be passing Saul's automotive lifeline en route. After all, the guy had been responsible for him winding up here in the first place, and, on balance, the whole adventure had been a positive experience. Only he, Beckman, had stymied it, effectively running himself out of town. For a guy who'd never fired a gun until today, he'd shot himself in the foot with commendable skill and impeccable comic timing.

Someone else stood on the sidewalk ahead, arm raised as if hailing a cab.

A large someone. A Buck-sized someone.

He checked his mirror. Was Clint behind, waiting to be hailed?

No.

Intrigued, he eased off the gas. Now he noticed Buck waving something. A beer bottle?

Then he wasn't waving it. He was tossing it.

Beckman saw into the future, and time fell to a crawl.

The green vessel arced gracefully through the air towards the road.

He had a good idea what would happen next because, as well as being a pretty decent salesman, he'd heard about something called Gravity.

The bottle tumbled towards the tarmac.

Again, he was way ahead of the curve. Not only was he A1 when it came to trashing the business dreams and love lives of, on reflection, mighty fine kissers in swing dresses, he knew that glass impacting on hard surfaces was A Messy Business.

The bottle shattered on the road twenty feet in front of the car.

In those twenty feet, he painstakingly made a mental list of things that could happen next. After the first suggestion, he ran out of ideas. No matter, he thought, you've got a fair chance of hitting the mark.

He didn't bother swerving.

Hell, I was going to call in on Saul anyway.

The front tire blew out.

He coasted to a halt.

No doubt about it: Buck was definitely on a kickback for this particular stunt.

Maybe Saul is gunning for Recovery Mechanic of the Year, and the deadline is today? He'd certainly have a shot at the prize. A lifetime in a sports bar with all the axle grease and Pirelli calendars a guy could want.

In school, Beckman had picked a fight with a boy half a head taller than himself and nearly had his jaw broken. He'd forgotten the reason behind the ill-advised manoeuvre. Buck Travis stood a full head taller than him, and as Beckman had no idea how far the nearest hospital was, he painted on a smile and swung open the car door.

'I brake for pedestrians too, you know.' He stepped onto the sidewalk.

Buck came over. 'Can't let you leave.'

His shoulders fell. 'Oh, snap.'

At least there was this; he wouldn't have to explain to Mr Malvolio why he'd failed to make the grade again. Plus, he knew Miss Broomhead would make sure a condolence card got to Mom.

So, this was it.

Number Two and out.

CHAPTER 25

A minute later, he was none the wiser about why leaving wasn't an option. On the positive side, he remained alive enough to be able to wonder, which scored as A Major Result.

Buck's bear arm lay around his shoulder, and they were walking—because when Buck's arm is around your shoulder, you do as he commands—down to his café.

The condemned man gets a drink. No contest for what to choose.

'If I leave my car on the street, it'll get impounded,' he offered, for something to say.

'Don't think so,' Buck replied, knowingly.

Beckman craned his neck round to where they'd come from. Saul was hitching the Caddy.

'Okay,' he peeped.

Momentarily, they were inside the familiar refreshment establishment. Buck walked them over to a table and, both hands *encouragingly* on Beckman's shoulders, bade him sit.

The aproned proprietor-slash-bodyguard-slash-possible-future-executioner went to the counter and breathed life into the gargantuan coffee production facility.

Beckman gazed out the window. Life in Sunrise carried on as usual. Neons glowed and flashed, people went about their business, a man in a dark blue car watched him.

A glass was deposited on the table. A person with a mug deposited himself on the seat opposite.

Buck eyed him for a time. A long time. Sipped his coffee. Beckman took it as a cue to drink, so he did. It was still nectar.

'You're an Okay Guy, Beckman.'

Huh? Did I skip a day? Guessing they don't kill Okay Guys?

'Thanks,' he mustered, brain in an overload like the last moments of a Bond villain's hideout before it detonates.

Damn, his coffee smells good from here. If this is a whole Hotel California thing going on, I guess I'll have to break my duck. Never see Coffee Planet again. But hold that thought.

'I couldn't break her heart before—you know that?' Buck said.

'But I could, huh?'

'You don't know her like I do. No, strike that. Maybe you know her better.'

Beckman flopped out an ironic laugh. 'Doubt it.'

'I do care about her.'

He slugged more root beer. 'I guessed as much.'

'But not enough to do the bad stuff. Or maybe too much. Not keen to tell her things she wouldn't want to hear, show her pictures she hate to see.'

'Can't blame you not wanting to break a friendship.'

Buck gave him a look verging on admiration. Or perhaps surprise. Possibly disbelief at the level of Beckman's bravado… or stupidity.

More likely stupidity.

'You did something nobody else in town would do.'

'Yeah, I broke the code.' He chuckled, recognising that a good word for his action would be "arrogance". He shook his head. 'I walked in and blew the lid off a perfect life.'

'And what happened? She hit you for it?' In contrast, Buck's face showed that he knew exactly what had happened not twenty minutes earlier.

'Word gets around, huh?'

'You need to know she's like a daughter to me. You don't have kids, Beckman. Neither do I. But I know one thing. You don't tell them who they should or shouldn't date, how they should or shouldn't live their lives. They don't like that shit.'

'Still, you said something to her yesterday—what changed?'

Buck took a healthy draw on his coffee. Beckman even saw satisfaction in the man's eyes.

This stuff must be good if the guy who's been making it for who-knows-how-many years still takes pleasure.

'I thought, "Why did Beckman do it?", "Why did he hire Reba to do that?", "What's it to him?".'

'I don't like cheats.'

'I got that. Then I wondered, going back aways when the guy screwed over Lolita for that Egyptian piece, would I have wanted to stop that if I'd known? And, hell yeah, I would. Look what it did to her. Putting up a wall to people like you.'

'Because I'm this Okay Guy.'

'Yeah. She'd have found out anyway about Carlton, right? It would have been worse then—break up a marriage. Better to prevent it now. So, if I ignored it—and knowingly let more heartbreak come to her—it makes me not an Okay Guy.'

'Let alone not an Okay Kinda Father.'

Buck gave a reflective shrug.

'I guess she did something pretty special to wind up with you watching over her,' Beckman guessed.

Buck played with his mug. 'What goes around.'

'What went around?'

'She looked over my numbers when things weren't so… easy.'

'There's a head under those curls,' Beckman agreed.

'Plus, I may have helped her along.'

'After her folks…?' Beckman asked. Buck nodded. 'You put her up? Gave her a shoulder?'

'I helped with the house.'

'That what put you in money trouble?'

Buck shook his head. 'A fat head on fat shoulders put me in trouble.'

'I did think it was a pretty impressive property.'

'Ginetta wanted out of town. Jack wanted out of bad memories. Lolita wanted a place.' Buck shrugged. 'Jack, had he not been an ass, would have gifted the house. Instead, he said, you've got such a great business head, honey, *you* figure a way to make the repayments. So, she did. Or she tried.'

'Jack reckoned without other people giving a shit.'

Buck's face was sober. 'Life works out. Sometimes water is thicker than blood. So, quit on all this Armageddon baloney, Beckman. Yeah, you're a butterfly. You flapped your wings, the universe'll carry on. She's bruised, we're still talking, but I didn't need to chop you into pieces and put you in one of those little brown boxes.'

'Which you would have.'

'On account of hurting her, absolutely.'

'You want me to leave you with an empty box for Carlton?'

Buck smiled. 'He knows how to tread. Plus, we've still got Reba, no?'

Realisation dawned. 'Shoot! I was about to skip town without paying her check.'

'Lucky that I dropped that bottle.'

'I can't believe anyone gets away without paying the check. I mean, they are P.I.s. How are you gonna hide?'

'I paid Reba.' He held up a defensive hand. 'Don't thank me. It's what a Kinda Father does for a Kinda Daughter.'

'I pay my way, Buck,' Beckman insisted.

142

'I know. So why blow town? Word is, this is a gold mine for you. Help you hit your target.'

'Because the "Number One" part is not supposed to follow a "Public Enemy" part. I'm not for treading on all you people just to get where I want.'

Buck reached across and grasped Beckman's forearm. Paternally, not crushingly. 'I pulled you over so you know not to leave on account of anything you did. All the same, you're free to go. Nobody is after screwing your goals, and no, not for any stupid revenge because you think—*think*—you did a dumb thing. We clear?'

'Crystal.'

Buck let go of his arm. 'So, here's the deal. I have a brother. I know— Mom was pretty brave to push out another oversized bowling ball a year after I popped. He works at the bottling plant. They have two hundred guys there. A lot of noise.' He looked Beckman in the eye. 'A whole lot of headaches, I'll be bound.'

'Sounds out of town. You may have noticed—I've only three wheels on my wagon.'

'*Your* wagon.' Evidently, Buck had heard about the vehicular carousel too.

'Pool car,' Beckman improvised. 'Same difference.'

'We'll take mine.'

'Honestly, Buck, I couldn't.'

The hand came back onto his arm. 'I think you'll find you could.'

They picked up Buck's Jeep and rolled down to Saul's, where they took on board a box of boxes. Buck insisted on paying in advance for the new tire.

Beckman said he couldn't let that happen. Then he found out he could.

At the Sunrise Bottling Plant (they'd been up many nights thinking of that one), Buck knew the shift supervisor, Grenville Dix. They had a tannoy system.

Beckman didn't believe they'd let a non-employee use it. Then he found out they would.

Not unsurprisingly, most people knew Buck.

They listened to his advertisement for Beckman's Magic Headache Curing Box. Then about half of them went back to work. The other half made a beeline for Dix's office, where the visitors had ensconced themselves.

Beckman collected the fives and tens. Buck stood beside him, still sporting his work apron, and doled out the boxes. In twenty minutes flat, they were cleared out.

As they walked back to the Jeep in the noon sunshine, Beckman turned to the big bear. 'I don't know how to thank you.'

'You stopped my Kinda Daughter entering into a sham marriage.'

'Isn't that Jack Milan's lookout?'

'Like he gives a shit. And if she'd never listen to me, she sure as hell wouldn't listen to him. Matter of fact, she'd do the damn opposite. So, enough with the gratitude, okay?'

'Okay.'

They trundled back into town.

This time, they sat at the counter in Our Buck's.

'Now, don't put your fat hand on my arm and say lunch is on the house, okay?'

'Fat?' Buck raised an eyebrow. 'It would only be coming out of my cut anyhow.'

'Cut, huh?'

'You want to make this Number One spot?'

Beckman's shoulders fell. Cards on the table time.

'It's like this. I'm guessing you know who Tyler is?' Buck nodded. 'He's a shoo-in. I have zero chance. He has the stock. He has the territory. He has the patter. I did the math. Unless Godzilla climbs out of the Colorado River in the next forty-eight hours and stomps down the freeway in search of a black Chevy with a hell of a lot of stains on the back seat, I'm just Ernst Schmied and Juerg Marmet.'

Buck's face creased. 'Who?'

'Exactly.'

CHAPTER 26

Buck, none the wiser, returned to the matter at hand. 'Like I said, you're free to leave. All I'm saying is, it would be a dumb move.'

'Why, you know some more shift supervisors?'

'I know everybody you need, Beckman. Or sit there and drink my root beer. I'm easy.'

'And hope for Godzilla, huh?'

'Remember Belcher?' Buck suggested. 'Shit happens.'

'Anything you *don't* know?'

'How to whistle up fictional Japanese monsters.'

'You know, this relentless concern for my career and wellbeing could get boring. Sure, not for a few weeks, but....'

Buck laid a hand on Beckman's shoulder. 'You did right by Lolita. I'm offering to do right by you. Aside from that, I have plenty of buddies already. I can take or leave another one. Your choice.'

'I'll take that list of buddies. I'm not a total idiot.'

'My cut is five percent.'

Beckman smiled at the apparent joke. Then he caught Buck's eye and realised the guy absolutely wasn't kidding.

His smile vanished. 'Take ten.'

'You are not a total idiot.' Buck slid a root beer across.

'I think that post around here is taken, anyhow.'

'Carlton can go be an idiot all he wants. Play in traffic, too, if he's not picking the prize rose.'

Beckman merely nodded. A gaggle of customers appeared.

'Go do your job. You won't make a living on five percent of half my day's work.'

Buck offered his hand. They shook, then he did as bid.

Beckman lingered as long as he dared with his drink, observing the comings and goings. Between serving duties, Buck dipped back to their position, making notes on an order pad. He also brought, unrequested, a ham and pickle on rye. Beckman slid a twenty onto the counter.

Slaked and sated twenty minutes later, he took Buck's completed list of potential customers, gave the man a nod, and wandered down to Saul's to collect the car.

He spent four hours spider-webbing between the town boundaries. Three things were consistent.

Neons.

Delmar.

Sales.

Something else stayed with him: the tiny voice in his head asking what he'd done to deserve such luck. Maybe the adage had a corollary that read No Bad Deed Goes Unrewarded.

He hadn't been sent to either Milan or EVI factories: Buck saw that much sense. Beckman didn't know Jack Milan, Walter, or Wanda Whack from Adam but he played the percentages that there was more to lose by crossing them than gained. Besides, by the end of his rounds, he'd sold most of his stock.

Maybe there'll be no need to work the whole weekend?

Yet he happily would, plus nights, if there remained a chance. Just a chance. But it was out of his hands. He could only run his race and hope Tyler fell short.

He rolled the Caddy into a space down the block from Buck's, went back inside, and found what was fast becoming his usual window seat.

The hands on the huge iron timepiece glided past five. Buck arrived. Beckman duly handed over ten percent of his sales money.

'Always a man of your word.'

'You expected different?'

Buck casually shook his head. 'No. What can I get you?'

'It's been a good day. Long Island iced tea.'

'What?'

'Long Island iced tea.'

'Who in the hell has those anymore?'

'Define "anymore",' Beckman suggested.

'The last few years.'

'Can you make it or not?'

'Sure.'

'Then I'll have one of those.'

Buck shrugged and lumbered off.

Beckman checked that Delmar was within spitting distance. Strangely, he'd be more worried if the P.I. dropped off the radar. It was a comfort blanket. If the tail weren't there, it would be like the birds falling silent before an earthquake. Now that he had nothing to worry about, this just counted as an amusing quirk.

Saul pulled over a seat. 'My favourite customer.'

'I may start taking the bus.'

'Don't have them here.'

'I didn't mean in Sunrise. I do have a life outside of this place.'

'Ah, more fool you.'

Buck set a glass down on the table.

'What's that?' Saul asked.

'Long Island iced tea,' Beckman replied.

'Who has those anymore?'

'You mean, in the last few years?'

'Yeah.'

'Well, Buck knows how to make them.'

Saul looked up at the proprietor. 'When was the last time you made one?'

'Last fall, some girl,' Buck replied.

'You said not in the last few years?' Beckman wondered.

Buck brushed it off. 'That's different.'

'Like how?'

Buck's mouth moved silently, then gave up. 'The usual?' he asked Saul, who nodded.

'So?' Saul asked when Buck had left.

'So?'

'Smart move—use Reba, find evidence, get the guy kicked into touch.'

Beckman's eyes widened. 'I'm going to say I'm not quite at the ball game with your sense of humour, Saul. It makes me sound like a scheming asshole. And we already have one of those at Pegasus, thanks.'

'If I'm yanking your chain, it's only halfway.'

Beckman set his face hard. 'This is not a conversation I want to have. Did no guy ever just do the right thing?'

'Because of guilt? Denial?'

He forced his breath to calm. 'Because my job. Because Sunrise is one of a million towns. Because my car is my home. Because no girl wants that—tall, short, rake, dumpster, blonde, brunette, swing dress or no. But because most of all, I come off like a heel trying to move in on her right now.'

'How about tomorrow? Sunday? Next week?'

'What are you, a dating service?'

Saul paused for a second, winking gratitude at Buck, who'd delivered his unidentified tipple. 'She didn't exactly kick your ass all the way down Main Street this morning.'

Word gets around.

'What am I suddenly? Required reading? Do I get my own column in the Beacon?'

'I'm just saying.'

'Look, I tried to do a nice thing for somebody, okay? Then it looked like it went to shit, and I felt like shit, and shit hit the fan, and I felt some more like shit, then Carlton as good as got the shit kicked out of him, and I thought I was *really* in the shit. Then it turns out everything I was worried about was for shit.'

'And she kissed you.'

He waved it away. 'Grateful, I guess.'

Saul flashed a smirk. 'Maybe I need to dick around with other people's lives some more.'

'Trust me—I don't think you're her type.'

'And what is her "type", Beckman?' Saul fixed the one good eye on him and took a slow draft of the clear drink.

'What do I know? You're the one who lives in this crazy town. I'd have to say, based on my *extensive* experience of her catalogue of boyfriends, her type is douchebags.'

'But everyone has their epiphany,' Saul suggested.

'What am I? Archimedes?'

There was a so-so of the head. 'You caused the epiphany. Technically, you'd be the water in the tub.'

'Saul, if you weren't the nicest damn tow-truck driver I ever met, I'd punch you on the nose.'

'I'd say that's not a good idea. Remember, when you try to do things to hurt people around here, they tend to end up kissing you, and being as we're all open and honest right now, you're *definitely* not my type.'

Beckman shook his head, smiling, dumbfounded. 'Now I *know* you're being an asshole about this.'

'You haven't had a date in, what, ten years?'

That remark took Beckman by surprise. 'Not that it's any of your beeswax, but yeah.' He worked the numbers. The evening with EJ didn't count—that had been a chance encounter, not a date in the true sense. 'Eleven, actually. Okay? That satisfy your warped curiosity?'

'You have not the faintest idea when a woman is into you, do you?'

'Saul!'

That came out loud enough for other late-afternoon customers to turn their heads. He knocked back the volume dial to a conspiratorial murmur.

'Whether or not I'm into Lolita, I can tell you for damn certain she is not into me.' He sat back and nodded his head firmly, that being very definitely that.

Buck walked up to them. A portable phone receiver dangled from his hand. 'Someone called for you, trying to track you down.'

His spirits nosedived.

Tyler Blowhard Quittle.

'Yeah?' he asked dismally, holding out a hand.

'Told me to give you a message.'

Beckman withdrew his hand. 'Yeah?' he queried, apprehensive.

'Lolita wants to know if you're free to come over to her place for dinner.'

He checked the café door was closed, lest tumbleweeds blow through. He fought not to look at Saul. He didn't need to. The tow-trucker's response wasn't a withering look—it was louder.

'You were saying?'

A hundred yards down the street, congratulating himself on a rapid exit that had trodden a good line between keen, courteous, and dismissive, a bell clanged in his thick head.

He slowed to a halt, turned carefully through a half-circle, and paced back to the café, an errant pupil hearing that detention was not over quite yet, young man.

Opening the premise's door as little as possible, he called, 'What time?'

Buck threw his hands up. 'Search me.'

'Oh, snap.'

He resumed the walk, checking the time. 18:19.

What time was a good hour for dinner? In Sunrise? For her?

Should he retrace his steps and seek advice? Ask if she had a... routine?

He might as well ask if he could borrow the car, if he looked smart enough, and what time he needed to be home by.

Get a grip, Beckman. It's not even a date. It's dinner. Heck, she already made you lunch once. What was that—first base?

All the same, what time? Seven? Seven-thirty? Eight's too late, surely? You'll look tardy. She'll think you've stood her up. Except you can't stand somebody up when it's not a date.

All the same.... Seven fifteen. Yeah, that'll do.

He unlatched the Caddy's door, started her, and eased up the street to Sunset Hotel, navy Lincoln in tow.

A late shift for you tonight, Delmar.

At the reception desk, he realised he'd taken a risk by checking out earlier. In hindsight, and had he not been such a yellow-bellied chicken, he'd have held Room 12.

Risking disappointment, he gave Kinsey a questioning look.

'Usual room, sir?' came the reply.

'You know, only if….'

'It's already made up, Mr Beckman.'

Word. Gets. Around.

He climbed the single flight of stairs, case in tow.

He unpacked methodically. First, hanging items in the narrow wardrobe. Then, folding items in the drawer. Next, ablution items laid out neatly in the bathroom. Shoes off. Jacket hung on the chair back. Curtains two-thirds closed. Air to 21 degrees.

Then, an evening shave—a rare occurrence.

As he'd alluded to Saul, it had been eleven years. Glenda Ramage.

He drifted off into reminiscence.

The blade hovered. The foam on his face began to tingle. Water burbled down the drain. Fragments of memory danced. There was a smile. A frown.

His hand sagged. The blade caught his cheek. He twitched in pain.

Eyes on the mirror. Darkest grey oozed from his skin.

'Oh, snap.'

He finished shaving at a pace, then washed down and examined the damage.

Damage caused by Ramage.

A small cut.

'Oh, snap.'

He kicked off his shorts and took a shower.

Routine complete, he rechecked the wound; noticeable, no doubt about that. In the bedroom, he used the flimsy ironing board and a doll's house iron to breathe some new life into his outfit.

What the hell are you doing? It's a good thing you don't own any cologne, Beckman Spiers, otherwise, you're liable to make an even bigger fool of yourself.

He imagined the scene:

'"Can I smell cologne on you, Beckman?'

Sheepishly, 'Yes.'

'Why, what do you think this is—some kind of *date?* I'm suddenly this easy woman, out of one man's bed and into another? How dare you! Of all the nerve! You can damn well turn around and walk right out that door, and don't stop walking 'til the county line. You're just like everyone else, Beckman Spiers. A self-serving, one-track-minded, opportunistic asshole. Get the hell out of my sight!'"

Cut to the quick, he snapped back to life, jerking the iron off his shirt as if it was hot. Which it was. Well, warm.

There was no cataclysmic imprint. He exhaled in relief.

Daydream on the crosswalk instead, why don't you? Maybe that'll bring an end to it.

He finished the preparatory routine, sending a good thought away to Mom as thanks for teaching him the basics of How To Get By In The World As A Single Guy Without Looking Like A Vagrant.

The clock on the nightstand read 18:56.

Why did he have butterflies?

The uncertainty. Curiosity. Unfamiliarity.

Events in Sunrise were never predictable. Lolita had to have a hidden motive here, didn't she? Belated revenge for him causing the breakup?

She would secretly cast an ancient Egyptian spell, designed to take effect long after he'd left town, ensuring plausible deniability on her part?

Maybe a welcome glass of wine, secretly roofied, followed by a quick mummification while unconscious?

Perhaps a trap laid by Carlton to set him up for a mob-style drive-by?

Or maybe it was worse! It all fell into place now. Pick on the nerdy new guy, entice him to a remote house for a dinner, which nobody, now he thought about it, had *explicitly* said would be a cosy twosome.

The swing dress. The neons. A brilliant guess as to his weakness, his worst fears….

'Oh, snap.'

It meant only one thing.

Dance lessons.

CHAPTER 27

Whatever fate awaited Beckman, he wasn't about to allow Lolita the chance of a cheap jibe this time.

His watch showed 19:14 when he jabbed the bell push and immediately remembered that the seven-fifteen call time had been a total guess anyway.

Idiot.

The door opened.

The dress of choice tonight was a restrained burgundy (at best guess), with a pronounced white V-collar and white hem. Her glasses, still tinted, had burgundy rims. Her hair was less… up, lustrous open brown curls falling to her shoulders. Makeup was more… demure.

This, apparently, was Evening Lolita.

He felt under-special. Evening Beckman was merely Regular Beckman with fewer creases.

'Hi, Beckman.'

'Hey, Lolita.'

His brain screamed Awkward Greeting Situation. A handshake would be lame. A kiss would be presumptuous. A hug risked Creasing The Dress.

He quickly opted for a loose buss on one cheek. It went down fine. Her scent was gentle, yet it washed over him like ambrosia.

She waved him through. He couldn't hear other voices in the house. But then, maybe they hadn't had to guess the arrival time? Maybe he was the first.

Except he wasn't.

In the kitchen diner, the table was laid for two.

He was the only.

Thankfully, there was no single stem in a vase, no solitary lit candle.

Does Sunrise do candles? Surely not. Too antiquated.

Dinner smelled good enough to cause riots.

'You like roast?'

Even if his answer hadn't been Yes, he would still have said Yes. It would be a dumb move to be impolite before the evening's hexing, mummification, or machine-gun attack had even begun.

'You may need a fork truck to get me home.'

She opened what he recognised as the fridge door. 'Aperitif?'

'Sure.'

She lobbed him a beer. Mercifully, as his high-school third-base coach would agree, he caught it.

'I gather you had a good day.' She tore the cap off her bottle and took a swig. Evening Lolita was still no duchess.

'Buck is—and I know the word is overused—a legend.'

'He's a pretty fine guy.'

'Don't know what I did to deserve this welcome. And support. And... leeway.'

She stepped in closer, held out her bottle, and they chinked necks.

'You helped a lot of people in town. You got a goal, a dream—we help you.'

'Yeah,' he said with resignation.

'Wow. Well, I can see you're real excited about it.'

'It's not that. It's just....'

'Tyler?' she wondered, eyebrow raised.

'He hasn't just pulled every trick in the book—they had to publish a Second Edition. Then he gets wind I'm on his tail, and he's like a mad wasp.'

She broke away into the kitchen. 'Keep talking.'

'The guy is lower than a snake's ass in a wagon rut.'

He stayed at a safe distance, to avoid getting caught up in the blur of Shiva serving dinner. 'He's the kind of guy who'd pull a starving kid off the street, put him in the car, go to a customer he wanted to break, and say, "Look at my poor son. Help me give him a good life".'

She cracked a laugh.

'One time,' he continued, 'I think he faked a heart attack in an office on his rounds, all to draw a crowd and pitch to them.'

'Maybe Tyler's simply more ruthless when it comes to reaching what he wants.'

'Yeah.'

Lolita was pretty driven too, he had to concede: getting success despite Jack's attitude, taking no prisoners with Carlton, and the small matter of engineering Beckman's prolongued stay in town.

She carried plates over to the table. They were piled with an array of deliciousness, and he wanted to take a dive off the high board to get right in there.

'Did he not have a career in phoney Egyptian artefacts back awhile?' she wondered.

That made him snigger. They sat.

He remembered how his tires had not escaped so lightly. 'He'd probably stop short of shooting a guy to make Number One, but I'm not after finding out the hard way.'

'He'd have to track you down first,' she suggested, tucking in. He followed.

'I'm not out of the woods. Carlton shoots, huh?' he pointed out, sensing retribution might still be lurking.

'Yes, but I think he'd plug me first.'

'I was joking, but now….'

She shook her head. 'He's a lowdown shit, but, come on, Beckman—he's an accountant for Chrissake, not Wyatt Earp.'

'I guess.' He shovelled in a mouthful with as much reserve as he could muster. 'Besides,' he said offhandedly, 'I've got a gun.'

She roared with laughter. His face must have shown something because she checked herself, though the amusement didn't entirely leave her eyes.

'I'm sorry. It's, well, you're no action hero, are you?'

'I guess…,' he began to admit.

'Hell, you just cut yourself shaving.'

Without ceremony, she reached across and lightly touched the tiny cut with her index finger. He tried not to let his face betray the slightest flutter of embarrassment and appreciation.

'Yeah, mornings, huh?'

'It wasn't there this morning.'

'Oh. Yeah.' He'd been caught in… what? Not a lie.

Why had he glossed over the fact he'd re-groomed himself? To avoid letting her know he cared about how she saw him, and that he wanted to give a good impression? Was it so verboten?

'In case you missed it, I got pretty close to your face this morning.'

'Oh. Yeah,' he mustered again, not meeting her eye.

Please don't talk about That Kiss.

That stuff is known globally as an Awkward Moment that usually necessitates the What Just Happened conversation.

This meal is too good for me to not feel like eating right now.

'I'm observant, okay? Lighten up.'

'You'd make a good P.I.'

'Maybe I'm only observant when I want to be. You know, little things. Not stuff like my boyfriend doing some industrial espionage shit and banging another woman.'

He shrugged. 'People keep hidden what they want.'

'Problem is, so did a lot of other people.'

'Sometimes people are too nice. Afraid of consequences.'

She finished her beer. 'Not you, though. Afraid, I mean.'

'I'm a curious person.'

'Like when you spotted my headache from across the room.'

'I guess.'

Silence fell for a minute while they cleaned their plates. When she put down her cutlery, it was with a non-sequitur of disdain.

Her voice had a hard edge. 'I can't believe he hired a damn P.I.! The nerve. The goddamn irony! It's not just spying on you—it's me too, by implication.'

'And he hired the cheapest one, too. How's that for a kick in the teeth?'

'He's a finance guy. It comes naturally. Always got to save a buck.'

'So, any chance his thing with Wanda is financially motivated?'

She looked pensive. She rose, took away their plates, then went to the wall and dialled down the lights.

Romantic Lighting Alert.

She laid her glasses on the table. He began to join dots and see beyond the possibility that the tints were for show. That she wasn't so shallow.

'The company is losing market share. Has been for a while. Carlton was supposed to turn that around. It kind of has, but EVI still have the squeeze. Said he had ideas. Didn't figure for infidelity, though. Maybe he's trying to find a way in and do something … I don't know. It's not like the Carlton I know. Knew.' She sighed. 'Thought I knew.'

'Is Wanda so dumb not to know she's being used like that?'

'Unless she's on a mission to screw over *her* father, too.'

'Bad blood?'

'I don't know. She's not exactly on my Christmas card list, even on a good day. She and Walter. The Milans and the Whacks, we're like Sunrise's own Montagues and Capulets.'

'So maybe Romeo is where he belongs?'

'We all know what happened there.'

'Carlton got off lightly with a ring toss,' he ventured.

'Lucky I didn't have him killed.'

Beckman sat back quickly. 'Jeez.'

'Take it easy, no big deal. It's about as easy to hire a hitman round here as a P.I.'

'I'll take it under advisement.'

'Just don't piss me off, okay?' She winked. 'Pie?'

He nodded vigorously.

She went to prepare the dessert.

He watched her, got lost in the view, then came back to reality, reflected on the *un*reality of it all, then gained some perspective.

It's another dinner in another town on another day. It just happens that it sucks a lot less than the others.

She set the plates down, and they dived in.

'Can I ask you a question?' he found himself saying.

'Sure.'

'Why am I here?'

'Do you not want to be?'

'No. Hell, no. You already said thanks for what I did. At least, I assume that's what… what, err, the kiss was.'

Her eyes met his, oh so briefly, yet she avoided a direct reply—and he noticed.

She gathered herself. 'After I saw Buck and he told me about the photographs, then I saw you on the street, I went home. I thought, "If this is true, I've lost a shot at getting the company." Can you believe that? Not Carlton. The company.'

'Interesting,' he said.

'I realised I can afford to lose Carlton—that's not the kicking. He's just a guy. I can get another guy! It's the inheritance. I was vindictive. Dad approved of Carlton as an heir, as a son-to-be. I decided, "I'll show you—I'll marry him. Then I'll screw you over like you screwed me. That'll show you what a woman can do." Beckman, my motivation was screwing someone over. I acted no better than a lying art salesman.'

She took a mouthful of key lime pie, reflective. 'So, I guess you made me a better person.'

'Let's not get carried away here.'

She didn't meet his eye. 'I do everything to piss off my father. That makes me not a nice person. Not an Okay Gal.'

'Could have fooled me.'

'I'd been carrying a flat for too long. You were my Saul. It was selfless and caring.'

'It was hardly deliberate.'

Now she finished her plate and met his gaze. 'We are what we show.'

'Lolita, this food is amazing. For one, that means you're a lot more than meets the eye.' Then he checked himself. 'Sorry, that was a cheap thing to say.'

'The whole bimbo in a look-at-me dress, huh?'

He pulled a sheepish face, digging furiously for a way out of the hole. 'For the first five seconds, maybe.'

'My father disapproves. That's some of why I do it. See a theme here?'

'Your real father. As opposed to Buck.'

She gave a smile of recognition. 'Yeah. Jack. Anyway, it works for me. Plus, I have great legs.'

In a flash, she stood and did an impromptu twirl, the dress hem kicking up and proving her statement to be wholly correct.

'Pretty hot, huh?' She grabbed the empty plates and took them to the kitchen island.

He chuckled, partly out of nervous embarrassment, as the question hung in the air, teasing.

Jeez, Beckman, get a grip.

'I'm a salesman. You know I'll tell you what you want to hear.'

She faced him, hand on the surface, hips kicked out slightly.

'Beckman, you're not any old salesman. You're as honest and well-meaning as the day is long. A pretty rare commodity.'

'I can't believe you're the kind of person who needs shallow flattery.'

Needing a distraction, he grabbed the empty beer bottles and set them on the counter.

'Indulge me. I've been through an emotional breakup.' She gave him a pointed look, tempered with a knowing smile. 'You may have heard.'

'Lolita, you look a million dollars.'

She cocked her head. 'Yeah, I do, don't I?'

He left that alone, so she smoothed her dress and continued. 'This is one of Buck's favourites. Never figured why, not with his color problem.'

His brow creased. 'Say what?'

'Buck is red-green color blind. Never tell from the café, though. I gave him a consult on the lights.'

'Yeah, it's a cool place. But I guess there are worse problems to have.'

'Tell me about it.'

Come on, you know it's killing you to ask. You gave her chapter and verse. She didn't hit you outside the house or on the street.

Why would she now?

'Forgive me—you have light sensitivity, don't you?'

'Yeah,' she said, somewhat reflective. Then she brightened and touched his upper arm. 'Thanks for asking.'

'Just curious. There are worse problems to have.'

'I'm sure.'

Do it, Beckman. It's not verboten.

'It's burgundy, isn't it? Your dress.'

She was perplexed. 'Of course. Why—you're not…?'

He gave a small smile. 'No. Nothing so easy. I have monochromacy.'

She eased back, her instant reaction one of shock and disbelief. A few expressions flickered over her face. She studied his attire, which helped make the sums work.

'You can only see black and white?'

'Shades of grey.'

'My God, Beckman, I'm so sorry.'

'It's not your fault. It's nobody's. It's… life.'

She bit her lip. Then she leaned in closer, looking at his eyes. 'You can't tell.'

He met her gaze. 'No.'

She was still processing. 'Wow,' she said slowly, sadness tinging her face. *Awkward Eyes-Meeting Situation.*

His mind sought a new direction. 'Thanks for dinner.'

She snapped out of the curiosity of inspection. 'No problem.'

'You realise I should be making *you* dinner. You're the one who started all this in Sunrise. First buyer. You spread the word. Gave me a real shot at my dream. I should be thanking you.'

'You cook?'

He smiled. 'Hell, no. I'd burn water.'

'No matter. I consider myself thanked.'

'Well, so we're clear,' he said and found himself pressing his lips briefly to hers, 'Thank you.'

Whoa! Where did that come from?

Not you, brain, I'm guessing. Somewhere lower. Somewhere rustier.

In her eyes lit the slightest surprise but mostly contentedness. 'You're very welcome.'

'So, we're even now.'

She nodded. 'Can I ask you a question?'

'Always.'

'Monday, when you saw me for the first time in Buck's, you were looking at me as a customer, right?'

He licked his lips, nervous. 'Honestly?'

'I don't know. I did think you were an honest kind of guy.'

He waggled his head, deciding. 'No. Not entirely as a customer.' He coughed. 'At first.'

'I see.'

'Yeah,' he replied sheepishly, confidence knocked back, looking away.

Her hand laid on his face, gently drawing it back to meet hers.

'Beckman?' she asked gently.

'Yes, Lolita?'

'Would you like to close the sale?'

Outside in the dimming light, a cheap private investigator in a dark blue sedan watched all the downstairs lights go out. Then a single upstairs light went on.

He reached for his camera, then paused.

Presently, that light also went out.

While not the sharpest tool in the box, he knew he wouldn't be needed again that night, so he started the car and moved quietly away.

CHAPTER 28

Beckman's bladder woke him.

A flutter of nervous unfamiliarity shot through his frame. What was the room?

In the near-dark, he didn't know.

A quick recollection. Lolita's place? Could it be? If the whole Sunrise episode had been a dream, this—right here, right now—was the standard-bearer. It couldn't get more dreamy, unreal, unlikely than this.

Yet, here he was, awake.

It felt real. Was it real? He lolled his head over. Someone else lay beside him in the bed.

So, it was real. A warm glow permeated inside and blew the nerves away. He bathed in it for a minute. A smile appeared and broadened across his face.

I'll be a son of a gun. A strapping great teenage line-backer offspring of a Sherman tank cannon.

His bladder reminded him why he was awake.

He carefully pushed the cover aside, remembered the newly-acquired bearings towards the ensuite, and padded across, hoping not to clatter anything in the near-dark.

Keen not to wake her, he gently closed the door behind himself and, in the faintest moonlit glow from the window, fumbled for the light pull.

His hand clasped it and yanked, closing his eyes to dull the imminent shock of illumination.

The world beyond his lids bloomed brightly.

He opened his eyes slowly to it. Then they snapped open, drinking in the color.

The color.

COLOR!

Involuntarily, he screamed.

CHAPTER 29

She found him perched on the edge of the bath, shaking, sobbing.

'Oh my god, Beckman, what is it?'

She sat beside him, cast an arm around his shoulder.

'It's color,' he said brokenly. 'Everything's color.'

She could only stare at his face, which was rent with anguish and disbelief and relief and joy and new birth.

'Really?' she asked, in a measure of shock.

His wide-eyed gaze took in the room. He wiped the tears away and looked again. All he could do was nod.

Her face ran a gamut of emotions, reflecting many that coursed through him. Neither of them understood. Neither believed, although they needed to.

Should he trust his own eyes? Why now, when he'd been unable to trust them for the last thirty-seven years and five days? Yet surely *those* were the bad days, not this one, not this astonishing moment?

'Tell me this isn't a dream,' he implored.

She laid a hand softly on his wet cheek. 'No. You're here with me. This is real.'

'Promise?'

She took his hand and laid it on her camisole top. More precisely, where it covered her breast. He stroked the sheer fabric and its contents.

'What color is this?' she asked.

He peered more closely. Countless hours of tutoring, practice and studying color charts were being put to the test. He knew all the words, all the possibilities that had always existed for everyone else, but this was the first time he had to match what was actually in front of him with what he'd only been able to presume for his whole life.

'Purple?'

She nodded. 'The towels?'

'Peppermint.'

She smiled.

It was just a bathroom, yet he engorged himself on the sight as if beholding the Taj Mahal, an alien world, the very face of God.

She could only watch him, consumed with wonder and care, as if a mother in that first post-birth embrace.

A tear ran down her cheek.

When he finally turned to look at her again, she said, 'I have an idea.'

She held his hand as they walked down the quiet road towards town. The moon glowed a crescent, clouds drifting, the night warm.

The mosaic of lights crystallised out of indeterminate visual chaos of color.

They reached Main Street.

Four a.m., and nothing moved.

He meandered, lost, Alice in Wonderland.

There was scarlet and imperial and crimson and cherry and orange and mustard and lemon and burgundy and jade and magenta and olive and maroon and navy and salmon and candy and violet and indigo and sky and brick and chocolate and turquoise and lime and taupe and tomato and emerald and cyan and gold and tangerine and fuchsia and plum and heather and cobalt and sage and mint and caramel and wine and teal and lilac and coral and rose and fawn and oyster and....

Joseph's outerwear had nothing on this.

As he gazed, rapt, she looked at him and at the symphony of colors that lensed through the tears running down his face.

Neither spoke.

Soon, they reached Our Buck's, and he drew her to a halt. They stood, looking through the window at the not-grey neons inside, which bathed the dim and empty room. He gazed at the bar, at the stool whereon this first of his customers had been sitting.

He stared, transfixed. 'This is where we met.'

He said it as neither question nor statement: a sleepwalker, a hypnosis volunteer. Yet, as a remembrance, like a person looking at an old photograph found in the attic, a pensioner returning to his alma mater.

'Yes, Beckman, this is where we met.' She trod on eggshells, unable to truly comprehend his state of mind.

He faced her. 'What's happened?'

She shook her head, horribly lost and helpless. 'Sunrise likes you?'

He, too, felt adrift and had no answer.

She retook his hand. 'Come home with me.'

He returned to reality, this apparent new truth of million-hued vibrancy.

For the first time, he allowed his gaze to linger on her face, take in the color of her skin, her hair. Her eyes were lined with faint creases of worry, a transparent display of empathy, which warmed his soul.

'Your eyes are blue,' he noted. She nodded. 'Are you an angel?'

She shook her head slowly, eyes now also searching his.

He eased into her, kissed her gently at first, then as if his life was at an end. Or a beginning.

The remainder of the night was destined to follow one of two paths: wide awake, brain wired, or dead to the world, brain fatigued.

Mercifully, he flickered back into life around four hours later but allowed his lids to remain in the shuttered position. He reached out a hand, and it touched flesh.

So, that part hadn't been a dream. What about the interlude?

He almost dared not think. He couldn't face the notion that his sight had returned to what he'd known as his own normal. Fear took him, almost more than it had earlier.

'Lolita?' he whispered.

The sound of her waking. A heart-warming sound, one he'd experienced all too seldom these past years. Decades.

'Hey,' she mumbled.

'I'm scared.'

'Why?' The concern in her voice was almost motherly.

'I don't want to open my eyes. What if…?'

He felt her wriggle and press closer. 'You need to.'

'I don't want this to end. I don't want it to be… a glitch.'

'Here's the problem. If you never open your eyes, you'll be a hell of a lot worse off. At least you didn't bump into things before.'

'I didn't mean…,' he began.

'I know. I'm fooling.'

He felt her lips on his. Her face stayed close. 'Open your eyes. I'm here,' she said, mollifying.

He took a deep breath and looked.

Color.

His eyes widened. His heart leapt. Her face, occupying most of his view, broke into a smile, knowing the outcome.

He kissed her.

They celebrated in physical, horizontal, fashion.

It was way past nine when he left the bed, the shower calling to him.

In the bathroom, he checked his reflection in the mirror. In color. He, Beckman Spiers, existed in color.

He leant in. His eyes were greyer than the blue grey he'd imagined. His skin was more tanned than the brown he'd believed.

Imagine if all those miles these last twelve years had been in a soft-top. I'd be marginally less charcoal than poor Belcher is.

The door opened.

Her face creased with intrigue as he regarded his visage so intently. 'I'd ask what's up, but….'

She stood at his shoulder. He saw a hand coming up to run fingers tenderly through his hair.

'Nothing's changed,' he suggested.

'Or everything's changed.'

'Perception is reality.'

'There was only one dishonest part of you, Beckman, and now it's gone. The part of you that lied, not to anyone else, but the rest of you.'

'Poetic.'

'I'm way more than a great lay in a crazy dress.'

He faced her and put his arms around her waist. 'Way, way more.'

'So, stick around? See if it's the kind of "more" that appeals?'

'Well, it *is* the weekend.'

'And after?'

'Don't get me wrong, but based on the last twelve hours, I'm not up for predicting anything. Okay?'

She did a so-so with her head. 'Okay.'

He kissed her. 'Okay.'

She tilted her head towards the shower. 'How are you with helping wash my back?'

'A little out of practice. You know, just five, ten years.'

'Let's work on that, huh? If you're not so bad, I might even let you do the front, too.'

CHAPTER 30

She threw open the vast wardrobe doors. 'Help me pick something.'

He wanted to say, "But the underwear is doing you just fine", then realised it would be fatuous and sexist and opportunistic and Pushing His Luck.

Lolita had a *lot* of swing dresses. If last night's walk had been an enchanting symphony of colors, this represented at least a concerto.

And the cost...

'How much do you *make?*' he wondered aloud, then cursed himself that the underwear thing would only have been a marginally less inflammatory comment.

'I cleared a hundred k last fiscal,' she said, as if stating her preference vis-à-vis muffin flavours.

He whistled softly.

She laid a hand on his cheek, tenderness with a trickling undercurrent of menace. 'But then, you're dating me for my brains as well as my body, aren't you, Beckman?'

He held up a palm as if taking the witness stand. 'On Esmond Belcher's grave. Well, urn.'

'Correct answer.'

'Back up. We're dating?'

'Or it was a one-night stand, and I'll tell Buck you planned as much.'

His brain reacted with commendable purpose. 'I don't think any girlfriend of mine would truly do that.'

She pecked him on the cheek. 'Correct answer. So?' She gestured theatrically, taking in the long row of spectacular attire.

'Are you feeling happy today?'

'Does Dolly Parton sleep on her back?'

'Then wear what makes you happiest,' he suggested.

'What a caring soul you are.'

He pecked her on the cheek. 'Correct answer.'

She corpsed.

The dress was blue and yellow in vertical stripes.

Over breakfast, she looked again in disdain at his ensemble. 'We have to do something about that.'

'But how will I stand out and find all the customers I need in this rainbow town?'

'You'll find a way, darling.'

What now? Terms of endearment? Already? Lucky that Bogie isn't a bunny.

'Starting now. Delightful as it would be to skip around town all day like the cat who got the cream, first, that's not me, second, I don't trust Carlton not to take forty-four calibre offence at the speed of all this, and thirdly, I have a sales target to make. *Darling.*'

'Well, *darling*, I have another hundred k to make, so that means an appointment with a buyer.'

'Not that my rounds will make any difference to our financial status.'

"Our"? Did you just say "our"?

That's the dictionary definition of getting ahead of yourself.

'Lighten up. Stranger things have happened.'

He nodded sagely. 'You could say that.'

Her brow furrowed. 'Are you okay?'

He puffed out a breath. 'Yeah. Just sensory overload, that's all. Forgive me if I wander round in a stupor for a while.'

He plucked an orange from the bowl on the table and turned it slowly in his hands, bathing in its retina-burning orangeness.

'It's a wonder I don't short-circuit. Or bawl my eyes out. I mean, getting you *and* normal vision on the same day? Heaven knows what I did to deserve that, let alone how I'll cope.'

She gave a comforting smile. 'I hope my presence will make it easier, not harder.'

'Your presence might have caused the damn thing. And no, I don't have a millimetre of headspace to even think about that. Daytime in town with all those lights is plenty enough. I hope my poor optic nerves can cope because if they burned out now, that would be a hell of a shame, as I wouldn't get to look at you, which is fast becoming my favourite pastime.'

She rubbed his arm. 'I don't think the town would do that to you. I don't understand a lot about this place, but it's not cruel to its citizens. Like I said last night, I think Sunrise likes you. It wants you to stay awhile.'

Her positivity was undeniable. Misplaced, but undeniable. He didn't dwell on the futility of today's sales calls and instead finished his home-baked bagel, which was delicious.

Downsides—what are the downsides here?

Lighten up, dummy.

'Maybe see you at Buck's this afternoon?' he suggested. 'If I get a break.'

'Then I'll help you bring your suitcase inside afterwards? You know, so this is at least a two-night stand?'

'I'll stretch to three nights. Deal?'

A voice inside him said he was semi-serious. The same voice that had said "our". He wasn't sure if he liked that voice. So, he told the voice to go take a nap for three days.

I'm on vacation from ordinary life, Voice.

'It's a good job I know you're kidding, Beckman. On that, I don't want to call you "Beckman".'

'"B" okay?'

If it's good enough for Wilbur and... well, just Wilbur really, then I'm hardly giving up privileges.

She put her arms around his neck. 'Go and close some sales. Just none lying down, okay, B?'

'On Belcher's urn.'

He kissed her good and long, pulled his still-charcoal jacket from the back of the chair, and set off.

No navy Lincoln sat outside her house. Sadly, it arrived on his tail as he pulled to a stop outside Saul's garage. It represented a new experience—visiting the place voluntarily. Vehicular activity on the lot was minimal, prime evidence being that the owner had found time for some illumination-related marketing activity.

Because why? Saul's is the best tow garage in town. Strike that, the only tow garage in town. New signage?

Oh, I get it. With your money, dufus. That and Pirelli announcing record profits this quarter. So, I guess he does owe you the favour you're about to ask.

Beckman strode to where a pair of snakeskin boots rested halfway up a ladder.

'You sly old dog, Beckman.'

Shoot. It's all over town already. And I'd hoped for better from you, Lolita.

He sighed. 'Yeah, I guess.'

Saul climbed down, screwdriver in hand. 'Can't blame you.'

'So, you heard.'

'I don't need to hear. I can see.' He held out both arms in a ta-da! 'You're still here.'

Beckman's poor brain navigated some switchbacks and a loop-the-loop for good measure. 'Oh. Yeah. That. Still here.'

Phew. He doesn't know about last night.

'So, what can I do for you this fine morning?'

Definitely fine. Certainly unprecedented, and not only the Company Of A Woman angle—this entire lack of universal black and white to the world.

Apart from the things which are actually black and white, of course. Like that black tire over there or the white walls on that white-wall tire, or...

Park it, Beckman. Stop looking at the blacks and whites and greys. Instead, maybe start with Saul's brown irises, which are awaiting a response from you.

'I don't mean to interrupt.'

'It's okay. Just putting up this new piece. Got a great deal out of EVI.'

The gentle clang of an alarm bell. 'EVI? I thought you were a die-hard Milan guy.'

'Well, you know, I got convinced.'

'Uh-huh.'

'They're on a Customer Welcome Program or some such. Anyway, pretty smart, huh?'

He gazed for what he deemed enough time to appear interested. His mind was elsewhere. 'Yeah. Smart.'

'So, what gives?'

'You know I've got my own Customer Welcome Program type affair?'

'Who *doesn't* know?'

Beckman gave a shrug verging on Gallic for its emphasis. 'Anyone not yet a customer?'

'Fair point.'

'So, I wondered—?'

'If I had any leads for you?' Saul interjected.

He pulled a guilty face. 'Kinda?'

An arm thudded across his shoulders. 'Come on in. I'll give you my whole database.' They began walking.

'Whatever one stop above Okay Guy is, you're it.'

'That I am, Beckman, that I am.'

He'd never made so many calls in a day. He covered a hundred miles without leaving the town.

Poor Delmar.

The difference was Delmar got squat.

What Beckman got was a sight he didn't ever recall witnessing before: the floor of his trunk.

It was Saturday, just past five in the afternoon, and he'd been cleared out. His sales year had wrapped with a day to spare.

For a second, he did curse Wilbur. There was at least another trunk full of untapped business to shift in Sunrise. Then, quickly, he recognised he was shooting the messenger. Wilbur babysat the stock; he didn't make the stuff or organise the deliveries. That was Mr Malvolio's job.

Why would a self-respecting CEO personally handle vendor management? Because stock lying idle cost money. Better to have a deficit of stock, and salesmen at each other's throats than tie up cash flow.

On days like today, Beckman thought it idiotic. But then, it was true that he (1) had a vested interest this year and (2) wasn't the one who'd successfully accrued $100m despite such apparent supply chain short-sightedness.

It would have to suffice, he consoled himself, as the Caddy pulled into the sloping driveway of 1002 Edison Avenue.

At least now you get Sunday off. In company. Man, just look at the company.

Was there ever a stranger (and more adorable) sight than a grown woman in a swing dress, ribbon in her hair, thick gloves on hands, and secateurs in her grip, tending to a young tree?

Unconsciously, a smile spread across his lips.

Yet more color. Green fingers.

She turned when the car door slammed.

'Hi honey, I'm home.' He couldn't believe he'd said it but hoped it would make her laugh.

It did.

'I would have thought, on a hundred grand, you'd have people for stuff like this,' he mooted.

'Ah, but this is special.' She pointed at the tree and popped him a kiss. 'Mom gave it to me before she left.'

'She could have sprung for a decent one.'

'It was fine. I think a wolf tried to eat it or fight it or screw it.'

Unarguably, it needed TLC. Maybe even a defibrillator. 'Fig?'

'Apple tree. Symbolises permanence.'

'After she left, huh?'

'Permanence for me, nimrod. Putting down roots.'

'Uh-huh.'

'Sound thrilled, why don't you?'

'Sorry. You know—me and roots.'

She gently bit her lip. 'Yeah. I guess.'

He steered the conversation away. 'So, are we painting the town red or a million other shades?'

'Together?' she asked with mild disquiet.

'Problem?'

'I just thought, you know, privacy?'

An a-ha washed his face. 'That's why Saul didn't know. About us.'

'Why would he?'

'Word gets around?'

'Only when I want. I'm not broadcasting it around the neighbourhood. Give me some credit. Besides, getting folks all excited over a one-night stand?' She smiled impishly.

'Or two.'

'You said three.'

'I may give you time off for good behaviour.'

She pushed in tight to him. 'What about bad behaviour?' She blew gently in his ear.

'Are you finished with that tree?' he gabbled.

'It'll keep. Why, will you not?'

'Blow in my ear much longer, and Delmar will have some interesting pictures.'

They turned, as one, to the road and waved. 'Hey, Delmar!' they chorused.

A figure behind the wheel sank, fruitlessly, lower into his seat.

CHAPTER 31

As he buttoned his shirt, there came a glimmer of self-consciousness for the first time, verging on despair.

His hands slowed to stillness.

Is this me? he silently asked the mirror.

And I thought she was the quirky one.

The second reflection paused what it was doing and walked over. Its arms wrapped around his waist.

'I'm going to Pretty Woman you like you wouldn't believe.'

He looked at the face over his shoulder. 'I don't need charity, Lolita.'

'It's not that. It's…,' she searched for another excuse. 'A belated birthday present.'

He turned within her grasp until they were in a standard embrace. 'Besides, that would make *me* the streetwalker.'

'I guess.'

'As it is, I'm Rebound Guy, and I'm not sure Rebound Guy is ever a good move.'

'Why, you breaking up with me?'

'Honey, I'm not that dumb.' He kissed her. 'I'm not dumping you until you've spent a ton of cash making me look awesome.'

Her eyes narrowed. 'I hope you're ticklish.'

'Money first, revenge later. Okay?'

'Whatever you say, Rebound Guy.'

Sunday mornings in Sunrise were quiet.

Few other cars mooched around on Main Street besides his (not really *his*) Caddy. A couple of vehicles were familiar. One of them had loosely trailed them down from the outskirts.

They visited five stores. In each, both were recognised. In each, they didn't cling to one other, neither did they act like strangers. In each, nobody passed comment. But then, nobody had passed comment on Carlton's unfaithful antics either. So, was their relationship the new unspoken rumour, a truth destined to remain under the surface?

Did he mind? The one person who should care either way was Carlton, and he'd be finding out via the medium of long-lens photographs. At a stretch, Jack Milan might be selfishly pissed because his daughter had forsaken an apparently Okay Guy for a scheming outsider. However, it would hardly alter his attitude towards her.

Ultimately, she conceded to shelling out half towards the various ensembles they came away with. She contributed a real insight into which colors suited him, as if he had his own personal shopper. At the very least, looking as radiant as ever, she was confusingly a prettier woman than his stab at the role of Pretty Woman.

Afterwards, they dumped the bags in the car and walked down to Our Buck's for "brunch".

He didn't recall ever having "brunch". He'd heard of the concept. At best, for him, it meant whatever particular candy-or-similar he had with coffee around that time of day. For Lolita, it was A Thing.

Another thing was that the world felt cleaner, brighter, sharper. Covered in fairy dust. The air was more wholesome, the passers-by more smiley, each step supplemented by a tiny spring.

For instance, there's a place I don't remember seeing: "Barber's".

Behind the tall plate-glass windows sat two guys having a haircut.

The fascia board not only spelt out the name of the establishment in neons but was also illustrated by a masterpiece of neon engineering, wherein, over four stages of illumination, a head of hair was trimmed by a hand holding a pair of scissors that opened and closed. It was stop-motion in red and white, an unmistakable advert that was in equal parts brilliantly clever, beautifully made, and appallingly kitsch.

Yet, something bothered him. He studied the name.

"Barber's."

'Your signwriter has Apostrophe Disease,' he pointed out.

She looked across the street, turned back to him, and shook her head gently. 'Oh, dear sweet Beckman. You've got a lot to learn about Sunrise. That's Unwin Barber's place.'

Ah. Nominative determinism. Easy mistake to make.

'You have a Joey Generalstore in town, too? A Lyle Haberdasher?'

'Go ahead, mock my little town. I can return those clothes pretty easily, I'll have you know.'

He beamed innocently. 'It's all just as charming as you, but only a fraction as wonderful.'

'Make me hurl on the sidewalk, too. Great,' she joked.

They nudged shoulders playfully, and then he retook her hand. As they continued walking, he couldn't help but feel self-conscious for the second time that morning. This was A New Beckman.

Beckman In Color.

The jacket was a deep burgundy, pants navy, shirt—the least offensive item to his sensibilities—a mid-grey. The one constant remained his existing shoes, which, as they were black, he'd insisted were just fine.

'Pretty sharp, Beckman,' Buck remarked as they entered the coffee and root beer parlour. His greeting for Lolita was a hug; for him, a nod, which was more than satisfactory. He wasn't an Almost Father-In-Law quite yet, nor even by the longest shot.

'Thanks, Buck.' No explanation would be forthcoming if it could be avoided. His eyesight was his own private matter and, though he constantly fought to suppress the notion, he remained unconvinced that the change was permanent. Besides, he didn't have a monopoly on ocular peculiarity round here.

'Pretty sharp, Beckman.'

Is there an echo in here?

Saul saluted from across the room.

'Guessing word gets around. I should probably spring for that promised ten percent,' Beckman said, excusing himself.

He pulled up a chair beside Saul, glancing over as Lolita and Buck struck up. He fished some bills from his wallet, did a ready-reckon, and handed across a slim sheaf of Andrew Jacksons.

'Gratitude is its own reward,' Saul said, not offering his hand.

Beckman leant across and jammed the notes into the other man's shirt pocket. 'It's like this. On a million-to-one shot I do make the top of the mountain tomorrow, I'd rather see you right today than have you ask for a cut after the fact because that would get pretty damn expensive.'

'Why, what's the Number One prize money?'

'Search me.'

'You're in line for a prize and don't even know what it is?'

An unrequested root beer arrived on the table.

Beckman guzzled it gratefully. 'There are a million different ideas of Heaven, but nobody knows 'til they get there.'

'Poetic.'

'Thanks. Guess I'm in a good mood.'

Saul flashed the briefest of glances towards Lolita. 'I'll bet.' Beckman didn't dignify that. 'So, how come nobody knows what this Valhalla of yours is all about? They all get too big and important to talk to the little guys once they've reached it?'

'Because overnight millionaires, as a class of people, are well known for sticking with their old friends?' he joked.

Saul shrugged and sipped his mug of coffee. 'Just saying.'

'Well, mister conspiracy, my old pal Charlie sends me a postcard on Thanksgiving. Does that satisfy your curiosity?'

'Gloating on his desert island, huh?'

Well, that's oddly accurate.

'He has… a better life now,' he replied hurriedly.

'When did this Charlie make Number One?'

'Three years back.'

'I could stick about a week on a desert island, and then I reckon I'd kill someone.'

'Well, when you come visit, I won't make you stay.'

Saul smiled. 'Thanks. Good thing you won't be lonely, anyway.'

Beckman followed the inference as easily as a trail of kernels leading to an oversized box of Acme Bird Seed in the middle of the highway.

The question was, if he took the seed, would an anvil land on him?

'Didn't take you for a dreamer, Saul. Because that's all there is. Every day here, I think I'm going to wake up.'

Saul's look towards the bar was deliberate. 'Looks pretty real to me.'

'At the risk of having my face Picasso'd, you're hardly twenty-twenty in the perception department.'

'I'm just completely wrong, huh?'

He sighed. 'I wish this was a dream—because no consequences. And, honestly, I have not the first clue what I'm doing.'

'Boy meets girl. Boy likes girl. Boy puts his—'

Beckman held up his hand. 'Boy has life. Girl has life.'

'Things change.'

'I wrote the book on that, you might know. Things like a different home to come back to every couple of years, a different school, making friends—,' he snapped his fingers, '—losing friends. Seeing a girl, getting to talk to a girl—,' he snapped again, '—pack the case, new county, new state.'

Saul nodded, understanding. He drank. 'New shirt, new town, new motel.'

Beckman shrugged. 'Things change. Every day.'

'Except Beckman.'

He drank, as a nervous defence. 'Some things have to stay the same.'

'Word is, you're not twenty-twenty, either.' Saul met his gaze. 'With your perception of things.'

'Nobody's perfect.'

'But we can all aspire, huh?'

'We can.'

Saul patted his pocket of scrunched bills. 'Then if I helped, that'd be good.'

'We gave it a shot,' he ventured.

'Good. I believe in giving things a shot.' He glanced towards Lolita again. 'Don't you?'

CHAPTER 32

Whilst his preconceptions that Lolita was nothing more than "kooky" had long faded, she continued to make scant effort to jump into the box marked Normal.

Exhibit A: late lunch was a picnic. On the back lawn. On a rug, no more than ten feet from a perfectly serviceable terrace.

'Can I open a fresh wound?' he asked, washing down the last of his meal.

'You're safe. My gun's in the dresser.'

'You... what?'

'Carlton used to go shooting with me too, you know. And not in a Bonnie and Clyde way, so get over yourself.'

He did. 'Why would he cheat on you?'

'If you're looking for logical reasons, I'm out of ideas. Because we both already know the "I'm hot, he's a scumbag" part.'

'Will Jack renege on the deal now it doesn't tie up so neatly?'

'You mean will my loss of a husband be less important to him than holding onto a successor? That's a pretty dumb question.'

'So why would Carlton do it?'

'Because he gets to keep his stature and bang a woman he's into more than me. Win-win.'

'What's Walter going to think?'

'I have no idea. But if EVI stays ahead in the market, and he gets a son-in-law who has a good job, he couldn't care less, I guess.'

'A son-in-law working for the competition.'

She shrugged. 'You said it already. Romeo and Juliet.'

'But if the outcome is that EVI buys your father out, where does that leave you?'

'Who needs a daddy when I've got my ancient mummies?'

'Because it's not what you want.'

'I believe it's called compromise.' She tousled his locks. 'I want a taller man with dark hair, but those are the breaks.'

'I wanted the office girl with the tight ass.'

'And...?'

He rolled his eyes. 'Tyler.'

'Always one step ahead, huh?'

He supped his store-bought, not-as-good-as-Buck's root beer. 'I agreed to meet her for… not even a date. A class. Kind of.'

'"Agreed"? But the rod was too far up your ass, huh?'

'It was a dance class. I was nervous, okay? You know the thing where you decide to do what *she* wants, to win affection? Well, I did that. I never danced in my life.'

'So, how d'you get on?'

'Tyler used her cell while she was in Malvolio's office, taking notes. He texted me to say, "Be there for eight". So, I turned up at eight like I believed she'd asked. The class started at seven. Tyler had an hour's lead on me. He barely needed half that. So, I left.'

'You ran away?'

'I… found something better to do.'

'Home, beer, ball game.'

'Yeah,' he admitted. 'But I made sure to let the air out of his tires on the way out.'

Her face lit from exasperated disbelief to a beaming smile. 'I never would have thought that of you.'

'Pyrrhic victory.'

'Well, he'll get payback.'

'He's charmed.'

'Trust me, nobody in this world is charmed.' She wriggled towards him. 'Charming, though….' She lay a long kiss on his lips.

'This is not going to lead where you think it's going to lead,' he replied when she came up for air.

'You're no fun.'

'Probably very true. But the dry-cleaning bill for grass stains on this dress will be criminal, so hold fire. I'll still be here tonight.'

'And for kicks before then?'

What to do for your last day in town? Especially when you don't want to admit to yourself—and especially your lady—that the situation is as cold as that?

'Show me some sights?'

'Okay.'

As they were dropping the hood on her Miata (she told him the color was "Eternal Blue"), he again noted the bumper of the Lincoln, pretty well concealed (for Delmar) behind trees on the road below.

'I wish we could do this without company.'

She followed his eye-line. 'Yeah.'

He pondered a minute. 'I have an idea.'

She listened to the idea. 'It might work.'

Delmar grew nervously self-aware as Lolita locomoted towards him. There was nowhere to hide. He knew he'd been made—he wasn't dumb—but hadn't bargained on actual confrontation, not with a Person Of Interest.

'Afternoon, Delmar.'

Reluctantly, he ran the window down. She put a hand on the roof and leaned down, body bent forwards at the waist. Nervousness danced in his eyes. He couldn't see *her* eyes because that's not where he was looking.

She asked how he was doing that fine day.

His voice said something, but his brain was busy processing what his optic nerves were offering him, and what they were offering him was much more compelling than mere words.

She showed interest in him for a good couple of minutes—flannelling small-talk and no searching assignment-related questions. For his part, Delmar even looked at her face a few times.

Then she suggested he have a nice day and sashayed back up the drive.

He watched as she climbed into the mid-blue soft-top, gave Beckman a peck on the cheek, then trundled the car down to the road and away.

He turned the key, slid the Lincoln into D, and span the wheel over. It felt very sluggish. Nonetheless, he eased in the gas.

An appalling rumbling, rushing noise came from under the car. The wheel felt like he was controlling a one-tonne jelly.

He stabbed the brake to a stop, shoved the selector in P, and leapt out, cursing to himself, as the Miata shrank to a blob.

He did a full three-sixty of the car.

All four tires were flat.

The wind of the open road tugged at Lolita's hair. 'I never would have thought that of you,' she giggled.

'You're the one who did the hard work.'

'That was runner-up for a world record for staring at my chest, I gotta say.'

'You keep score?'

'Felix Venturi, high school. A whole math lesson, I swear.'

'Boy's got taste.'

'He should be so lucky.'

'Well, I know *I* am.' He jiggled his eyebrows deliberately.

'Brain's just a bonus, huh?'

'That and the money.'

'You're a bad, bad man, Beckman Spiers.'

With that, she gassed the convertible, and it tore down the highway like a startled impala.

Oh yes, she liked to drive. And if any cops came calling, he felt sure they would enjoy a similar conversation to Delmar Spinkle.

You're a bad, bad woman, Lolita Milan. And that's just fine.

Fifteen minutes and no new scenery later, she eased them to a stop in a roadside parking spot mercifully shaded by two brave trees.

She turned to him. 'Confession. I don't think there are any sights.'

'This is your backyard. I'm not looking for the Eiffel Tower or the Hanging Gardens of Babylon. I'll take a haunted motel, an abandoned gold mine, or, I don't know, a rock shaped like a six-foot wiener.'

'You won't believe this, but I don't get out of town much.'

'You won't believe this, but I believe you.'

'Hell, I never even crossed the state line.'

He laughed. Then he saw her expression. 'Apart from on an airplane, right?'

She shook her head.

He felt a little sad inside. 'You never left the *state*?'

'I just, you know, had other things to do.'

'You know how close we are?' She looked sheepish. He unbuckled himself. 'Out.'

'Pardon me?'

'Out.' He walked round to her side and opened the door, thumbing towards the verge.

She complied. He took the wheel, and she slid in beside him. 'Straight on?' He turned the key.

'Honestly, you don't have to.' A hint of apprehension in her voice.

'Straight on it is.'

'What if…?'

'There Be Dragons?' he scoffed. She didn't reply.

He rolled the seat backwards a couple of notches, checked the mirror, and nailed the gas. Ten minutes later, the Nevada sign loomed large, and he slowed to a respectable pace.

'It looks great, thanks.' She nodded nervously. 'Road, fields. All good. Thanks. We can head back now.'

He rolled to a stop with the bumper in line with the border notice.

He took her hand. 'I promise you won't turn into a pumpkin.'

She squeezed his hand as he tickled the throttle, and they rolled into the undiscovered country.

'Oh my god! Lolita! You're starting to swell up and turn orange!'

Her look was mock anger overlaid with good humour. She loosened her hand and jabbed it playfully into his ribs. He retorted. In a moment, the car began weaving under the influence of their sparring. His pulse quickened, the air crackling with eagerness.

He did the only sensible thing and pushed the throttle to the stop.

Two minutes later, a building rushed towards them. It was an abandoned gas station.

He speared the Miata off the tarmac, bounced onto the rutted ochre ground, and round to the rear of the building. The brickwork was crumbling, the shade merciful and the silence deafening.

Lolita enjoyed something she'd never done outside the state before.

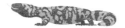

Delmar wasn't there when they returned to the house.

Poor guy is probably feeling deflated.

The sun hung low in the sky, and with every additional degree towards the horizon, the butterflies in Beckman's gut mated with growing intensity. Sunday would soon be Monday: Judgement Day.

He showered away the desert dust that had blown over them (and maybe sneaked into a few places not generally exposed to the elements), found a new pair of slacks, and searched out his girl. A familiar shape stood at the kitchen worktop, her back to him.

He crept in. She didn't flinch. He sprang forwards and threw both arms around her waist. Her waist felt narrower than he'd remembered. His hands kept moving. A lot narrower. His hands met.

Laughter erupted behind him. He span.

She descended into tucks. 'Oh, that's a slam dunk in the keepsake box!'

He flicked his hands through the unreal image. The light danced off skin, fluttered in his eyes. Then it vanished. She dropped the remote control onto the kitchen island, still giggling.

'I'm sorry, B, I couldn't resist.'

He shook his head, smiling. 'Milan Enterprises are in the hologram business, too.'

'Pretty impressive, huh?'

He embraced the real shape. 'It was always going to be pretty and impressive.'

'Aw, shucks.'

Then she really kissed him, really cooked dinner, and they really ate.

The Awkward Conversation drew nearer.

They retired to the terrace, a set of tall solar lamps glowing in the half-light of evening, cicadas distantly chorusing. They sat down together on her swing set.

'What happens tomorrow?' She'd fired the gun.

He took a breath. 'I go back to the office.'

'Why?'

'My job.'

'Uh-huh.' She was holding in disquiet. 'And you come back when?'

He shrugged. 'I have no idea.'

'Here, let me loosen my dress a little, so it's easier for you to rip my heart out,' she said derisively.

'Lolita, I have a job. No, it's not big, it's not clever, and it doesn't pay a hundred grand, but it's mine, and it's what I like.'

'Because any other way, There Be Dragons, huh?'

He smirked at the echo in her rejoinder. 'You're acting like this is fun for me. It's not.'

'Then don't go.'

'Here's how it works. Come nine-oh-one tomorrow, with the absence of a call from Malvolio, I go back to the office to fill my trunk for the next fiscal. Same as every year, start off on the right foot, maybe next July the First I *will* get Number One. And I have a shot, too—Tyler will be gone, Belcher has really slowed up his work rate since Sunday, and I'm feeling pretty good about my chances.'

'And, come nine-oh-one, you *do* get the call?'

'Hypothetically?'

'Yeah.'

He pondered. Light music drifted out from the house.

'Okay, very, very hypothetically, I punch the air, I kiss you like you wouldn't believe. I may even cry. I'm a sensitive guy—you probably noticed. Then, I go back to the office to see what it's all about.'

'And then?' She searched his eyes.

'What does anyone do when they get what they've been chasing their whole life?'

'Enjoy it? Re-evaluate their priorities? Start another, better life?'

He took a long draw on his beer. 'I wish I knew.'

'You scare me, Beckman,' she observed softly.

'Yeah,' he admitted, 'I scare myself sometimes.'

She pushed closer to him on the swing set. 'Success scares you?'

'That would mean I've chased something scary for twelve years. Pretty dumb, huh?'

'Dumb is doing something out of spite. I should know. Not out of goals or happiness, for you or whoever.'

'It's why I do what I do. Everybody wins.'

'Come nine-oh-two tomorrow, does everybody still win then? Every last—important—person in your life?' She raised an eyebrow expectantly.

He sighed. 'Ask me at nine-oh-three.'

'But you'll still leave.'

'I'm here now.' He embraced her gently.

They sat there for a long minute, whereupon she raised her head towards the house. She listened intently, then grabbed the radio's remote from nearby and clicked the volume up.

'Jeez, memories,' she said nostalgically.

He didn't recognise the tune, but it had a romantic, loping rhythm.

She stood and offered her hand. 'This is a dancing song.'

He shook his head gently.

She nodded in reply. 'This is a dancing song.'

'I don't dance.'

'Not even for me? Tonight?'

He puffed out a breath, torn, and pushed himself to stand.

She drew him out onto the terrace, put one of his hands on her waist and another on her shoulder. 'Dance with me.'

He felt a total heel, fighting himself, sowing these memories for her, feeling with every fibre that it could only be a keepsake she wouldn't want in the box.

'You deserve better than this, Lolita.'

She held him close. 'Shut up,' she said, softly yet firmly. 'Shut up and dance with me.'

CHAPTER 33

Morning dawned too early.

He didn't want the anxiety, the suspense. Only to be asleep in a warm, unending embrace that he knew would end.

Fleetingly, he wanted to rewind to last Monday, to the shard of glass rending his tire, to have tapped Decline, to have passed the invisible road to Sunrise. To arrive at the next town, make a few sales, find a motel, get up on Tuesday, hit the road, find a Coffee Planet, find a stop, make a sale. Rinse. Repeat.

It killed him because his head wanted it, and to deny it would be a lie. And he wasn't a liar.

"You know, Beckman, you may be the most honest guy in town."

He gazed at where she lay close, breathing lightly, chocolate curls bedecking the pillow.

To hold her would be to wake her, which would be selfish. The clock glowed 06:01, and there were a full three hours before he needed to wake her, whatever the outcome of the call.

Sliding quietly out from under the sheet, he pulled on briefs and padded downstairs. He indulged himself with a glass of warm milk and meandered around the house.

She looked about sixteen in the family photographs, her attire remarkable in its normality: this was pre-Fifties Girl. The sharp eyes were still there, the curls, the slightly crooked smile.

In the background stood the factory, bearing the legend MILAN ENTERPRISES.

He felt surprised she kept it on show, a reminder of what she could reach at but never grasp. Jack Milan would be an asshole if he weren't proud of what she'd achieved despite him.

Would Marlon Spiers be so gratified?

Guess I'll never know. Got to get there first, anyhow.

He checked the wall clock: 06:33.

Returning carefully to the bedroom, he went to his roller case and slid a hand into the lining pocket, drawing out the two items that rested there.

One was a postcard:

"Hey, Beckman. Another year. Another twelve months in nirvana. No rat race, no targets, no cane. It's all worth it, buddy. Hold onto that. I know you can do it. Best, Charlie."

All the corners were dog-eared, the nondescript photograph of paradise long since faded.

He absentmindedly fingered the edge of the card, gazing at the handwritten words, the quirky script.

Then he brought over the more recent card, toyed with it a while.

At least you'll be grateful, Mom.

He went to the nightstand and checked his cell had full charge—no point in missing the call of a lifetime.

Would Malvolio ring anyway to commiserate? If nothing else, Tyler would, to gloat.

If she remembered, Mom would call to enquire, in habitual faint hope, about career progression instead of relationship developments.

He lay down gently and worked through a few choice excuses, witticisms, and comebacks for when the inevitable happened.

A perennial late riser, Lolita woke after eight. He did the decent thing and allowed her to be the little spoon. Neither had much to say.

A metaphorical bottle was arcing over the road again, and they foresaw what would happen next.

At breakfast, he declined coffee, as ever.

'You're a strange fish, B, a strange fish.'

He shrugged. 'When you find something you like, you stick with it.'

'Present company included?'

'It's been less than a week.'

'A lot can happen in a week.' She checked the clock. 'Or ten minutes.'

'Don't be disappointed, okay? Number Two is my best yet. And it's all because of you.' He kissed her.

'I do what I can.' She put a hand to his cheek.

For those ten minutes, he paced nervously, without knowing why. It wouldn't make a difference to the outcome; that ship had long sailed.

He would never forgive Tyler for snatching victory at the last, for using Scoot's good nature to fuel his rise. He'd never forgive Scoot, either. At least he'd never meet Tyler again, so perhaps there was a silver lining in all this. Plus, Tyler wasn't a postcard kind of guy. Unconsciously, he crossed his fingers and willed Tyler to win so that the man would be out of his life. He wished the lead car to slipstream him down the home straight, retire gracefully at the line, then allow Beckman a victory lap next time around.

Hell, he might even return to Sunrise at the end of next year if his numbers needed a late boost.

His cell rang, stupidly startling him. She rose from the sofa in expectant support.

He thumbed Accept, heart pounding.

'Congratulations, Spiers.'

His brain instantly went into Overload. Red lights flashed. Klaxons blared. Sparks flew. He feared a total system shutdown.

'Mr Malvolio?'

Because this was a Tyler prank call, as sure as the sun rises, wasn't it?

'Yet you still play the fool, Spiers. Mercy on us all when people like you can make Number One.'

'Number One?' he parroted. Across the room, Lolita's face bloomed joy.

'Yes! What did you think? This was a social call?'

'Number One? Are you sure?'

'Of course, I'm sure! Take me for incompetent, do you?'

'No, sir, no, only… Tyler?'

'Tyler Quittle fell at the last. Well, not fell, was pushed.'

'Pushed?' Beckman queried, lost.

'In front of a street sweeper. Yesterday, Sunday, I hear.'

'Holy smokes.' He drank it in. 'Holy smokes. Is he…?'

'He'll live. Miss Broomhead insisted we send a card anyway. So, you won by a nose, Spiers. I'd imagine congratulations are in order.'

Beckman waited for the congratulations to be forthcoming. And he waited. And waited. And realised Mr Malvolio was waiting for him to say something to indicate a reaction to the Stupefying News of the Number One Prize. Because what could be more sensible than prolonging a brain-addling phone call in not the middle of the morning when you're standing with a disarmingly lovely woman in nightwear, in her kitchen, in an unmapped town in the middle of nowhere on a Monday?

'So, I'll see you at the office, sharp as you can. Then we can get this over with. The world keeps turning. Nine hours into the new fiscal already, and the boxes won't sell themselves. Isn't that right, Spiers?'

'Yes, sir.'

'Not that you'll be selling anymore.'

'No, sir.'

'Your future will be very different.'

'I'm sure.'

'All speed, Spiers.'

Then the line cut.

His arm fell, glacially, to his side. Mouth hung open. Time froze.

Number One. I'll be a son of a gun.

In his glazed vision, a shape moved towards him. At the acknowledging movement of his head, she darted forwards and threw her arms around his neck.

He remained a statue, his mind a sphere of clay that nothing would sink into.

'Congratulations, honey.'

Presently, that filtered through. 'Thanks,' he replied, dumbfounded.

'Didn't I tell you?'

'Yeah,' he said, still distant.

'I knew you'd do it.'

What was that in her voice? A layer of...?

'Well, that's more than I thought.'

'I understand. Sometimes I guess a girl just knows.'

Now he spied something in her eyes. He didn't like it. He eased her away. 'How did you know?'

'Intuition. Faith.'

'Really?'

'Sometimes things work out for the best.' She took his hand. 'So, you know—you and I....'

Alarm bells clanged in his skull. He took his hand out of hers. 'You did this.'

'It's all right, now. You can stay. No more door-knocking. No more slave labour. No more striving, hoping—'

'You did this!'

'Things happen for a reason.' She pressed on, regardless.

'You put Tyler in the *hospital!*'

She brushed it away with a swat of her hand. 'Come on—the guy sounds like a major league ass-wipe.'

'You put out a *hit* on a guy? Over this?'

She stepped back, hands coming rudely to her hips. 'And a lot of gratitude it's gotten me.'

'I don't believe this. You rigged the salesman contest to get what *you* want?'

'You want it, too,' she protested.

'Damn right, I want it, but not like this. Can't you see? I got it by cheating.'

'Technically, you got it by *me* cheating.'

'Like it makes a difference. What are you *on*, Lolita?'

'Happiness. With you,' she cooed. 'Besides, this Malvolio guy will never know.'

'No, but *I* will. Tyler will.'

'Is that so bad? You got what you wanted. Your life's work. The dream. So, now you have it, you can do what you need to. Stay here. Be with me.'

He shook his head, paced as if in a trance. 'I can't believe I'm hearing this.'

'So, what, you want to carry on traipsing the country for ten bucks an hour? And what about me? I'm supposed to follow you around like a puppy?'

'You?'

'Hell yes, me. Or anyone. Or does some other Mrs Homemaker keep the house just the way Mr Perfect likes it, hoping one day he'll actually call by and spend a night in between his precious motel rituals?'

'You know, this is sounding less and less about me with every word.'

'Hey—you got Number One, okay? Or did you lose sight of that already?'

'No. And now I'm taking my case and taking my keys and going to find out what I get.'

'You made it,' she pleaded. 'That's what you wanted. You're the best. You did it. That's all you need to know. Come on, Beckman, you know that—in your heart.'

'I didn't spend twelve years of my life aiming for a prize and then never find out what it is! It would eat me up. It'll be in my brain for nights, weeks, years,' he implored.

'If it's money, I have that.'

'Because that would make me feel *so* good, using you like that,' he jibed.

'Look, I'm sure there's a job somewhere in Sunrise.'

He rolled his eyes. 'Sales, I suppose.'

'Why not? You're obviously good, and every company needs a salesman.'

He stepped away, giving himself physical and mental space, and calmed somewhat.

'Lolita,' he suggested, 'Let me just go back, for curiosity.'

'And if the prize is more cash and easy women than you can shake a stick at?'

'I'll come back,' he vowed.

'Look at Charlie. Look at the others. They didn't come back. Why should you? How are you so much damn better than them?'

'Because the word is, I'm an Okay Guy. Because honesty. Because you.'

She sneered. 'There's always an antidote. Especially money. Look at Carlton.'

'You know I'm not the same as him.'

'We'll see,' she scoffed, turning her back.

He threw up his arms in exasperation. 'What can I say?'

She faced him. 'Just… stay. It's easier.'

'And you said *he* was possessive.'

'Yeah, and a douche. I thought you weren't. Maybe you really are just like all the others. The patter, the quick in-and-out, doing it all for yourself. All about the commission, the bragging rights. Name on a plaque, a pin on the tie. You found me. You got your word of mouth. You had a quick fling, got your prize, then you're history.'

'Says the woman who was planning to screw over her father for her own end. I don't take life lectures from people like that.'

Her face went from cumulonimbus to nimbus in an instant. She stepped forwards, and a hand cut across his face. 'Then screw you, Beckman.'

As the stinging radiated through his cheek, he waited for the thunder and lightning to start. The dark grey clouds held there, simmering on the edge of a deluge.

She turned away, seething.

His world lay broken at his feet; he was out of conversation. 'I'm going to pack.'

The words rested with her for a moment. She didn't face him.

Her voice had calmed when she spoke. 'I'll give you five minutes to get out. Then, if I never see you again, it won't be a day too soon.'

CHAPTER 34

He'd never seen a cop in Sunrise but didn't want one to appear like Saul, genie-style, so he kept the needle hovering on 35.

He dearly wanted to put pedal to the metal like never before. Worse case, he'd blow a tire. Best case, and as likely as anything in Sunrise, he'd hit 88 m.p.h. and wind up in 1955. The good news would be he'd get a do-over. But with his luck, he'd bump into Lolita, looking entirely not out of place, and she'd probably clock him again.

Was there ever a guy in history who felt so like shit on the day he achieved his dream?

His body see-sawed between feeling fashioned of lead or feathers. His mind pulled apart the paradoxes, rebuilt them, searching for answers. It presented him with entirely zilch.

Our Buck's passed, then Saul's, then the town thinned. The road climbed out of town. Behind him coasted the perpetual shadow. He felt dazed.

'Running away, Beckman?'

He looked lazily to his right. 'What?'

'Why are you running, son?'

'What's it to you?'

'Doesn't seem very smart, leaving behind what you want.' The sun's rays caught his father's uniform insignia and created a lustre its owner didn't deserve.

He snorted. 'You'd know about that.'

'Break up with another girl?'

'You have a better idea? I'm about to make a grade you never did.'

'It's not all about grades,' came the terse reply.

'I'm doing what makes me happy.'

'You don't look happy.'

'Well, I am. Look.' He pulled a beaming smile and pointed at it. 'See—happy.' Then he let his face fall sullen again.

'Are you sure? You can't get out of here fast enough.'

'I have a prize to claim, in case you weren't paying attention.'

'Really? Running *towards* that or *away* from something else?'

'You are so full of shit. You spent your entire life running away like a kid who saw a ghost. Why the hell couldn't you just stay and fight for what you wanted?'

'This, coming from you? Now? Even in a dream sequence?'

Beckman puffed impatiently. 'Then give me some fatherly advice, for once in your damn life.'

'I don't need to. You're a bright kid, Beckman. You'll figure it out.'

'Thanks for nothing.'

A sudden glare bounced off the rear-view mirror. He winced, then checked it again. The Lincoln's windshield was reflecting towards him.

He checked the empty passenger seat. 'I must have been a real little asshole.'

He shook his head, sighed. Ahead, the town boundary sign read,

You Are Leaving
SUNRISE
Come Back!

He'd never noticed it before. He scoffed.

Bet she put it there just now. Or called Buck to rush out and do it.

Unlikely. Didn't seem she wanted you to stay—or return. If so, she could have gotten Buck to toss another bottle.

He dismissed it. Mr Malvolio had said "All speed", so he prepared to gun the engine.

The sign slid past.

The world flicked black and white.

Aghast, he jammed both feet on the middle pedal, and the Caddy screeched to a halt in a cloud of spent rubber.

'You are kidding me!' he railed at the universe.

He rammed the lever into R and screamed back a hundred yards. In the mirror, a startled Lincoln made a similar manoeuvre.

The car crossed the invisible line. Color leapt into his retina.

'Oh, SNAP!' he rapped, smacking his hand on the wheel.

His heart rattled away, nerves jangling, mind racing.

He yelled a primal scream that almost burst his eardrums. Closing his eyes, not only to shut out the horrible lies they told, he forced deep breaths into his thudding chest.

Lost for any better answers, he selected D and tickled the gas. The car rolled out of town.

Life drained monochrome.

He wanted to cry.

Instead, he nailed the gas.

He didn't stop, not even for Coffee Planet. The last stamp on his card would have to wait. There were more important things to attend to. Like destiny. He'd torpedoed one future and wasn't about to scuttle the other. The two paths were incompatible—so he'd have to make sure he achieved one of them.

The Caddy swung into the Pegasus lot shortly after noon.

Small mercy: Tyler wasn't there. Big result: his lovely white Buick was.

He sighed with relief: normality again. More than that, he experienced a whole new feeling: it would be a positive experience to see Mr Malvolio.

Miss Broomhead rose when he entered the outer office. He felt like a King.

If this is the New Life, I like it. I like it A Lot.

She shook his hand. 'Congratulations, Beckman.'

"Beckman", now, is it? Please don't curtsey; that would just embarrass us both.

'Thank you, Miss Broomhead.'

'Mr Malvolio will see you now.'

If he does so much as smile, I'll probably have a fit or throw a party.

As rote, he knocked on the door and eased it open.

Mercifully, Malvolio didn't smile. Or stand. He looked up, which counted as A Major Event.

'Well done, Spiers.'

Would he be offered a seat?

He would not.

All he could do was sidle away from Bruno, who eyed him with suspicion. Maybe Beckman had an invisible glow of greatness about him now.

'Thank you, sir.'

'Can't say I'm not surprised.'

Ah, there we go. Damned with faint praise, even at the last.

'About that, sir—winning by default. Is that even allowed?'

Talk yourself off the top step of the podium, why don't you? After all, today's already been a real World Series win when it comes to saying dumbass things and pissing in your tent.

'You forget, Tyler Quittle appropriated the stock of another employee,' Malvolio clarified.

'You know about that?'

'I know everything, Spiers.'

His spirits bombed. 'Including Belcher's stock.'

'That is a different matter. That was lateral thinking. Laudable, in fact. Belcher was no longer an employee, more....'

'A vase?'

'Exactly. Appropriating *active* stock is expressly forbidden in your terms of employment.' For illustration, Mr Malvolio opened his desk drawer and dumped something marginally slimmer than the Braille print version of *War and Peace* onto his desk.

'So... Tyler—bad, Beckman—good,' he inferred.

'Crudely, yes,' Mr Malvolio granted.

Beckman waited. For balloons to drop from the ceiling, a marching band to enter, the presentation of a cake with a woman jumping out of it.

A cake *without* a woman jumping out of it? A ticker-tape parade?

Maybe?

He waited.

A crown? A sash? A cheque?

He waited.

A... handshake?

Instead, Mr Malvolio opened his other desk drawer. Beckman's heart hopped up a step.

Car keys? A thick wad of Benjamin Franklins? Airline tickets?

In his hand, Mr Malvolio carefully held a small trophy. It was no bigger than his hand. It was silver-colored.

Beckman's heart dropped a few steps.

'Well done, Spiers.' Malvolio proffered the prize .

Beckman steadied his hand against the imminent weight of a solid silver ornament.

He took it. It weighed like tinfoil. It looked like tinfoil. It was probably made of tinfoil. Was it engraved for posterity with his name? He peered at the base.

No.

His heart tumbled down the entire cold, concrete, piss-odoured flight to the basement.

Unspecified time passed as he stood there in a stupor.

What do you do when you can't get angry? What do you say to a man like this who won't care what you say?

How do you react when your decade-plus dream is as broken as an R45 lightbulb on the side of a deserted highway?

'Thank you, sir.'

'There's also a financial bonus you'll find in your checking account this afternoon.'

He brightened. Then he dimmed, because asking the value of said bonus would be rude. Mr Malvolio might react badly. Which could cause Bruno to react badly. Which could mean deadly jaws on his leg. Which could mean he'd end up in the same hospital as Tyler was currently visiting. Possibly the same floor. The same ward. Which would truly suck.

'Success is its own reward, sir,' he replied through half-gritted teeth.

'I'm sure the small stipend will help.'

'Wonderful.'

There was no reply for a few moments, then, 'Thank you for your service, Spiers.'

His mouth opened and closed like a fish.

Okay, how can I be tactful? Remember: rudeness = Bruno = hospital = Tyler.

'Charlie didn't mention anything about the exact nature of the stipend, but I assume...?'

'Charlie's doing very well for himself—you must have heard. Happy as Larry. And Larry's pretty happy too if memory serves.'

'Yes. Absolutely. The thing is, sir, this all sounds oddly... final.'

'Well, I should hope so. You've seen the postcards—you know the life you can look forward to.'

Charlie sent postcards here, too? Really? To a man he despised as much as I do? Perhaps nirvana does that to a man—makes him repentant, Zen-like, grateful to those who catalysed his elevation to the higher echelons of life satisfaction.

'Of course. Well, I won't keep you. Like you said, new fiscal, boxes to move, etcetera, etcetera.'

'Good man, Spiers, and again—well done on Number One.'

'Thank you, sir, it's been...,' he searched feverishly for words that were neither a barefaced lie nor offensive to his overlord, '... a real ride.'

Like the Titanic.

Mr Malvolio offered the weakest of smiles, fluttered a liver-spotted hand, and Beckman closed the door. A sigh gushed from his lungs.

As Miss Broomhead tap-tapped away on the old typewriter, he gave himself an almighty pinch on the back of his hand. Nothing changed.

This was reality.

The pot at the end of the rainbow was full of pure liquid cowshit.

CHAPTER 35

The typewriter's Ding! nudged him as if from a reverie.

Miss Broomhead swivelled in her archaically modern chair.

'This is for you, Beckman.' She tendered an envelope. Lovingly attached to it was a plain typed label; "Mr B. Spiers".

Perhaps this contained the cheque? Had Mr Malvolio delivered a deadpan downbeat performance worthy of an Oscar? Had this all been a giant ruse? Would laughter fill the office the moment Beckman stepped outside?

Could there be a joke even sicker than the apparent reality?

He took the envelope. 'Thank you, Miss Broomhead.'

She gave a sad half-smile. 'Good luck, Beckman.'

Again, with the forename. So, only now, at the end, some sense of friendliness. The cherry-shaped turd on the crap cake.

That apparently being that, he went for the door, clutching his tiny trophy and mystery envelope, head still not entirely straight, yet with a slight sting which told him this was Really Happening.

Twelve years for this? Eleven other pour souls have experienced this crashing disappointment and yet shuffled on to greater things?

He glanced around the room.

'Miss Broomhead?' She looked up from her machine. 'Did you get the cards from Charlie, too?'

Her eyes darted. Nervously? 'Charlie? Cards? Received—here?'

'Oh.' He smiled weakly. 'Never mind.'

With that, he left her to minister to whatever she had to minister to. He trudged mournfully down the corridor, absentmindedly turning the envelope over in his hand. Music drifted in. He stopped.

Rude not to say hello. And Goodbye.

In the warehouse, Wilbur was beatboxing. To his credit, he didn't stop before the end of the stanza.

'Beckman!' He moonwalked over. 'Did you not open it?' He looked at the missive.

'I hardly dare.'

Wilbur pointed encouragingly at the card, but Beckman was distracted by today's cap, which read, "INSERT SLOGAN HERE". Reluctantly, apprehensively, he fingered open the envelope, careful not to let anything loose fall out. Like a million-dollar cheque, as a wild example.

Inside was a card.

On the front were the words, "WELL DONE".

Below the words were a joyful cartoon man bearing aloft a trophy twice his size and, as Beckman held his own prize near the thick paper, apparently nearly as big as the real thing.

His sigh could have whisked Dorothy away.

He opened the card. It was festooned with a plethora of upbeat messages.

Well, three.

Malvolio had scrawled, like Dracula himself, "Well Done, Spiers".

Miss Broomhead had beautifully penned, "Congratulations, Beckman".

'I always knew you could do it, B!' Wilbur piped up, peering over Beckman's shoulder.

He grunted.

'See.' Wilbur pointed at the third message.

It read, "I always knew you could do it! Wilbur".

'Thanks, Wilbur. You're a pal.'

They stared at the card; Beckman from still being in a stupor, Wilbur because he didn't have anything better to do.

'Miss B has a great hand, doesn't she?' the warehouseman noted. 'Real art.'

Beckman couldn't deny that the secretary's writing was the most caring aspect of the whole card. The entire prize situation, in fact. As he studied it, something piqued his interest. Little men with wings on their shoes charged around his brain, seeking answers, but came up breathless and empty-handed. Still, there was an unsettling aspect to it, and it… unsettled him.

'Wilbur?' He snapped out of this navel-gazing. 'Did you ever get any cards from Charlie? Or other Number Ones?'

'Not one. But then, they don't have what we have, eh, B?'

'Shoot.' Beckman hung his head.

'Yeah,' Wilbur replied, mirroring his colleague's downbeat sensibility.

'Calls?'

'No.'

'Shoot.'

'Yeah.'

'They never sent anything here?'

'No. Not that I saw.'

'Shoot.'

'Yeah.'

He rechecked the card.

Wilbur dangled a set of keys in his peripheral. It caused the smallest ray of light to penetrate the black hole of Beckman's entire being.

'Had it valeted, too. You know, on account of Number One.'

More rays appeared. He laid an palm on Wilbur's shoulder. 'Wilbur, you're a stand-up guy.'

'Yeah.'

'Thanks.'

Now I'm all set. I can take my stupendous card, vast winnings, veritable ticker-tape parade, burgeoning soul, spotless car, and drive the whole damn lot off the nearest cliff.

'Two hundred bucks,' came Wilbur's voice. Beckman shot him a look. 'You know, a favour's a favour, but the garage ain't a charity.'

Bills were duly sought, during which Wilbur absentmindedly moonwalked and cut a few moves.

'You should give classes,' Beckman offered.

'It's an idea. Need seed capital, though. Cut me a hundred grand out of your winnings, and I'm there.'

He struggled for a reply. He hadn't the faintest idea what level this "stipend" of Malvolio's constituted. If it made such a sum a drop in the ocean, then (1) he'd be delighted and (2) he'd willingly bequest a chunk to the guy.

'No promises, okay?'

'Sure, B, sure.'

'So, I should check on flights to Acapulco and such.'

'Send me a postcard.'

'Count on it.'

Wilbur handed over the keys. 'Beckman, it's been a pleasure.'

'You too. Don't let Tyler pull any tricks this year, huh?'

'Count on it.' Wilbur fired an impromptu salute and pirouetted away.

So, here's the thing, he considered as he trudged out to the parking lot. *The unspoken word is I'm no longer an employee here. What does that say? There must be a lot of zeroes in my checking account right now. The golden goodbye.*

So, how about not acting like the world is ending, huh?

Lighten up, Beckman. You did it. You made Number One. Mom will be thrilled. Lolita is already thrilled. Hell, even Dad is probably thrilled—in his own unique way. Albeit in your head, but still. If he knew, he would be. Maybe.

He dumped his case in the empty trunk of the gleaming white Buick, dropped into the familiar worn seat.

First order of business: celebrate.

Coffee Planet and their most heinous of muffins, here I come.

He burbled through the suburbs en route to the most local outlet, his mind churning. Something didn't add up.

Was he simply being a pessimistic, ungrateful, distrusting SOB? Why did it feel like he was being cast on the scrap heap? Was it the self-induced collapse of a romantic notion of celebration, mounds of gold coins, and executive adulation he should never have harboured?

Was he looking for a conspiracy where none existed? One cheating fiancé in one strange town does not suddenly make the world full of reprobates.

In the parking zone at Coffee Planet, he paused before heading into the building and pulled the two cards from his shoulder bag. He looked at them, comparing. The niggle remained. He studied harder.

'I'll be a…' he breathed.

The writing on both missives wasn't totally identical, and yet….

That "g".

The curl on the tail was unmistakable. He scrutinised it more intently. Other similarities crystallised out of other letters.

His mouth hung open. His mind raced. Where did this rabbit hole go?

He pulled his cell from a jacket pocket, reminded himself that this imminent spike of annoyance was worth it for a shot at more answers, and dialled. He instinctively winced, anticipating the end of the ring tone.

'Beckman.' No insult, no venom, just a flat tone.

'Tyler.'

A pause. Then, 'Congratulations.' Nevertheless, he heard a hint of spite, maybe ire, in the voice.

'How are you, Tyler?'

'Broken, bruised. Defeated. Why the call? Don't strike me as the gloating type.'

'No. I got lucky,' Beckman said with honest reflection.

'And I got shoved. Must be mistaken identity. What did I ever do? Punk asshole. I'm suing him right up the wahoo. So maybe I'll get a million after all.'

Looks like you need to hire better hitmen, darling. Ex-darling? One thing at a time.

'I need to ask you something,' he said.

'Well, I got nowhere else to be but this bed.'

'Did Charlie ever get in touch?'

'Why the hell would he? He hates me almost as much as you do.'

Tyler was oddly self-aware. Beckman considered checking he'd dialled the correct number. 'Hey, come on, I don't *hate* you.'

'I piss you off big time, though. Don't blame you. Hell, I piss off a lot of people. Even Fate herself, it seems like.'

'There's always next year,' he said helpfully.

'Not that you'll be in touch. Nobody has any time for that,' Tyler snorted.

'Why wouldn't they? At least one of them would have to be a gloater?'

'It's a "Sayonara" deal, don't you get it? Why in the hell would they come back after hitting the jackpot? Why write, either? Or call? Hell, you're only on the horn to me after asking about Charlie. That's a lot more than I would be with you. I couldn't drop this crap fast enough if I won.'

He sighed. 'I guess. So why do it? This crap?'

'It's a step on the ladder. To get out from under....'

'... circumstances?' Beckman suggested.

'Circumstances.'

'We all got moms.'

The response was a long pause, then, 'Have a good life, Beckman.'

'You too, Tyler.'

Silence, so he hung up. Still, it had been the most civil conversation they'd ever conducted. Somewhat enlightening, in a head-scrambling kind of way.

He again scanned the two scrawls on the papers.

It didn't make sense. Had Miss Broomhead genuinely been forging Charlie's cards? If so, was it for Beckman's sole benefit or were there more skeletons? It smelled more rotten than Fresh Kills Landfill, NY.

One answer would swing this mystery to either Fine But Odd or a far worse Not At All Fine. To either a glorious Who Gives A Crap Anymore or an infinitely more unpalatable I Am So In The Crap.

He hopped out, locked the Buick, and, bypassing Coffee Planet on his more critical quest, went to a nearby wall ATM. Because, of course, those nice folks at Coffee Planet didn't want you rocking up without the means to pay, did they?

The machine took his card, accepted his PIN, and gave him options. He chose Recent Transactions, heartbeat quickening. Was Malvolio as good as his word? Had the "stipend" arrived?

The list flashed onto the screen. His eyes widened.

There was a one, and there were zeros.

Four zeros.

His blood began to boil. He wanted to scream until his lungs burst.

$100.00

He yanked his card from the slot, pelted back to the car, slammed the door so hard it nearly shattered the window, and buried his head in his hands.

It can't be? Can it?

It had to be a keying error. Miss Broomhead's fingers must have slipped. This joke was so sick, not even the worst stand-up would face telling it. How would any of the winners build a new life on a hundred lousy bucks? Why would Charlie write every year to say life was peaches and cream?

Except he hadn't. Miss Broomhead—undoubtedly under Malvolio's instruction—had done that.

Why wouldn't Charlie set the record straight? Or any of the previous Number Ones?

He felt nauseous. There could be only one logical explanation. One situation where you could do absolutely nothing; no communication you could provide, no move you might make.

His hands scrabbled to fasten the seat belt. It clacked mercifully home. He wrenched the key in the slot. The engine fired. His foot jammed the throttle to the stop, and the Buick tore crazily out onto the road.

Get out. Run. Now.

The intercom on Miss Broomhead's desk buzzed.

'Sir?'

'Make the usual arrangements, would you?'

'Certainly, sir.'

A pause. 'What letter are we up to now?'

'"I", Mr Malvolio.'

'Excellent. Thank you.' The line clicked off.

Miss Broomhead dutifully but resignedly went to a wall cupboard, unlocked it, and drew out a file.

It was marked "Terminations."

CHAPTER 36

With every fibre of his being, Beckman demanded calm and reason to take hold.

Sadly, calm and reason were busy clutching onto each other like frightened children and unable to help.

Somehow, he reached the freeway without distractedly ramming—or getting rammed by—other people with lesser problems than he.

Logic screamed to drive as fast as humanly feasible, to get as far as possible from the clutches of Mr Malvolio and whoever was coming for him. Because someone was, weren't they?

Sense told him not to take risks; he just needed to keep moving. Getting pulled over, spending a night in a cell in Pegasus' town—that would surely keep him uncomfortably close to Certain Danger. He couldn't go home; the Terminator would definitely try to acquire him there.

Keeping to the speed limit was a feat of superhuman endeavour, exceeded only by his ability not to detonate like Little Boy.

The miles passed, and as hard as he examined the situation logically and from different angles, he always ended back at the conclusion that there was Something Fishy Going On. And he was the fish. And a line had been cast.

The "trophy" lay like a toy on the passenger seat, a trinket a child might spot at an amusement arcade and vainly chase with The Claw. He tutted. He'd not even retained the presence of mind to withdraw his hundred bucks. What were the chances Malvolio would suck the "prize money" back out of his account if it weren't claimed immediately? Beckman wouldn't put anything past the duplicitous toad.

After a half-hour, the subconscious autopilot had put him on a familiar course, and he congratulated autopilot on a job well done. If there was one place where he might have a slim chance of dodging doom, it was a town that allegedly didn't exist. He checked the tank; there should be enough gas to get him there. Worst case, he'd stop at Earl's.

He was soon on Infinity Highway. Counter-intuitively, he'd calmed himself by playing a fun new game he'd invented, called Check The Rear-

View Mirror Every Ten Seconds. The game's result had been that if someone was tailing him, he could say for sure it wasn't Delmar.

What felt like a week later, Earl's slid past. On the lonely road, he alternated between feeling pleasantly solitary, then worrying about being easy to spot. As the apparent Tow Away Zone neared—to his best judgement— nerves increased. Would he make it over the finish line before the invisible pursuer struck?

Without slowing, he strained over and pulled the revolver from the glove compartment. Instantly, he felt safer yet more apprehensive. He wasn't anticipating a gun battle, but if it came, would he stand a chance? Lolita had correctly inferred that he was no action hero.

He hoped it wouldn't come to that. Then, he prayed that he was being a jerk about the whole mess. Surely, someone would set him straight, offer an infinitely more plausible explanation. Some sane counsel, someone from a place where odd was normal—they would tell him if his own normal was actually odd or merely irate misunderstanding.

One way to find out.

Checking the mirror, still jittery, he ran down the driver's window and switched the gun to his left hand.

Then he rechecked the mirror.

Maximum driving. Minimum stopping. Minimum exposure time.

He breathed deeply.

He jammed on the brake, leant out the window, took rough aim, and fired three quick shots.

The tire detonated with an eardrum-rattling alarm. The wheel wrenched in his hand. He dropped the gun in the footwell like it was hot, hastily grabbed the steering with both hands, and fought the car.

The battle was short and violent, rent with rubbery screams and a torrent of Mom-unapproved words.

The car won.

It slewed across the road, fishtailing. He howled in anguish, cursed his stupidity, begged the fates that he hadn't prematurely done the invisible pursuer's job for him.

The Buick nosed onto the margin, slid parallel to the roadside, and hit a dip. It was enough to buck the car up.

Beckman's horizon went straight, forty-five degrees, then vertical.

'Oh, snap!' he yelled, wincing, anticipating the cacophony, the hurt, the repair bill.

With the discord of a million nails on a million blackboards, the car smashed onto its roof. Then the driver's side, then the wheels.

Beckman, shaken like a charity collection tin, begged the chaos to stop. Stitches, bandages, and dollar bills rattled through his vision like the drums of a one-arm bandit.

The car tipped, oh so teasingly, onto the passenger side again, then the roof.

The passenger window exploded.

The noise was abominable.

He tensed for another roll.

But the Buick had had enough. It lolled towards the driver's side, tarmac ballooning into the side window, then fell back, rocking once, twice, coming to rest.

Quickly, the loudest sound was the blood roaring in his ears. Which was a good thing. The best sound ever.

It meant he was alive.

He counted his limbs. Check. He counted his head. Check. He counted his luck. Major check.

He dangled upside down for a minute or so.

What does a person do in this situation?

He looked around for options.

A pair of snakeskin boots appeared at the side window.

He checked the rear view in the truck's big door mirror. The Buick had come off much worse than he had. This would run to way more than a hundred and twelve bucks, not counting the cost of any necessary sessions with Miss North to tend to his own fleshy crumple zones.

The classical music in the cab ebbed.

Saul lowered his hand. It was safe to speak.

'You picked me up.' Beckman hadn't meant to sound surprised.

'Always. Lot better than scraping you up. What happened?'

Better let things pass for a while.

'Long story.'

'I'll bet.'

'I thought I was barred.'

Saul's brow knitted. 'From town? On account of what?'

'What happened with Lolita.'

Saul shook his head. 'That's her battle. You didn't pick a fight with me. Besides, I'd be an idiot to turn down a repair bill like this.' He flashed a toothy grin.

'I may make Customer of the Year, let alone month.'

'So, why come back?'

He sighed. 'Long story. Again.'

'Guess you're stuck here for a while unless I sell you another car. Then it's Customer of the Decade.'

He let that sink in. 'She say anything?'

'No. But you may want to stay an arm's reach from Buck.'

'Shoot.'

Reflective silence fell.

The town sign appeared. He was about to heave a sigh of relief, of sanctuary, when something more impossibly revelatory happened.

The entire vista sprang into blues and greens and yellows and oranges and reds and every other shade the world truly consisted of.

Involuntarily, he gasped.

Saul looked across. He understood. 'Welcome back, I guess.'

Beckman could only nod. Literally, this marked the brightest spot in the darkest of days.

Soon, they rolled onto the familiar forecourt.

Saul unhitched the battered Buick. 'So, what you gonna do?'

'Walk everywhere. Starting with heading up to the Sunset Hotel. I can't say I want to see anyone. I already escaped with my life once today.'

'You'll be SOL for a room. Conference in town. Shame you burned your bridge with Lolita, otherwise....'

'We both started that fire.' He shook his head. 'So, I got nowhere to stay, and I got no way to leave, even if I wanted to, which I don't. What did you say about Hotel California?'

Saul pondered for a second. 'You're welcome to lay your head in the office tonight.'

'That would be doing me a solid.'

I bet it's no feather bed, but anything more comfortable than a coffin is a major break.

'Or... I guess I could find a spot at home.'

'I don't want to impose.'

Saul shrugged. '"Best Customer".'

'Thanks.'

'Plus, you could do me a favour and go see Lolita tomorrow.'

'You have a vested interest all of a sudden? Why?'

'You came back here all of a sudden. Why?' Saul retorted.

'Long story.'

'Long evening,' Saul suggested.

Beckman weighed it. 'Sure.'

'I'll get one of the boys to jemmy something open, get your bag out. Wait up inside. Five o'clock sharp, we'll head out.'

He peered in through the cracked side window. His shoulder bag and roller case lay strewn on the back seat. In the front footwell, the tiny silver trophy mocked him.

He curled his lip in aggravation.

Encased within the cheap plastic inch-square pedestal, the GPS transmitter continued to mark its position to whoever was listening.

CHAPTER 37

As they pulled up outside the impromptu overnight rest spot, it appeared as if Saul lived in an Airstream. A cosy night was in store. Perhaps too cosy.

The engine on Saul's Ford Ranger rumbled to a stop. They climbed out, and Beckman tugged his valise to the ground.

Quickly, it transpired the accommodation consisted of more than an Airstream. It was an optical illusion with unexpected depth. Behind the facade, the rear part of the vehicle didn't exist. Instead, it morphed seamlessly into a single storey home that put Beckman's meagre apartment to shame. The detail was exquisite.

It was RV as designed for Doctor Who.

He became aware of Saul watching his gaze. 'Sorry,' he offered.

'It's meant to catch the ladies. But you're welcome, too.'

'I don't know you that well.'

'Conference is three days. I have a date tomorrow. So, you need to patch up or ship out. The air in the office rattles pretty bad, so you won't get much rest there.'

'I'll make something work.'

'I'll make food.' Saul departed to the kitchen area.

Beckman toured the place, taking in the period detail, the myriad photographs of muscle cars, Airstreams, and what appeared to be Saul with someone who might have been his daughter. That was a conversation for another day. If he survived another day.

Saul's culinary skills stretched to beef tacos. Hardly Lolita levels of acumen, but (1) at least he was on speaking terms with Saul, (2) he'd skipped lunch and could have eaten roadkill, and (3) they were pretty fine tacos.

There was beer, too. On draft. Saul had a small bar, complete with a chilled keg. Perhaps it wasn't only ladies who got to experience this particular style of hospitality?

Saul washed down the last of his meal. 'So, do I have to jemmy it out of you?'

Beckman owed his host nothing less than chapter and verse. So, he gave it, keeping a lid on the hypothesising and anguish.

Saul let it sink in, then summarised. 'You're hoping nobody in Sunrise wants to kill you more than your own boss?'

'Out there,' he jerked his head, 'I didn't do anything wrong. So, I'm pissed as all hell. Here? Worse case, I've been a stubborn SOB and given a girl good cause for false hope. I'd rather it was *her* face behind the gun—if it comes to that. It would serve me right.'

'Lolita would no more shoot you than she would Carlton, and Lord knows she had reason for that.'

'Just Buck, then.'

Saul shook his head. 'He just thinks you're an idiot.'

'Wait 'til he finds out about this.'

'So, why d'you leave town?'

Beckman shrugged. 'Certainty versus uncertainty.'

'I think you got them switched.'

'I kept this job twelve years. They kept the prize, the tease, twelve years. I never had a girl for more than six months. I know uncertainty, okay?'

'Why in hell d'you want more of that?'

'Because the big thing about uncertainty is being certain it'll be uncertain.'

'You scare me, Beckman,' Saul observed.

'Yeah, I scare myself sometimes.'

'What you should do is feel like an ass.'

'Because Lolita is this great girl, and it seems everyone in town wants us to settle down, yadda yadda.'

Saul shook his head. 'The universe just proved you don't know shit about chasing a future that ain't there.'

Boom.

'This is my fault how?'

'Malvolio is a salesman. He's selling you guys a dream. He's taking the dues upfront, then handing over an empty box. Lolita's not taking anything, only giving. I may not be married, but I know some about giving love.'

Beckman eyed the photograph but let the topic lie.

Saul rose, jabbed a thumb towards the relaxation area, and they took seats—comfier ones.

'Her name is Katherine, like Hepburn.'

'I didn't mean—'

'You gave me chapter and verse, Beckman. You don't owe me nothing.'

'I owe you picking me up.'

'I pick anyone up.'

'Don't doubt it. It's what an Okay Guy does.'

Saul drank, shrugged. 'What goes around.'

'Someone pick you up?'

Saul's mind drifted away into a world like the one he visited in which Beethoven, Brahms, or any other of those dead acoustic magicians serenaded.

'Ten two sixty-nine,' he replied eventually.

Beckman didn't follow. October '69 what?

'On the highway,' Saul elucidated. 'A week-old baby with an eye missing.'

A cloud passed across Beckman's heart. 'Someone found you? On the highway? You mean near where you…?'

'Neighbourhood of there.' Saul drank again, robotically.

Beckman whistled softly at the revelation. 'Sounds like you damn near invented karma, doing what you do.'

'Maybe I'm deep down hoping they'll come back.'

'Never knew them?' Beckman suddenly found the relationship with his parents to be a warm hug compared to Saul's newborn abandonment.

'Nor found them. And it's not like I didn't try. All the big cities. I took the world's longest road trip, soon as I finished high school. I kinda turned it into a game. So, I'm forty-nine for fifty on state capitals.'

He whistled softly. 'Anchorage?'

'Honolulu.'

'I guess not many roads lead there.'

'The old wagon outside, she took me. Three times round the clock. Met a lot of people. A girl, for a time.' His eyes went to the photograph, then his head fell.

'But no luck?'

Saul shook his head. 'So, you think you've travelled? You're small fry.'

'In a lot of ways.'

'But I'd always come back.' He patted the arm of the chair. 'I worked long years chasing that dream, then realised there were more important things.'

Beckman let reflective silence hold sway for a few moments.

'So, when I crawl back to Lolita, d'you reckon hands and knees or the full belly-drag?'

'I'm not your mom, okay? It's your life. Hands and knees, belly, go back on a white charger, in a Dodge Charger, on a unicycle, on a damn unicorn. Or not at all. You just gotta decide one thing. Did you come back here on account of saving your life or *making* a life?'

'Saving,' he admitted.

'So, if there's more zeros on that bonus cheque, you're not here?'

'I don't know.' His head dropped. 'I don't know.'

'Did you make her a promise?'

'She threw me out of town.'

'Did you make her a promise?' Saul repeated.

His brow furrowed, remembering the previous evening. 'Yeah,' he said sheepishly.

'Then I've had you wrong all along? Maybe you're not this Okay Guy.'

'Maybe I'm not.'

'If I believe this cockamamie story of yours, if I throw you out of town, then I'm killing you, you know that?'

'So, you'd rather I walked out into No Man's Land by choice.'

'By choice, I'd want nobody hunting you down.'

'Because I'm this Okay Guy?' he ventured.

'You tell me, Beckman. You tell me.'

CHAPTER 38

Beckman woke in the morning, which was immediately A Big Plus. He'd slept like the dead and woken like the living—exactly how he liked things to be.

He saw in color, which scored a sizeable bonus.

Shave. Shower. Dress. Pack.

A much less regular motel than usual, but still—any port in a storm. Especially a Category 5 Hurricane.

Saul, conversely, was prepping for another regular day. 'Coffee?'

'I don't do...' he tailed off, considered his options. 'Can I buy you breakfast?'

'Least you could do, I guess.'

The ride into town was short but tense. Beckman couldn't help scanning the road ahead, beside and behind, hunting for the dark cloud of doom he felt sure must be stalking him.

At least you're not checking the sky for ravens, vultures, or search helicopters.

Nevertheless, other demons closer to home needed to be conquered, too. An olive branch was required.

Halfway along Candela, he spied an opportunity and asked Saul to pull into a parking lot. The driver duly waited while his passenger entered the store and returned with an object that provoked an interested query. Not quite a branch, and certainly not olive, but he'd given it his best shot.

Soon, Saul nosed the Ranger into a kerbside spot near Our Buck's. 'You want me to bodyguard for you?'

'You'd do that? Loyalties and all?'

'Buck should hear why you're back.'

'Doesn't mean he'll believe or give a rat's ass.'

'That stop you trying to explain?'

'Guess not.' Beckman opened the car door. 'Carlton is still walking after what he did, so my chances are better than even.'

A couple of yards and a deep breath later, he swung open the café door. Buck stood stock still when they entered.

High Noon.

Saul quickly broke the impasse. 'Morning.'

'Coffee's out,' Buck snorted. 'Machine's on the fritz.'

Beckman noted that there were undoubtedly fewer customers than he'd expect at oh-eight-thirty.

The silence was oppressive. The stand-off remained.

Androcles glanced over at the lion's injured apparatus. 'Can I take a look?'

That received precisely the expression he expected: *Are You Kidding Me, Sonny?* Then Buck's gaze moved to Saul.

Whatever passed between the men, Buck instantly woke as if from a dream. His posture softened, and he cast a gesture, still unmistakably dismissive and antsy, towards the counter.

Beckman took a wide arc round, staying well beyond the long arm's reach. Buck and Saul watched, intrigued—as if they expected him to flap his arms and lift six feet off the ground—as he examined the beverage-making behemoth.

Quickly figuring the issue, he decided to risk it all. If this were to be his last day on Earth at the hands of any number of opponents known or unknown, large or small, apron, pants, or swing dress, he'd at least be able to say he went out with a good deed.

Remind me how you're faring on the results of good deeds around here?

Evens, okay. Evens.

He located the right spot and gave the machine an almighty whack with his fist.

Buck instinctively took a half-step forwards, a swan protecting its young.

Saul's hand came up gently as a barrier.

The machine belched a magnificent burst of steam, missing Beckman's ducking head by inches.

He stood back and cordially waved the swan back to its nest. Warily, it approached. It examined. Seeing its singular charge in good health, it gave a querying look to where Beckman stood, on tenterhooks.

'Fort Bragg, ninety-eight,' the fixer-upper elucidated. 'Carey Mulholland. Had eyes a boy could get lost in. Did get lost in. Worked a coffee shop off-base. If I'd gotten to know her body half as much as I got to know how she made coffee, I wouldn't be standing here.' All three eyes remained fixed on him. 'So, I guess I got lucky on that.'

If there had been such a thing as indoor tumbleweeds, there was time for a few to blow through.

Finally, Buck took his eyes off Beckman and checked a couple of gauges.

'What'll it be?' he asked, almost cordially.

'The usual,' came the tow-trucker's reply.

Buck's gaze alighted on Beckman again. He reached for a glass on the counter. 'The usual?'

'Coffee. Please, Buck.'

Buck was thoroughly taken aback, then waved them to a table. Legs the steadiest they'd been in minutes, Beckman followed Saul over, and they sat.

'Kill or cure?' Saul asked.

'I have no idea. Whatever I do in this town is wrong. So, I guessed I'd do the opposite of instinct. Or maybe it was time for some karma.'

'If Lolita has a busted coffee machine at home, I'd say you were in the box seats.'

'Fortune favours the brave.'

Two cups were deposited on the table. 'Your drinks, gentlemen.'

Beckman tried to peer behind Buck's eyes. Curiosity was the guy's overriding state of mind.

Whether or not it was the lack of other customers to serve, Buck remained rooted to the spot. Suddenly it felt like chaperoning. Or Beckman was sitting a term paper. Or the priest had just finished asking the "Do you, Beckman Spiers…?" line.

A penny dropped. He took a lingering mouthful of the brew.

'Saul, who's the most honest guy in Sunrise?'

'You are, Beckman.'

'Buck, that is the best coffee I've had in my entire life, bar none.'

The attentive barista extraordinaire nodded, and a small smile appeared. 'Why'd you come back?'

'I could be honest and say someone is going to kill me if they ever find me. But I'll be honest. There's another reason, too. A heck of a lot nicer one.'

Buck's gaze wandered to Saul, saw something, and wandered back.

'Stay as long as you need,' he said.

CHAPTER 39

When they re-emerged onto Main Street, Saul tossed Beckman the keys to his Ranger.

'Roll it, and there definitely will be someone out to kill you.'

'Loud and clear.'

The snakeskin boots clacked away down the gentle incline.

Beckman climbed into the cab and headed in the opposite direction. Naturally, a navy Lincoln fell into line.

Has Carlton forgotten to pull the plug on this charade? No matter. So long as it doesn't cross the line into voyeurism, or I'll have to inform Buck what's happening to his Kinda Daughter, and four flat tyres will be the least you can expect, Delmar.

The journey was short and nervy.

Whether or not she'd sensed his approach—notwithstanding he'd come in vehicular disguise—she didn't turn around.

He tugged up the parking brake and gazed on the scene.

Her dress was lilac and cream. A lilac bow bedecked that waterfall of chocolate. Thick gloves were on her hands, which wielded a fork.

Well, nothing this good comes that easy. Plus, you're the one who put yourself in this position, remember?

With a deep breath, he hopped out and walked up the drive.

She remained stock still, without turning. Her tone came unyielding. 'I will give you ten seconds. Then I will turn and throw this.'

He froze. His mind raced. The one time when word needed to get around town, it hadn't. He'd be brokering this deal from scratch.

Sell, Beckman. Sell. You're Number One, remember?

'If I leave town, I'll die.'

She let the implement's talons rest on the ground. 'It's original, I'll give you that.'

'Plus, I think I'm in love with you.'

A moment for that to sink in. 'No dice. Choose one.'

Think fast, dummy.

'Easy. Staying alive. You'll find I'm a lot less fun to be around when I'm dead.'

There was a sharp crease in her body. A chuckle?

'Your ten seconds are done.'

He gulped. 'Be sure and throw with one hand, like a javelin. If you use two hands, it might drag your aim off.'

Still, she didn't turn her body, though her head twitched. Another awkward silence descended. He'd attracted a lot of those recently, like flies round shit.

He glanced around. The gift from Lolita's mom had been dug up and removed.

'You give up on the tree?'

'I tried to save it, but I failed. I was selfish. Trying to make it put down roots when it couldn't.'

'Best to start over, I guess.'

Now she turned. His spirits leapt.

She saw what was in his hand. 'Did you …?'

'It was worth a try.' He offered her the takeaway cup emblazoned with "Our Buck's". 'It's pretty fine. Fact is, it's damn fine. I could get used to it. Like a few things around here.'

She hesitated, then stepped forwards, slipped off a glove, and took the cup.

'Buck says you rolled the car. Lucky escape.'

'Dying while trying to avoid getting killed—it would be one hell of an epitaph.'

'You want to fill me in?' Quickly, her eyes narrowed. 'Metaphorically, Beckman. For now.'

'The prize for making Number One is a bullet in the head. Or more. Probably doesn't hurt too much after the first one. I'm hoping not to find out first-hand.'

She shrank back in revulsion, then looked curious. 'Says who?'

'Two and two make four.'

She sipped the coffee pensively. 'I'll bite. Thousands wouldn't.'

'I thought you should know that helping people has unintended consequences.'

Her face hardened. 'I don't like the inference.'

'Then I hope like hell my math is wrong.'

'I was only trying to give you the dream.'

'Number Two was fine. Number Two was *me*.'

'I know you don't believe that.'

'Okay. Number Two and you.'

Her face softened again. 'But anything except Number One means life on the road.'

He shrugged. 'You see the problem. Academic now, huh?'

'You're planning to stay?' There was clear hope in her voice.

'Right now, selfishly, because if *I* can barely find this place, I'm hoping the same goes for whoever is bringing the bullet.'

'That's a big if.'

'Too right.'

She nodded. 'So, no cash bonanza?'

'Hundred bucks.'

She whistled a soft sigh like a sad, deflating balloon. Then shrugged. 'Something, I guess.'

'I blew it already.'

'Your prerogative.'

He held up a finger for her to wait, and went to the Ranger. He pulled the peace offering out of the rear footwell, and carried it back to her.

She looked the gift up and down, cocked her head.

'For starting over,' he said.

She bit her lip, looked at him, then at the sapling. 'Apple, huh?'

'They say it symbolises love, too.'

'I heard that.'

He held it outstretched. 'So, will you accept it?'

The silence, the pregnant pause, was a lifetime. The contract stood in limbo, offer without acceptance. Blood thundered in his ears like an approaching storm.

She smiled. 'How long d'you think you've got? You know, before…?' She put finger and thumb to her head, cocked her thumb.

'Hours? Days? Weeks?'

'Hmm.'

'Kinda new to this fleeing-certain-doom game. But I gather a red laser spot on your forehead is not a good sign.'

A nod. 'You should avoid those.'

'I'll try to stick with things that are good for me.'

He looked down at where his hand held the sapling and tried not to betray that it was making his arm ache.

Mercifully, she took the young tree and set it carefully on the ground. Then she gently clasped his hand and gestured towards the house.

'Do you want to come inside?' She peered over the top of her sunglasses. There was a glint in her eye. 'You can fill me in.'

CHAPTER 40

Lolita sat propped up in the bed, examining the two cards.

Beckman's head lay contentedly in her lap, mentally and emotionally anchored by the gentle rise and fall of her chest under the cover.

'This is all the evidence you've got?'

'I know I'm not up to Taylor's level of casework.'

She set them down on the bedsheet and stroked his cheek. 'Would you have come back anyway?'

'This is such a tower of cards. I *did* come back. Can't that be enough?'

'Sorry. What happened before has me hung up on motives.'

'Carlton's or mine?'

'Anybody's.'

He carefully sat, looked her in the eye. Then he gently laid a finger on the tip of her nose, ran it over her chin, vertically down her neck, bisected the breastbone, over her stomach, then lifted away.

'There. I've drawn a line. Okay?'

'Okay,' she agreed.

'Just two motives now. One: stay alive. Pretty fundamental, but worth saying. Kind of a prerequisite for motive two.'

'Go on.'

'Fall in love with you a little more every day. Or at least while you still put up with me.'

'I can run with those.' She kissed him.

'Looking over my shoulder all the time is gonna be a bitch.'

'Anyone comes for you, they'll have to go through me. And Buck. And Saul.'

'Or it's all in my head. I could use that break.'

'You have a nose for things. Subterfuge. Like with Carlton.'

He puffed his cheeks. 'Yeah. Now I have to watch my back for him, too. Serves me right for making that bed.'

'Think about it. You kind of started this. You pulled the surveillance stunt, and you wound up with me. I rigged your career and you felt the burn of the cross-hairs.'

'Think Carlton's a bygones-be-bygones kind of guy?'

'If he wanted revenge, you'd think he'd have taken it. He has a hand on the company rudder. He has a girl. Maybe that's enough.'

'Doesn't answer what the hell he was doing choosing that girl over anyone else.'

'He's up to no good.'

'The ship sailed on that long ago.'

They fell sober.

'I bumped into Reba earlier,' she remarked.

'You want to look where you're going.'

She rolled her eyes. 'Funny man. She gave me the skinny. Guess where that engagement ring wound up?'

Beckman snorted. 'Wow, he's a real classy guy.'

'That's Carlton—it's always about money.'

'What do you care? Ancient history.'

'I'm just surprised Jack's cool with it.'

'You care about that all of a sudden?'

'I'm not the stone-hearted bitch you take me for.'

'Or maybe just not *anymore*?' he suggested.

'Yeah, yeah, you made me a better person, okay?' she replied sarcastically.

'I know Reba doesn't do theories, only evidence, so…?'

'EVI are trying to poach our customers.'

'People like Saul,' he said, remembering the new installation of bulbs. 'So, Carlton's pillow talk isn't flowers and weekend plans. It's selling data.'

'That doesn't wash. He'd be running his employer into the ground. Or he'd try, then it'd get noticed, and he'd be out the door faster than—'

'—than you threw me out of town?'

She reached under the covers and grabbed his attention. 'Pardon me?'

'Nothing,' he squeaked.

She let go. 'So, it can't be that. He's not that dumb.'

'But he could be that pissed off. If he can't take revenge on you or me physically or emotionally, he can do it financially, and if not on you directly, on your family and their assets.'

'For what reason?' she wondered.

'Maybe he's seen the numbers and reckons Milan are heading for the toilet, he jumps ship to the competition. That's why he's not so pissed about losing you. He's got Wanda. Maybe he has Walter's ear on the side, and he's trying to ingratiate himself into *that* inheritance by fattening the goose he's hoping to dine on.'

She gritted her teeth. 'Trying to bring down the company from within. The shit.' She closed her eyes, and blew anger out in a heavy breath. 'My father's not a violent man. Hell, he gives to Save The Whales. But if this is true, and he gets wind of it, it'll make Tyler's problems look like a paper cut.'

'So, tell him.'

'Why? Revenge on Carlton or loyalty to Jack?'

'Depends what's in here.' He touched his index finger to her chest.

She eyed it. 'Watch that finger, mister.'

'The finger's not the problem. It's the hand that's got ideas above its station.'

He formed a palm and slid it inside her camisole. Their eyes met. He made no effort to stop what he was doing.

'I'll give you about a week to cut that out,' she smirked.

'Let's say this is real, Carlton's agenda—whatever it is.'

'As real as you think your mystery assassin is?'

'Yeah,' he agreed.

She nodded down to his hand. 'You're going to keep doing that, huh?'

'You just gave me a week.'

She shook her head gently but had no desire to protest. 'You're saying we should think about the consequences of blowing the lid on it?'

'If you expose Carlton, he'll know his job is gone, probably his life—in Sunrise, anyway.'

'Because word gets around.'

'He'll be poison.'

'He'll leave town.'

'You wouldn't bat an eye over that, would you?' he asked.

'Making men leave town is my speciality.'

'You may have a stone heart, darling, but the stuff wrapped around it is a lot softer. And warmer.'

'And I've given you a week to find out for certain.'

'I have no chance of lasting a week with this. In fact, I'd give you about ten seconds to get out of this bed or suffer the consequences.'

She lifted a hand, slowly counted to ten on her fingers, then pursed her lips suggestively.

'Oops.'

CHAPTER 41

The pristine 1980 Corvette burbled into the gas station.

Randall Ickey was pretty pleased with himself. Two bucks a gallon. He eased out of the car and stretched his legs. An old-timer walked up.

'Two bucks a gallon, huh?' Ickey said.

'That's what the sign says.'

'I'll take twenty bucks.'

'Sure.' The guy unhitched the pump and carefully eased the nozzle into Ickey's prize possession.

Ickey scoured the horizon for signs of life. 'Where's the nearest town?'

The owner jerked his head down the road. 'Yonder.'

'Far?'

'Depends how fast you're going, I guess.'

That messed with Ickey's brain a spot, so he gave up. 'Pretty quiet, huh?'

'Just enough.'

'You do coffee?' Ickey asked, changing tack again.

'We do gas.'

'Where do I go for coffee?'

'Coffee place.'

'Uh-huh,' Ickey was none the wiser for the third strike.

The guy re-hooked the nozzle, then subtly moved to stand in front of the display. 'That'll be twenty bucks then, sir.'

Ickey fished a crumpled note from his equally careworn 501s and slapped it into the waiting palm.

'Thanks.'

He swung open the long door and sank into the mottled leather.

'Have a nice day,' the attendant offered.

Ickey gave a casual wave, slammed the door, fired the engine, and punched the throttle. Dust kicked up, then the car hit the tarmac and accelerated with even more vigour.

Earl pulled the rim of his hat further down. 'Asshole.'

Ickey checked the rear-view mirror. 'Asshole.'

His brow furrowed as he checked the fuel gauge. Must be a fault. He gave up on doing the math.

The pin on the geolocator map drew closer; this could be a one-day deal. Was it ever this easy earning big money? He had a photograph, a note of the license plate, a tracer, and the guy sounded like a do-gooder who'd never carry a gun in a million years because it would offend his sensibilities.

He relaxed back into the cruise, the road arrowing straight ahead, his gaze alternating between the tracer screen, the road, and the first-person shooter game on his phone.

Fifteen minutes and three levels later, the tedium began to bite. Worryingly, he noticed the trace dropping out with increasing frequency.

He cursed, leant over, and tapped the screen. It made no difference.

'Son of a bitch.'

If the signal died, he'd actually have to work for this paycheck. He peered at the locator map, trying to memorise the geography. Pretty tough without much geography in this part of the country.

The Corvette wandered across the road. He corrected it, returned to the task at hand.

The car strayed again. He jammed his elbow into the door card to lock his arm and thus the steering angle.

The pin dropped out. He cursed again.

Motion outside caught his eye. He yanked the wheel over, wincing as the shape disappeared under the hood, and braced for the thump of tire on wildlife.

None came. He checked the rear-view mirror: the lumbering armadillo had gotten a lucky escape.

'Dumb animal,' he murmured.

Counting his luck, he returned his attention to the target when a light winked in the road ahead.

Yet there was no car.

Again, it flashed, undoubtedly a reflection of the sun on glass, then it arrowed straight into his right eye. He snapped his head away.

The car drifted. Wheels went onto the margin. He inhaled sharply, the clatter of loose stones doing untold damage to his precious ride. He steered violently back onto the tarmac.

Too late.

Something unfriendly impacted his radials, and a report rang out.

He wrestled the wheel and jammed on the brake.

The now less-than-perfect Corvette came to rest in a cloud of Arizona.

Dust and silence descended.

Then the quiet was broken by a hail of expletives, which turned the black road, green cacti, and burnt yellow ground all violent blue. He pounded the steering wheel, horn blaring angrily across the open scenery.

Reluctantly, the mad dog climbed out into the searing noonday sun, confirmed his suspicions at the rear of the car, redundantly checked there was no traffic in the vicinity, then opened the trunk. Deep inside sat the jack and the spare, which he began to heave from its recess.

A shape appeared in his peripheral vision. Instantly, he regretted leaving his Magnum in the front of the car. He grasped the tire iron, allowing his hand to fall behind him as he stood and turned.

But the guy just stood there, six feet away. In snakeskin boots and an eye patch. Behind him was a tow truck.

This was too much for poor Ickey's brain.

'What the Sam Hill?' he breathed.

'Where you headed?'

Ickey dragged his attention away from the non sequitur of the cab's interior tranquillity.

'You know, wherever the work is,' he replied with practised vagueness.

'What line of work you in?'

'Contracts,' came his stock answer.

'Uh-huh.'

'How d'you get here so fast?'

Saul looked across. 'I could tell you,' he said with deeply buried humour, 'But then I'd have to kill you.'

Ickey was about to reply along the lines of that ironically being his line of work when the self-preservation layer kicked in again.

'Anyway, glad you did.'

'No problem.'

They swung off the highway onto a road which he hadn't spotted. The town sign passed.

Ickey's mouth fell open, processing the almost magical appearance of a conurbation that he didn't recall seeing on the map. But a conurbation meant one crucial thing. Well, two, if he counted his job of work.

'You have Coffee Planet here?'

'Not sure. You'd have to ask Buck. He's the coffee guy in town.'

'You get a lot of passing trade? Guessing not.'

'We do okay.'

'Travelling salesmen, stuff like that?'

Saul gave him a good long look. 'They get everywhere, huh?'

'Sure do.'

'Like vermin. Hear what I'm saying? Bullet's too good for them?'

Ickey nodded. 'You're right on that.'

The sights of Sunrise soon flooded the eyes of the newcomer, and Saul again saw a brain trying to work it all through.

'You guys like your lights, huh?' Ickey noted.

'We pretty much supply the whole country.'

Ickey checked the geolocation monitor he'd brought out of the car. The trace pin had vanished, yet it wasn't far away—probably even in this very town, especially as little else showed on the map.

'That what causes the GPS to go on the fritz?'

'Do I look like a rocket scientist?'

Ickey reckoned he looked more like if Snake Plissken met Roy Orbison. 'No matter.'

The tow truck and its cargo crossed the dropped kerb and stopped on the forecourt.

'Thanks for the pickup.' Ickey grabbed his knapsack containing *essential* items.

'It's what I'm here for.'

'How long?'

'Couple hours. Complimentary inspection, too.'

'Well, thanks.'

'Then you can be on the way to your... contract.'

'That'll be fine.'

'Buck's place is up the street. Say I said "howdy".'

'Sure.'

As Ickey turned to go, his gaze swung across the forecourt, past the office, and into the open frontage where vehicles were being attended to. At this distance, his vision was 20/20.

There was a white Buick in the shop. It looked pretty messed up but still wore its rear license plate.

He smiled.

CHAPTER 42

Ickey paused. 'You won't believe it—I went to college with a guy who had that same plate.'

'That so?' By which Saul meant, "You went to *college*? For what—asshole lessons?"

'Yeah. Beckman, I think the guy's name was. Strange fish. Wore a lot of greys.'

'That right?' Saul replied noncommittally.

'He in town?'

'If you say that's his car, guess he must be. I don't make all the ride bookings.'

'Uh-huh. Well, maybe I'll bump into him. That'd be something.'

'Sure would.'

Ickey suspected the guy would give the gas station attendant a run for Mr Non-Congeniality.

'So, I'll take that walk.'

With that, he nodded a farewell and set off along Main Street.

Saul walked into the office and picked up the phone.

Ickey strolled the sidewalk, drinking in the endless shapes and colors, keeping eyes peeled for his quarry.

He became aware of a car keeping pace with him. Irked that *he* was supposed to be the one sloping around, he turned to face down the driver. The car was a cab. Suddenly, things were less worrying.

'Need a ride?' the cabbie called, window already rolled down.

'No clue where I'm heading, thanks.'

'Well, right now, you're on Main Street.'

'I got that. Thanks.'

The cabbie adjusted the vent and took a lungful of cool, conditioned air. 'Nice day for it.'

A bead of sweat rolled down Ickey's forehead. He sighed.

'You give a ride to a grey guy? Maybe from the recovery place?'

The cabbie stroked his chin, steering with the palm of his other hand. 'Yeah. Guess I did.'

'Motel, huh?'

'Matter of fact, I think it was.'

'Take me there?'

'Sure.' Clint eased to a stop.

Ickey climbed in.

Clint flicked on the meter. 'Here for the conference?'

'Does it look I am?' Ickey said, bemused.

'Not really. Passing through?'

'Here to meet someone.'

'Grey guy,' Clint suggested.

'Yeah.'

'Motel's full. On account of the conference.'

'No problem. I'll be out of here in a shot.'

'Quick meeting, huh?'

'If it all goes to plan.'

They pulled to a halt outside the Sunset Hotel. Ickey reached for the door handle.

'Shoot,' Clint said.

'What?'

'Just realised. Grey guy's not here. Couldn't get a room.'

'Then where?'

Clint pondered loudly and deliberately. 'Maybe at Lolita's? That possible?'

'How in the hell would I know?'

'You want to try?'

'Sure.'

Clint pulled a one-eighty and headed for Edison Avenue. 'Flat, huh?'

'Yeah. Dumb luck. The guy I need to meet is here anyway.'

'Someone smiling on you.'

'Doubt it,' Ickey mumbled.

Inside two minutes, they were slowing outside 1002. There were no vehicles on the drive.

'Ah, shoot,' Clint breathed.

'Strike two.'

'You not arrange to meet this guy anywhere?'

'Call it a surprise visit.'

'If only the guy had a GPS in his shoe, right?'

Ickey chuckled. 'He been in town long?'

'Couple days.'

'Seen him around?'

'Sometimes he goes to Buck's.'

'So, let's go to this "Buck's" place.'

'Your money,' Clint said, concealing glee as the meter ticked on.

After purposefully taking a long route round, he pulled up outside Our Buck's. Clint shielded his eyes from the sun and peered across the sidewalk into the café.

'Strike three. You want to wait inside?'

'You got a better idea?'

Clint made a pantomime of thinking, then offered, 'He could be at the Milan factory.'

'Rate we're headed, he could be on the goddamn moon.'

'Sorry, I don't go that far.'

'Wiseass.'

Clint remained even. 'You want out, or you want the factory? No skin off my teeth.'

Ickey shook his head in annoyance. Why *didn't* Beckman have the damn transmitter in his shoe? No mind. These expenses were chicken feed.

'Factory,' he rapped.

A few more satisfied chickens later, the cab slowed to a halt outside the building adorned with "MILAN ENTERPRISES".

Clint pointed at a blue Miata. 'Home run.'

Ickey tugged some bills out of his decade-old wallet. 'Thanks for the tour,' he grouched.

'Hey, you got your guy.'

'Nobody takes Randall Ickey for a ride.'

'Next time, I won't pick you up, I guess.'

'Wiseass.'

Ickey climbed out and slammed the door. He surveyed the parking lot. A ton of regular sedans, a nice Mercedes—the boss', he guessed—and a handsome '65 Mustang. That would be the easiest to boost later, but ultimately, he'd take whatever he could to get back to the recovery place, then he'd grab the 'Vette and blow town.

Ahead, the Reception office looked like the kind of place he'd have to give name, rank, and serial, which wasn't ideal.

As the cab eased away, he headed off to circle the building.

Passing around the corner, he was oblivious as a figure emerged from a navy Lincoln, fired off a barrage of redundant shots with his Canon, and took distant pursuit.

That figure was also unaware as a woman with cropped hair eased out from behind an outbuilding, snapped with her Minolta, assessed the geography, and moved off.

CHAPTER 43

Ickey climbed the steep, metal stairs of the fire escape, crossing his fingers that the Health and Safety guy knew his job.

On the top step, he noticed a few cigarette butts.

Finding a centimetre gap between door and jamb, he pushed a muscled finger into the space and prised the door open.

He smiled. Batter up.

He checked around and, seeing nothing, not even the shoes of a P.I. hiding behind a border fencepost, he opened the door wide enough to squeeze his broad shoulders through.

Harsh sunlight disappeared. He'd arrived on a wide, metal walkway that formed a mezzanine on four sides. Below, through a large, central space, lay the warehouse. Up on this level stood continuous shelves on three sides. He reckoned Milan had outgrown the original site and been forced to line the walkways to avoid the need for bigger premises.

From both ends of the room, wide stairs led down inwards to the ground floor. Above, a series of ropes and pulleys crisscrossed the eaves. At the far end from his position was a line of offices with glass on both the warehouse and parking lot sides.

Soft music played; otherwise, the place was quiet.

Drawing the .44 to his face, he pressed against the corrugated outside wall and inched towards the offices.

He prayed there wasn't a board meeting in progress. Anyway, what would a loser like Spiers be doing in there? He was only a salesman. No matter— worse case, Ickey would do an extraction here and the deed later.

Halfway along the walkway, he saw only one of the office modules was occupied. A few seconds later, he recognised one of the two people inside. A grey man.

Bingo.

Around, all remained quiet. In a few steps, his line of sight fell perfect. The office door stood open; the bullet wouldn't even have to navigate glass.

He took careful aim.

The grey man and the striking woman in the swing dress continued to look intently out of the front window. For a man of Ickey's relative talents, a stationary target at this distance was easy meat.

His finger curled the trigger. Squeezed.

The bullet ripped through the air, bisected the target's head, and crashed into an office cabinet. Noise bloomed through the space.

But the figure remained upright.

'What the?' he thought.

He fired again.

Same impact point.

The figure continued chatting.

He ran forwards, keeping his gun commendably steady, cracking off the remaining shots, aiming for shoulders and back.

All seemed to miss their target.

Randall Ickey had never missed a target, not by the third shot, let alone sixth.

He burst into the room. The figures didn't even turn.

Instead, a floor-to-ceiling stationery cupboard burst open behind him.

Alarmed, he turned.

The nose of a gun came to his ear.

'Drop it,' a female said.

Internally, he cursed apocalyptically. But as his chambers were empty and the gun's owner knew the same, he complied. There was always Plan B.

The gun backed off.

A second figure, the grey man, appeared through the doorway and scooped Ickey's discarded gun from the floor.

'Sorry, Ickey,' said the woman in the swing dress.

The facsimiles continued to look out the window. He frowned, mind cartwheeling.

Lolita brought up the remote and clicked the image off. 'Don't believe everything you see.'

Inside, he boiled. Nobody took Randall Ickey for a ride, certainly not twice in a day. He waited for Plan B to present itself.

Thankfully, for the second time that day, someone smiled on him.

The clatter of the fire exit door made Lolita and Beckman jump.

It was all the incentive Ickey needed. He shoved her hard against the wall, backed off, and bent down, drawing the backup .22 from his leg holster.

Beckman stood rooted to the spot, eyes wide, hands jelly.

The gun came up.

Lolita was floundering, a mass of chiffon and shapely leg.

A shot rang out. The partition glass shattered. Lolita screamed. Beckman hit the deck.

Ickey span, seeking out the source.

Emerging from shadows across the mezzanine, a woman with cropped hair had hands together, outstretched in front.

He returned fire. Six feet from the target, a box of glass exploded. Reba winced, stepped away, fired again. She missed, the bullet thudding into the cupboard door near Beckman.

Ickey caught sight of another figure scuttling towards him down the nearer walkway. He shifted aim, and the gun spat at Delmar.

A box of glass erupted.

He span and fired at the woman. More glass.

Instinctively, he checked the room. Lolita was six feet away and taking aim.

Cornered and unable to hit three targets simultaneously, Ickey made the most logical choice. He bolted. Out of the office and along the end walkway. Glass showered ahead and behind. He returned fire in both directions, then ducked behind what looked like a laundry trolley standing near a door leading to an internal stairwell.

Enraged, Lolita yelled, 'Leave my boyfriend alone, you asswipe!' and darted from the office, taking position behind a shelving unit. Her aim sought a clear line of sight to Ickey as he crouched, trapped in a three-way pincer with Reba and Delmar. She cracked off a warning shot to show she meant business.

Beckman recognised this instantly. In fact, he'd known it for about half an hour, during which she'd spun this scheme. He thought her ballsiness had peaked in the last thirty seconds with her ice-cold disarming move. He'd been wrong.

Boyfriend, she said. Well, shouted. Hmm. It sounds weird now that she's said it out loud. Sounds weird, period.

In your eye, Mom: I've got a girlfriend. She's got bangs and swing dresses, and she's packing heat. That's my girlfriend over there: crouching tigress, hidden dragon-slayer.

Another shot rang out, shaking him.

Hey, brain, get with the program.

He'd seen enough. Two things were true: (1) his fears about being a hunted man were as real as the shards of glass that littered the floor, and (2) he was damned if he was just going to stand there. Sadly, there was a (3), which he'd unknowingly made a bad call on. Having failed to count the shots already fired from the gun that now warmed his hands, and believing himself to be armed, if not exactly dangerous, he stuck Ickey's Magnum out in front and charged from the office with his best bloodcurdling scream.

Ickey immediately cracked off a wild shot at this moving dervish.

Three feet behind Beckman, more bulbs exploded. Still, he continued, bearing down on poor Delmar, who'd gotten so far out of his depth a submarine would have struggled to mount a rescue. The P.I. instantly turned on his heels and ran straight down the walkway, his erstwhile investigative target now in pursuit.

Except Beckman had no motive for pursuit, let alone using the gun. Worse, he hadn't the faintest clue what he was doing. His girlfriend—

Wow, girlfriend.

—was taking good enough care of herself. Reba was effectively playing his very own sidekick. Delmar offered minimal threat.

Which left Ickey, who stood no chance. Someone in the office would have called the cops.

Beckman reached the far corner of the warehouse, having run pretty much the length of a football field, and came to a stop, panting. Delmar had vanished.

At the far end, a standoff had developed. Ickey couldn't go to his right; he'd encounter Reba. He couldn't go left; Lolita barred the way. Even if he clattered down the steps to the warehouse floor, he'd be out in the open for too long, facing odds of three-to-one against. Lastly, the door behind him was entry controlled; a red light glowed on the wall pad.

Beckman scanned around for options. What he needed was a distraction, a stall, an intervention, a plan until the cops or any kind of cavalry came.

There was nothing enlightening on the mezzanine level. Nearby, the long flight of stairs led down through the atrium, mirroring that in front of Ickey. Below were crates, trolleys, a huge cardboard-sided pallet structure filled with discarded packaging. Whatever else Jack Milan was, he also recycled.

The tension was unbearable. Everyone was mulling the same quandary. Beckman begged Ickey wouldn't go all Butch and Sundance.

But Ickey, who hadn't been receiving the mollifying vibes, sprang into action. For a stocky man, he moved fast and vaulted well. In five steps, he reached the walkway rail. In a single bound, he was airborne.

Beckman winced in misplaced sympathy: death or glory. Well, a long spell in the ER or glory, at least.

Gravity doing its work, treating assassins as it did beer bottles, Ickey's flight came to an end. His frame mashed the pile of empty boxes, cushioning his plummet, though not without a howl of discomfort that carried the length of the warehouse.

Reba fired. The bullet vanished into the cardboard melee.

Lolita didn't have a line of sight to the floor below, so she inched along the walkway, taking the recently vacated spot behind the wheeled trash trolley.

Ickey pulled himself from the heap of detritus, casting boxes aside like The Hulk ripping off his shirt, and rolled into a crouch, seeking cover.

Lolita stood and fired, almost certainly blind.

The door behind her burst open. She'd barely turned before the door swiped into her, catching her feet. She unbalanced, toppling forwards into the trash trolley.

Beckman watched as Carlton, for it was he joining this party, raised his gun. The impromptu skittling of his ex went unnoticed.

All we're missing here is Doc Holliday.

Ickey was secreted now, tucked behind shelving on the warehouse floor. He fired up at this new target. Carlton hit the deck, spindly legs flailing and kicking into the side of a trolley.

Lolita screeched. The trolley slid forwards.

Reba fired. The glass beside Ickey detonated. He ducked his head out and returned a shot. Glass erupted beside Reba.

Carlton gathered himself, rolled to the walkway's open side, reached his gun over the edge, and fired two half-blind shots in Ickey's direction. More of Milan's stock died in a shower of shards.

The trolley reached the edge of the steps, rocking as Lolita tried vainly to sit.

Beckman was the only one with a clear line of sight to Ickey. He raised the gun. There was scant hope of hitting him at this distance, but he had to try. At least it would draw Ickey's fire.

Draw his fire? Are you nuts?

Shut up, brain. You're the one who started this.

But kill a man?

It's kill or be killed, dummy.

He took careful aim at Ickey's bobbing head and squeezed the trigger. The revolver clacked. He squeezed again. Nothing.

Again and again. Nothing.

Furious, he tossed the gun aside.

Eighty yards distant, the trolley crested the edge of the top step, slanted thirty degrees, and bumped down. Lolita's head appeared, then disappeared.

Below, Ickey fired up at Carlton, the bullet zinging off the walkway stanchion and punching into a box with a sympathetic whump. Carlton fired. An open box of fluorescents disintegrated.

Beckman looked around in panic.

'Figuring to run, I guess,' came an imagined voice.

'Not now, Dad.'

'Look what you did to all these people.'

'This is a really bad time. Kind of trying not to get killed, in case you didn't notice.'

'You ran away and left her in the lurch, didn't you?'

The trolley was on the third step. In a heartbeat, it would be in Ickey's firing line.

'Because you'd know all about that,' Beckman spat.

'Just trying to get ahead, son.'

'Well, I did. I made Number One. Satisfied now?'

'Question is, are *you*?'

'If I keep the promotion and the woman, that'll be one better than you, huh?'

'You're a snide little wiseass, Beckman.'

'Thanks, Dad. Now piss off.'

The air cracked as Reba fired, missing Ickey again. Carlton was on his feet, scrambling round to take proper cover. Something caught his eye. His head darted.

Beckman looked round. Delmar appeared fifteen feet away, took aim, and let fly at Carlton, who replied instantly, clattering a shot into a wall-mounted light fitting behind Delmar's head. The P.I. shrieked and fell back into the shadows.

Beckman spotted the overhead pulleys. He lunged to the nearest open cardboard box, yanked out a three-foot fluorescent, and went to the wall. He tugged the rope from its mooring, tested its integrity with a heave, then ran at full pelt to the top step.

The trolley careered through the halfway point, a tangled mess of limbs and swing dress flailing inside.

Beckman lifted into mid-air, swinging the long bulb between his legs and clamping it tight, both hands clutching the rope as it took him out over the warehouse floor thirty feet below.

Ickey saw him, turned his aim, and let fly. Beckman winced as the bullet flashed past.

Reba returned fire. Carlton took aim at Ickey and loosed two shots. With a metallic howl, both rapped into the girder beside Ickey's chest.

Beckman was falling now, his weight drawing down the rope, the pulleys clattering. He'd be on the floor in seconds. But he'd planned that.

Ickey altered his attention away from Carlton, gave Reba a warning shot, then turned his aim on the trolley.

Beckman opened his legs. The tube crashed to the floor close to Ickey and exploded in a million fragments. Ickey scrambled away and let fly with some words that Mom would have blushed at.

Reba joined in, putting a warning shot into the floor near Ickey's feet. His response was to retake aim and squeeze the trigger. A bullet flashed up and tore through the side of the canvas trolley.

Beckman, twenty feet away and ten higher, still falling under tension, held his breath.

Somewhere to his left came a tinkling sound.

A head of chocolate curls crested the trolley. 'Son of a—,' she yelled.

But Ickey's aim had shifted. Beckman could almost see down the barrel as he slid past. He winced.

Ickey's finger squeezed.

Click.

Squeezed.

Click.

'—bitch!' Ickey launched the empty gun in the direction of the airborne salesman.

It missed by a yard.

Beckman continued to plummet. Ten feet. Five feet. He braced for impact.

His feet rapped the floor, and he willed his legs to support him. He jammed his arms out in front, and the trolley smashed into them, jarring his bones, the momentum sliding him backwards on his feet. The cargo, however, was not subject to the same brake and continued, forwards, forwards, up.

Because you don't mess with Newton's laws of motion, he let go, toppling backwards, as Lolita plopped out of the trolley, limbs akimbo.

He threw his arms wide, and she thudded into him, sending them both careering backwards and collapsing into a pile of packing wrap, the huge translucent rolls skittling away across the floor. Her head rapped painfully into his chest, her gun arm remaining outstretched towards Ickey, who scanned nervously for an escape route.

Beckman and Lolita came to rest.

'Don't move, asshole!' Reba yelled from on high.

But Ickey wasn't beaten yet. He needed Plan C, and fast.

Beckman gazed into Lolita's eyes, his chest heaving. 'You okay?'

She gulped her breath back. 'Yeah. My action hero.'

A shot rang out. Their heads flicked sideways as Ickey scrambled behind shelving, his feet quick on the concrete floor.

Another box exploded as Reba fired again.

It was too late. The hitman was halfway along the side wall, a retreating shadow passing between towering shelves of boxes.

Heart pounding, Ickey bore down on the fire exit at the end of the building and hit the door beam at full tilt, praying this door was also unlocked. Two broken arms would make a few glass cuts seem like an angel's caress.

Mercifully, he burst with a bang into the harsh sunshine, eyes wincing against the glare, but pushed on, free, arms pumping as he rounded the corner of the warehouse....

CHAPTER 44

… and slammed straight into the side of the waiting cab.

His chest and stomach erupted into pain.

'Going somewhere, Randall?'

A hand grasped the neck of Ickey's shirt and hauled him to one side. Buck raised a single eyebrow. Randall Ickey wanted to die.

Buck looked the miscreant up and down. 'You're right, Saul—he is not an Okay Guy.'

Saul's one eye locked onto Ickey's red face.

Ickey sighed. Then he winked.

Saul frowned.

Ickey winked again. Then blinked. Put his finger to his right eye. Prodded the lower lid. He winked. Blinked.

'You okay, Randall?' Buck asked, nonplussed.

'Think I… think I dropped a contact.'

'Yeah, right.'

'Damn thing.'

Buck roughly clutched Ickey's upper arm, then without warning, gave him a sturdy pat-down that would have any border guard shaking his head in embarrassment.

'He's clean.'

Ickey was still pantomiming with his eye. 'Yep. Definitely. Not here.'

'You have it inside?' Buck asked.

'Totally.'

'He runs, you total him,' Buck instructed Clint.

'Absolutely.' The cabbie raised a hitherto unseen .38 from inside the car and pointed it at the hitman. 'Under-eighteens thirty-yard field medal, Arizona state. Ninety-nine scored out of one hundred.' He eyed their guest. 'I also drive.'

Ickey's face told them he understood.

Then all three dropped to their knees and began crawling the nearby tarmac of the parking lot.

Lolita and Beckman walked out of the main entrance, hand in hand, and stopped dead.

'What's wrong with this picture?' She cocked her head.

They watched for a few seconds.

'They're grazing in a dumb place? Weeds are over yonder.'

They gaped a moment more.

'Why'd you go all Calamity Jane on me?' he asked absentmindedly.

'Why'd you go all Tarzan on me?' she replied, without looking at him.

'Well, you were being Jane, so I thought....'

'You're a piece of work, Beckman Spiers.'

'And you're a piece of ass, Lolita Milan.'

She shook her head slowly. 'Jeez, I created a monster.'

'Yeah. But *your* monster.'

They kissed.

'Found it!' Buck yelled.

The two men performed a kneeling re-enactment of Michelangelo's The Creation. Then Ickey moved his finger to an eyeball.

'You think he'd at least clean it,' Lolita suggested, wrinkling her nose.

'Yeah, he seems like this careful, conscientious guy,' Beckman retorted.

'You want to punch him first, or should I?'

'And you seemed like this careful, conscientious girl.'

'One day, darling, one day, I really will swing for you,' she joked.

'Good luck. I'm a pretty fast runner. I'll run from pretty much anything.' He jerked his head towards the building. 'Exhibit A.'

'Except you always wind up back with me.'

'Yeah. Need to work on that.'

'Don't you dare.' She whacked him on the ass.

'So,' he looked at where the trio stood. 'Any bright ideas?'

'Reckoned it was your turn.'

'Sure.'

He reached down and relieved her of the still-loaded Luger, then strode over to Ickey, regarding the tanned and stubbled guy for a moment.

'Woman or man's voice on the phone?' he asked nicely, touching the muzzle to the hitman's forehead.

Ickey swallowed. 'Woman.'

Beckman tutted. 'I expected better of Miss Broomhead. How much?'

'Hundred grand.'

Buck whistled.

'I'll bet every cent it's paid on completion,' Beckman guessed.

'Ninety percent.'

'Free advice, Ickey. You're about as likely to get that ninety grand as I am to take up nude skydiving.'

'Looks like I'm dead anyway, so who gives a shit?'

'You got the ten?' Saul interjected.

'In the car,' Ickey replied.

'From what I hear of this Malvolio, I'd go counterfeit.'

Beckman nodded in agreement.

'I got some here.' Ickey dipped his eyeballs to his pocket.

Saul rummaged around and pulled out a thin wad. Then he held a note to the sky, smoothed it flat on the cab's roof, ran his finger gently over it, closing his good eye.

'Sorry, Randall.' He handed it back.

'The double-crossing son of a bitch.'

'Welcome to my life,' Beckman added.

'Nobody takes Randall Ickey for a ride.'

Clint snickered.

'A ride would be the best you could expect,' Beckman said.

'Yeah, I know—a bullet. Go ahead. Guess I'll die poor, too.'

'This?' He waggled the gun. 'Saul, pulling the trigger now—that an Okay Guy thing?'

Saul shook his head. Buck followed suit.

Beckman lowered the gun and casually tossed it towards Lolita. She caught it and jammed it down her cleavage.

'I'll take a wild guess here, Randall. But you ought to know I'm two for two on wild guesses right now, so you might want to listen up. If you go back to Malvolio with me still breathing, you're a dead man. But, if you go back with me *allegedly* dead, you might get your hokey ninety grand, and you'll find out it's a con, you'll be pissed off, you'll go back to Pegasus again, and that's a risk Malvolio doesn't take. So, my guess is you get your ninety grand, and Miss Broomhead makes another call the second you're out of the office. Catch the drift?'

Ickey swallowed.

'So, on balance,' Beckman continued, 'It's dead or dead. Sucks to be you, huh?'

'Why do bad things happen to good people?' Lolita mocked.

'I killed a guy called Hallam last year. Same woman. But the cash was real.'

Beckman's eyes flickered in thought. 'First time, you kill last year's guy. Next time, you kill this year's Number One. Then you're toast. Malvolio only pays out once. It's a solid scheme—I'll give him that.'

'What's my move?'

'You run, play innocent, and suck up the loss. Or you tell him the game is over.'

'What would you do?'

Beckman pursed his lips, pensive. Looked around for inspiration. Found none. 'I'd think about it over coffee. Maybe there's a third way?'

Saul laid a heavy hand on Ickey's shoulder. 'Coming for a ride, Randall?'

Ickey didn't disagree. He, Saul, and Buck climbed into Clint's cab.

Beckman crouched down at the open window. 'I'm not a violent man. Neither are these guys. But I'm sure we can make exceptions. If you killed me for money, that's a job. Everyone's got to earn. I get it. But if you kill me now, it's because you're no better than the lowlife double-crosser who hired you. And he's dead. So, enjoy the coffee and don't get ideas.'

He rapped on the roof, and Clint eased them away.

Lolita slid her hand into his. 'You bump your head when you rolled the car?'

'You have such a low opinion of me, huh?'

'I just…. This past week is so messed up. Maybe I shouldn't figure anything as screwy anymore.'

'I kinda thought, throw a grenade in and stay.'

She smiled.

'Spiers!' rang out loudly behind them.

Carlton was trudging away from the main doors, a cardboard box in his arms.

'I've got this,' Lolita murmured.

'Spiers! You're a dead man.' Carlton came to stand ten feet away, his face like thunder. Poking from the top of his effects was a framed photograph of himself and Lolita.

'Why do bad things happen to good people, huh? But I guess I'll have to suck it up.'

'Get bent, Lolita.'

She levelled the gun at him. He shrunk back, whimpering.

'Left leg or right leg?' she asked.

'But… but….'

'Left or right?'

'I know you, Lolita, you wouldn't.' He offered a pleading smile.

'Like I knew you? Loyal fiancé, Dad's trusty abacus guy?'

'I can explain!'

'Left or right?'

Beckman stepped forwards. She fluttered her other hand for him to stay back.

'This was not the plan!' Carlton implored. 'I wanted the best for Milan. And the best was—'

'Bored,' she rapped, dropping her aim towards his knees.

He backed off further. 'I didn't mean to fall in love with her!'

'Still bored.'

'You're not that person, Lolita!' he begged.

Her shoulders fell. 'Who am I kidding? You're right—I'm not.'

His sigh was visible.

'But I am *this* person,' she added, snapping right, raising the gun, and firing.

Fifty yards away, the windshield of a beloved '65 Mustang exploded.

He yelped in anguish.

She let the gun fall to her side and strode to him. 'If you even breathe near either of us, I call Ickey. He *is* that kind of person.'

Carlton nodded meekly. His look went to Beckman, who just shrugged.

'Call off the dogs, okay?'

Carlton gave a sanguine smile. 'Jeez, Delmar sucked.'

'Telling me.'

Smiles broke out.

'He couldn't hold down a secret affair for five minutes,' Lolita suggested.

'He could barely catch himself doing it,' Carlton added.

A chorus of chuckles.

'Well, this is all very cosy, isn't it?' she said.

'Yeah,' Carlton reflected.

'Now get off our property.'

CHAPTER 45

'I expected your dad to be more of an ass. It's almost like he loves you.'

'Yeah, but like a daughter, not a son.' She tugged stray hair from her face as the wind eddied around the Miata's open cabin.

'We just stopped his wannabe son selling him down the river. Little gratitude would have been nice.'

'He believed us. Trust me, that's a victory.'

The convertible gassed out of the turning and onto Main Street.

'Think he'll change the inheritance?' Beckman asked.

'I'm counting exactly zero chickens.'

'How long is Jack going to hold a grudge?'

'He hasn't spoken to Mom since she walked out on him fourteen years ago. There's your barometer.' She dipped her head just low enough to give him a schoolmarm look over the top of her shades. He recognised it as Lolita's that's-an-end-to-it cue.

She parked in a manner that put an inked-in full stop to the conversation, and they went into the cool air of the café.

Buck, at the counter, offered a silent greeting and prepared their usual while they joined Saul and a circumspect Ickey.

'What's it to be, Randall?' Beckman asked.

'I go back, shoot this Malvolio guy, and that's an end to it.'

'It won't be with our blessing.'

'I couldn't give a shit.'

'You want to get paid?'

'Even though you're walking tall?'

'Call it out-of-pocket expenses. I'm pretty sure Jack Milan will want to sue you at least a hundred grand for criminal damage.'

'And believe me,' Lolita piped up, 'He's a real ass about things like that. And things not like that.'

'Blackmail Malvolio?' Ickey wondered.

'Take the money out of his safe,' Beckman said, enthused by the hitman's suggestion.

'After shooting him.'

'No shooting.'

Ickey pulled a face. 'And if he doesn't give me the cash or the safe combination?'

'Malvolio may be a greedy SOB, but if it's his money or his life, he has more money to spare than lives. He's a smart guy. If he lives, he lives to fight another day.'

'And find another way to even the score?' Lolita worried.

Buck deposited two coffees on the table and sat. 'I'm sure Randall can make Malvolio understand it would be a bad idea to mess with a hitman.'

'Randall understands that's the result we need. Don't you, Randall?' Saul laid a heavy hand on Ickey's shoulder.

Ickey conceded wordlessly.

'Randall also understands he should come back here with the money directly afterwards.'

Ickey nodded again.

'Because my Lolita is not averse to hiring guys to take out double-crossers,' Beckman added.

Lolita beamed innocently.

Ickey nodded vehemently, then, sensing no further interrogation or demands were forthcoming, took a slug of the coffee. His face lit.

Beckman pointed. 'A lot better than dying, huh?'

'This is, like, the best coffee in the world.'

'We have the best coffee, the best root beer, the best folks.'

'And the best women,' Lolita stressed.

'That P. I. —Reba is it?—now that's my kind of gal,' Ickey said.

The rest of the table exchanged glances.

Beckman waved it away. 'I'm sure she's not the kind of shallow gunslinger who'd be swayed by a guy just because he had a million bucks to his name.'

'A million…?' Ickey began.

'I said, you want to get paid?'

'Buys a lot of coffee.' Buck heard the register ringing in his mind.

'You like kids?' Beckman asked, remembering Reba's single mom status.

'Yeah, my sister has three.'

'She in the assassination business too?'

'Nothing so noble. She's in real estate.'

Saul laid a hand on Ickey's arm. 'I'm sorry to hear that.'

'She still makes a killing every week.'

They all laughed.

'I'm sure Reba would settle for a sense of humour, too,' Beckman murmured.

'Where you staying?' Buck checked the wall clock. 'Hotel's full.'

Realisation dawned on Ickey's face. 'By rights, Beckman would be dead, and I'd be back on the road.'

'Believe me,' Saul said, 'If you'd just killed my friend, there'd be no way you'd be leaving town in your car or any kind of vehicle. Well, maybe a hearse.'

'It always works out,' Ickey replied.

'You want to sleep in the churchyard?'

Ickey's face drained.

'You got company tonight, Saul, buddy?' Beckman interjected.

'Oh no,' came the defensive reply. 'No way I'm babysitting. I've got company. Expectations.'

They all caught his drift.

'You could reschedule your… evening?' Lolita said knowingly.

'Plus, Randall can pay bed and board, can't you, Randall?' Beckman asserted. 'In arrears, of course. Say, ten grand?'

Ickey scanned the faces and decided that agreeing was the best course of action.

Saul reluctantly saw which way the wind was blowing and threw his arm around the hitman's shoulder.

'I'll put the nice linen on for you, okay?'

CHAPTER 46

'You're actually doing this?'

Beckman's finger hovered over the Dial key. 'You'll think less of me for doing the right thing? How d'you figure, after everything that's gone on?'

'When did Tyler ever do right by you?' Lolita bit into her breakfast bagel.

'The guy's an ass, but I don't want him dead this time next year.'

'He'd be dead right now if it wasn't for me.'

Beckman couldn't argue. 'Yeah—he'd have got Number One and been Ickey's unsuspecting victim.'

'Absolutely—without the benefit of some friends, and a pretty awesome gal with a head for cunning schemes.'

'I wouldn't ask him to thank you. Because I know how he'd like to do it.'

'Maybe I'm not his type,' she ventured.

'Check your wrist. Got a pulse? You're his type.'

'Come on—nobody is that one-dimensional.'

'Oh, I'm sure he has a lot of good qualities. Works a soup kitchen on Saturdays, helps little old ladies cross the street, goes to the opera....'

'Now who's the ass?' She raised an eyebrow.

'I'm a chip off the old block, okay? Everybody has reasons for what they do. Even my old man. Tyler needs to be given a break.'

'Is this about you trying to make amends for what I did to him?'

'I'd bet my hundred bucks bonus that Tyler's Mr Perfect cheekbones have escaped a few fist swings in the past. So he lives at home? Norman Bates lived with his mom, too—so we all got lucky that Tyler's wit is the sharpest thing he carries.'

'So you'll forgive all his years of baloney?'

'Someone has to be the better man. Besides, I can't live with myself if I let all the other saps at Pegasus carry on like there's a real prize to aim for. And who's most likely to be gunning for it this coming year? Tyler.'

'You feel *sorry* for the guy?'

'Like you felt sorry for me? Helping the underachiever across the line...?'

'Maybe because you're not an ass?' she said.

'I'm not Freud, honey, but the school bully is always compensating for something.'

'Next, you'll tell me you're forgiving Malvolio too!'

'Now who's being the ass? Darling.'

She stuck out her tongue. He just shook his head gently and hit Dial.

'Beckman?' said a surprised voice.

'Tyler. How you doing?'

'I'm on my feet. What gives? Change your mind about gloating?' There was a weariness to the jibing, which had Beckman almost feeling sorry for the guy. Almost.

'There's something you oughta know.'

'You cheated?'

'Get bent.' He calmed himself. 'Malvolio cheated.'

'What?'

Beckman walked Tyler through the facts, then the suppositions and the dots that joined them. When he'd finished, the line fell quiet, which was unusual for Tyler. Then came a few choice words, which was less remarkable. Then silence again.

'So, you might want to start checking the job ads,' Beckman suggested.

'Why are you doing this?'

He hadn't gone so far as to avail Tyler of the truth behind his hospitalisation; otherwise, he would have admitted "Guilt", despite him being innocent of anything, at least directly. Could he help it if Lolita had cared enough to grease the wheels of his journey? At that moment, he'd have the rejoinder anyway—Tyler may have been put in hospital, but ultimately it had saved his life. So, it became apparent that no good would come of the truth, the whole truth, and nothing but the truth, so help him God.

'Because even assholes don't deserve injustice,' he said.

Tyler sighed. 'You ever get bored of being a nice guy, Beckman?'

He looked over at Lolita in her duck-egg blue dress. She pulled a Marilyn Monroe pose and blew him a kiss. He hadn't the faintest idea why.

'No,' he replied.

'Want me to tell the other guys?'

'If they all up and leave, Malvolio will get suspicious. Ickey'll give him a fright today. Draw the line there. Maybe next year it *will* be an island beach and a few more zeroes.'

'Then maybe I'll stay.'

'Your call. This is a heads up, is all.'

'What are you gonna do?' Tyler asked.

'Start living.'

'Take it from me—it's the way to go.'

'Thanks. Take it easy, Tyler.'

'You too.'

'And don't do anything stupid,' Beckman said firmly.

There was a pause. 'I catch your drift.'

'Because I saved your life today. And I didn't need to.'

Another pause. 'Bye, Beckman.'

And the line cut.

He turned to Lolita. 'Why the kiss?'

She shrugged. 'Happy.'

'For why?'

'Had an idea.'

He sidled over and put his arms around her waist.

'Not that kind of idea,' she clarified.

He pouted.

She rolled her eyes. 'I created a monster.'

'Yeah. But *your* monster.'

CHAPTER 47

Ickey kept low in the car. He checked the time: 12:29.

He checked his .44: loaded.

He checked his mood: apprehensive.

A sigh. He, Randall Ickey, had butterflies about *not* killing someone. Such an odd occurrence. What if things went wrong and he needed to resort to terminal force?

Why did he feel worried? He was hardly likely to get blackballed at the next meeting of the Guild of Assassins. Chiefly because no such organisation existed.

But extortion? It just wasn't him.

Unless...? Was there a Guild of Blackmailers and Extortionists?

He pondered. What would the logo look like? A pair of thumbscrews? Nah, the Guild of Torturers would have called dibs. A stack of bills? Not specific enough. A gun to a head? The Assassins Guild would want that—if they existed, which they didn't.

He drummed his fingers on the Corvette's wheel.

The building's door opened. A woman, matching the description he'd been given, emerged, right on cue. She walked to a nearby sky-blue VW Beetle and pootled away.

He gave her a minute, then went to the door, hoping things would pan out infinitely simpler than they had in Sunrise.

As predicted, the office was quiet and low rent, which dovetailed with what he'd learned about Malvolio. It also reaffirmed why he'd never be a desk jockey.

He eased open the outer office door. Miss Broomhead's room was, of course, vacant. No sounds were coming from behind the partition door to where the CEO sat. He drew his .44.

There was no reason to open the door quietly; it wouldn't prevent Malvolio from seeing him.

So he opened it smartly, gun coming quickly to its mark.

The target was, unsurprisingly, surprised. Malvolio's hand went to the cane. Bruno sparked into life.

'Erp!' Ickey cautioned. He couldn't remember warning a target before, at least not with anything that weighed less than 240 grams.

'Who in blazes are you?'

Ickey's brain didn't compute. Malvolio had an air of almost British disdain to both his manner and voice—a fact Beckman had either failed to impart or never noticed. The less said about his appearance, the better. Exactly how many years on Earth, on the spectrum of 55 to 70, had the guy accrued?

Ickey forced a conciliatory tone. Again, with a target, that marked a first. 'Randall Ickey. You hired me to kill Beckman Spiers.'

A moment for the penny to drop, then, 'Ah. And?'

'He's worth way more than a hundred grand.'

'Since when were you in a position to bargain?'

'Since Elmer Keith had his brainwave.' Ickey waved the gun casually.

'I don't negotiate with thugs.'

'Then don't hire them.'

'If Beckman's dead, I have your balance fee.'

'No dice. I want more.'

'I'll warn you—Bruno can kill.'

Ickey eyed the lizard. 'If he can outrun a bullet, then you're in luck.'

'Miss Broomhead will have you tracked down.'

'Miss Broomhead will be the one who winds up on a list.'

Malvolio sighed a phlegmy sigh. 'How much?'

'Fifty.'

'As opposed to ninety? We must update our list, make sure they're all dumb as chalk.'

'The ninety is hokey, like the ten.' Ickey tugged a sheaf of hundreds from his pocket and confettied it onto the desk. 'And it's million. Fifty million.'

Malvolio's mouth moved like a ventriloquist's dummy whose operator had a stutter.

'Pretty generous, I reckon—leaving you half,' Ickey continued.

'Half? What a load of—'

'Truth?'

Malvolio's mouth jiggled like a VHS freeze-frame. 'This is preposterous!'

'It's a choice. Your money or your life.'

'This is highway robbery!'

'Yeah. Except this time, you're the Dick.' Ickey smiled at his wordplay.

'I won't do it.'

Ickey levelled the gun at Bruno and began to squeeze the trigger.

'I don't have it here!' Malvolio lied.

Ickey withdrew the threat, stepped to the wall and yanked a painting from its mooring. Unsurprisingly, and to Malvolio's surprise at the fact that it didn't surprise Ickey, there was a safe door neatly set into the wall.

'Game's up, Malvolio.'

'You'll shoot me anyway.'

'I've killed seventeen people in my career. You've killed twenty-two, we've guessed. Well, you had them killed. So let's not play moral high ground. I know a pretty good safecracker. I shoot you, I call him, we take the full hundred mil. You'll wind up dead *and* poor. You give me fifty, I leave, you get on with what is the dictionary definition of the Devil's work. I don't give a shit either way. Question is, do you?'

'You won't get away with this.'

'I will if you're dead. So live, and prove me wrong.'

Malvolio thought about it. He gingerly reached for his cane. Ickey warned him off with a gesture. He reached for Bruno's leash. Ickey tutted loudly.

Malvolio's shoulders fell.

Ickey's gun watched him with its unblinking eye as he went to the safe, obscured the combination, turned the wheel, and opened the door.

'If you turn around fast, it's because there's a weapon in there,' Ickey countenanced. 'Consider that a warning.'

Malvolio turned slowly, a wad of bills as thick as a cheeseburger clenched in his wizened fingers.

Ickey's heart rate quickened.

Malvolio put the wad onto the edge of his desk, then carefully repeated the manoeuvre, building a sizeable pile.

Ickey peered into the safe. It looked modest, not hundred-million capable. He smelled something rotten, and it wasn't Bruno's leftovers.

'Where's the rest?' he demanded.

Malvolio eyed him with disdain. 'Only a fool keeps all his assets in currency.'

With remarkable caution and restraint, he took a small pouch from the cubbyhole, deftly pinched open its drawstrings, reached two fingers inside, and drew something out.

Ickey was smart enough to recognise the clear gemstone.

Malvolio returned the jewel into the bag with its brethren and removed more such bags from the safe. 'Each bag is worth one million.'

'Why the honesty?'

'Because you'll never get out of here alive.' Malvolio fixed the thief with a direct glare from his dark pupils. Then he closed the safe door and locked it. Retook his chair.

Ickey worried that this was all too easy. Still, he pulled a folded heavy paper bag from his pocket and tossed it over. Malvolio filled it with the pouches and cash, eyes flicking between his task, visitor, cane, and pet. Ickey's gaze did likewise.

The bag was brimmed. Malvolio sat back.

Ickey stepped forwards to the table.

'Kill!' Malvolio shouted.

Bruno lazily wondered what the matter was.

'Kill!'

Ickey raised the gun. With startling speed, Malvolio took up the cane and wielded it with alacrity, rapping it down on Ickey's wrist, the gun clattering to the floor at Ickey's feet.

The cane's sweep caught the tabletop phone handset, sending it crashing into pieces. Bruno hissed in alarm.

Ickey bent for his gun.

Malvolio shoved his chair rudely sideways, hand grappling for a desk drawer.

But the chair's castor squished against something living, and something living was not best pleased. Another hiss erupted from the floor.

Malvolio spooked. 'Kill!' he urged in vain.

Bruno simply knew that its enemy was the one who had crushed his tail, and its head whipped round, sinking jaws into the gap between an expensive black cotton sock and an immaculately tailored trouser hem.

Malvolio bawled in pain.

Ickey snatched up the Magnum, tugged the bag off the table, then flattened himself against the door.

Malvolio wailed, grabbed his cane, and rapped the end against the floor near Bruno.

'Not me, you imbecile, him!' he begged.

But the jaws held fast as Malvolio scrabbled the chair backwards, trying to draw the attached lizard to the end of its mooring chain.

Ickey knew it was time to leave.

'Nice doing business with you,' he smirked, closing the door softly behind him, quietening the hissing and cries of pain.

He focussed his task-oriented professional mind. He'd gotten what he came for; anything else that transpired would be a bonus. He'd not broken the golden promise he'd been beseeched back in Sunrise.

On the wall in Miss Broomhead's anteroom hung a series of large pigeonholes, labelled with names like Spiers, Quittle, Belcher, Pippins.

Ickey pulled an envelope from his pocket, counted a predetermined thickness of Benjamin Franklins, and slid them inside, next to the folded handwritten note. He sealed the envelope and slotted it into the lower corner cubby labelled "Wilbur".

Then he took another envelope from his pocket, checked it was already sealed, and deposited it into "Quittle".

He re-folded the top over the paper bag, grabbed it like the most expensive takeout lunch, secreted the gun in his waistband, and left.

His watch read: 12:38. Not bad for eight minute's work.

As he walked down the short corridor to the exit, all was quiet apart from the faint strains of feet on concrete and the beat of Ottawan's D.I.S.C.O..

CHAPTER 48

Tyler Quittle's Chevy pulled into the Pegasus lot at 13:19 and took the space second nearest the door, adjacent to the black behemoth that Malvolio piloted to and fro his Transylvanian castle. Probably.

With morphine-supported effort, he climbed out, winced at the remnant pain in his injured leg, patted his pocket, and went inside the offices.

The place was almost deserted. The rest of the salesforce, whipped into action by Malvolio's regular missive of the new financial year, were out on the road, seeking the best start on the journey to being the next Number One.

The fools, he mused.

Miss Broomhead was out at lunch. That wasn't news. In his pigeonhole lay mail; a rarity. He slid the envelope into a pocket, went to Malvolio's door, and took a deep breath.

He knocked.

A weak 'Help' was returned.

Intrigued, he carefully opened the door.

Mr Malvolio was on the floor in a corner, slouched with his back to the wall. His cane was outstretched like an arrow to Bruno, who strained against his anchor chain. The lizard's jaws were opening and closing slowly, about six inches from Malvolio's foot.

'Help me, Quittle.' The man was weak. There were bite marks on his ankle.

Tyler sized up the situation. The safe door was closed. There were no bullet holes anywhere.

'I've been robbed,' his cut-throat superior moaned.

'*You've* been robbed?'

'I'll give you anything you want.'

'Promises, promises.'

'Kill, Bruno, kill,' Malvolio ordered half-heartedly. Still, the lizard remained focussed on its master.

Tyler held out an envelope. 'This is my resignation letter, Malvolio.'

'Help me up, Quittle.'

He ignored that. 'But, on reflection, I'm not sure resigning a good plan. I reckon I might do better staying with the company. What do you think?'

'You'll make Number One, Quittle, I guarantee it.' Malvolio smiled weakly. 'Just deal with Bruno.'

'Hmm. Number One. Most senior. The top step.' The salesman nodded slowly. 'That sounds like a good idea.'

'It's yours, Quittle.'

'Yes,' Tyler said, 'I believe it is.'

He stepped around behind Bruno, taking a wide berth, and went to where the chain was attached by a sturdy karabiner to an iron ring set into the wall. He pulled some slack, careful not to antagonise Bruno, then released the chain from the mooring.

Bruno lunged forwards.

Tyler stepped back around, opened the door narrowly, squeezed through, then methodically locked it behind him. The yelps died away as he walked painfully down the corridor to the exit.

The air outside smelled cleaner, the sun brighter, the nearby traffic quieter.

He pulled the mail envelope from his pocket. It was handwritten on the front: "Tyler".

It wasn't Miss Broomhead's script, which intrigued him. He fingered it open.

Inside lay a single key attached to a fob bearing the number 12 and a sheet of A4, formatted like a page printed from the web and entitled "Care of your Leopard Gecko".

He pursed his lips in pensive exhalation, stood rock still, taking everything in.

A VW Beetle swung into the lot and chuntered to a halt nearby. He pocketed the rather startling envelope and watched the driver climb out and head towards the door.

Halfway there, he made a decision, stepped across, and gently intercepted her.

'Miss Broomhead,' he said with cordial grace. It was the first time he remembered doing anything with cordial grace. But then, this was not a typical day.

'Mr Quittle.' She eyed the bruises on his temple with almost motherly concern.

'Can I ask you a question?'

'You can ask me any question, Mr Quittle, so long as it's connected with the Pegasus Corporation.'

That intrigued him, but as his Intrigue Quotient had already been used up for the day—in fact probably the month—he passed over her oblique words.

'Excellent. Do you know the combination to Mr Malvolio's safe?'

She took a half-step back. 'That's not information I'm prepared to divulge.'

'You know, in case of emergencies or whatever.'

'That's privileged, Mr Quittle.'

'Miss Broomhead,' he touched her upper arm supportively, 'There's been a development during your absence.'

Her brow furrowed. 'Over lunch?'

He nodded. 'A change of ownership.'

'Here? At Pegasus?' she queried with disbelief.

'Your position is secure. In fact, more than secure. The new management would like to offer you a raise.'

'Mr Quittle, I—'

'Tyler, please. Say, one hundred percent?'

'I don't see how….'

'I appreciate this must be something of a shock.'

She flustered, her eyes unsettled. 'I'll need to speak to Mr Malvolio.' She turned to go.

'Miss Broomhead.' He retook her arm, gently restraining her for her own safety. The proceedings inside the office were probably not something a flower like Miss B should witness. 'Amaryllis. I've just come from Mr Malvolio. He's given all employees the afternoon off. Extraordinary circumstances.'

'I still don't—'

'Most, *most* extraordinary. That was his last word. He was forthright. You know how Mr Malvolio can be… uncompromising. Yet also generous. In his way.' He gazed into her eyes and turned up the Patented Tyler Charm all the way to 10.

She softened. 'Well, I suppose, if you're sure.'

'We wouldn't want to cross him, would we?'

'I suppose not.'

'Or Bruno. Bruno can be pretty vicious when he's riled.'

She looked pensive. 'This… takeover. Was it sudden?'

'It was… unexpected. Can I fill you in?'

'I… I suppose.'

'I've gotten a raise, too. Certainly enough to spring for cocktails.'

She checked her wristwatch, the red bangles clanking against it. 'At one thirty-five in the afternoon?'

'Sometimes, it's just that kind of a day.'

She cogitated. 'What will Mr Malvolio say?'

He guided her towards his car. 'Not a great deal, Miss Broomhead. Not a great deal.'

CHAPTER 49

Ickey climbed out of Saul's passenger seat.

'Here, let me see you right for last night.'

He cracked open the new briefcase he'd purchased en route and took out the pre-stuffed envelope. Saul, one hand on the tail winch that lowered the Corvette to the ground, took the payment with a grateful nod.

'And for the tire. Plus tip.' He drew five C-notes from his pocket and tendered them too.

'You know, Randall, you may be an Okay Guy.'

'For a man in my position, that's good to know.'

'I'll put you with the next mechanic,' Saul said. 'We'll have you on your way in a half-hour.'

'No rush. I got promises to keep.'

He clicked the case shut, adjusted the new Aviator shades that the briefcase store had also carried, and paced off up Main Street with the mid-afternoon sunshine on his back.

In Our Buck's five minutes later, he dropped onto the chair beside Beckman, who'd been passing the time knee-deep in the World's Best root beer. He set the case on the table and clicked it open with creditably little theatrics.

'Sheesh,' Lolita breathed.

'I can't believe he gave it up,' Beckman said.

'What?' Ickey blustered.

'Take it easy, Randall. I guess you have a way with people.'

'Money focuses the mind.'

'Which was Malvolio all over.' Beckman counted out Ickey's share. 'Will he live to regret it?' he asked, locking his gaze.

Ickey nodded. 'I never laid a finger on him. Hand to God.'

'I don't think God will give a shit either way. Us, however....'

Lolita gingerly opened a pouch and peered inside. Her eyes widened.

Beckman pushed the requisite piles of bills across the table. 'Where you headed?'

The café door opened. Reba went to the bar and popped onto a stool.

'Ask me tomorrow,' Ickey said absentmindedly.

'Saul gonna stand you another night?'

Ickey didn't look round. 'Depends how this evening goes.'

Beckman and Lolita exchanged a glance. Then Beckman's cell rang, so he whipped it from his pocket. Both of them saw the name.

'He's like Medusa,' she ventured. 'Except you can't even kill him with kindness.'

He answered nonetheless, primarily out of curiosity as to how the day's developments would be received.

'Hey, Beckman.'

'Tyler.'

'You're a generous guy.'

'I'm a practical guy.'

'So am I. Need to meet with you.' Tyler's words leaked from the speaker.

Lolita shook her head. Beckman gave her a calming look. It mostly succeeded.

'Why?' he asked.

'A proposition.'

'Thought it was only women that got those.'

'Bygones, okay? Or at least I reckoned it's what your envelope meant.'

He licked his lips, unsure but also enjoying a remnant layer of root beer. 'Shoot.'

'Meet, Beckman. *Meet*. So you'll know I'm straight on this.'

'Why does this sound too good to be straight?'

'Because maybe now you're suspicious of anything that goes on at Pegasus.'

'I've got a good reason, from nearly dying.'

'And I've got good reason on account of you maybe saving my life.'

'It's the kind of thing not-an-asshole does.'

'So is mine,' Tyler said.

'Can't say I'm a hundred percent that this isn't a chain-yank.'

'Listen. You ever had your life flash before your eyes and think, "Jeez, is that really me?"?'

He thought about his own desert road that had gone Damascene. Lolita shook her head again. He stroked her hand. She remained unconvinced.

'I'll ping you the location,' Beckman said.

'Okay.'

'No tricks. My colleague is ex-SWAT.'

'Whatever,' Tyler sighed.

This time, Beckman hung up the call.

There was a ton of questions in Lolita's eyes. The first one from her immaculately cardinal lipsticked lips was, 'Who exactly is ex-SWAT?' She looked around the coffee bar.

'That'll be you, darling.'

'In a pig's eye.'

'If there's one thing decent about Tyler, he'll never hit a lady. Much less shoot one.'

'That true?'

'Almost certainly.'

Fixing the signpost in a suspicious glower, Tyler pulled off the road and eased the car to a halt beside the pump.

The door of the dilapidated building opened, and a check-shirted old-timer trundled over.

'Afternoon.'

'Two bucks, huh?' Tyler asked.

'That a problem?'

'You tell me. Broke your ladder?' He imbued it with as much concern as he could muster, but it had still come across pretty curtly. He needed to work on that.

The man's eyes fixed him directly. After an interminable age of apparently being sized up, he was availed of a response.

'No. Sciatica.'

'Okay. Gas is what, three twenty?'

'Call it three bucks even.'

'Fill her up, okay?' He put a "please" in his eyes, if not in his words. Which was a start.

'Sure.' The attendant began the process.

'Ladder out back?'

'You fixing to be running this place?' Eyes were narrowed in disquiet.

'No. I'm "fixing" to fix you not fixing people up.'

'Maybe I don't like the inference.'

'Maybe I don't like cheats.'

The old-timer moved in a step. 'I absolutely don't like the inference.'

'Nobody ever takes offence at the difference between the sign and the bills going into your hand?'

Tyler was fixed in a glare again, and then the guy looked away.

The pump's whirr was the only sound for a few moments.

Tyler looked around again, then up at the sign. 'Ladder out back?'

A gentle nod of the head. Tyler strode away.

'Number cards in the back store,' came a reluctant growl.

A minute later, Tyler returned to find the pump holstered and the guy with hands on hips.

He held up the trio of foot-high numerals, which were the best he could find.

'You got a three and an eight and a six.'

'Kids.'

Tyler did a slow full three-sixty, looking for any kids.

'Kids who call in,' the attendant continued. 'Create a distraction. Take something. Drive away laughing. Plenty over the years.'

Tyler pulled a straight face, understanding why the store cupboard was so bare of numerals—and hence why the guy might have a decent reason for not putting the correct price up. At least it was some excuse for the deception—Malvolio had no such mitigating factor for his snake-like behaviour.

He nodded. 'Thieving's not too far from cheating.'

'Or being an asshole, whatever age.'

Tyler got the implication, but he was doing a good deed, so maybe the guy would think twice.

Tyler held up two numbers. 'So, eastbound, we'll use the three, westbound I duct-taped the eight up for a three.'

Old-timer gave the faintest of smiles.

Tyler hefted up the ladder, took it over to the tall sign pole, and, grunting in echoes of pain, leant it vertically. Then, ignoring the pressure on his strapped left ankle, he ascended on both sides in turn, switched out the number cards and returned to the pump with the pair of twos.

'You be okay on three bucks even?'

The guy nodded. 'You care for why?'

Tyler shrugged. 'A guy died today. Directly for being an asshole. False promises. Dumb way to go out, I say. Maybe sometimes doing the right thing ain't so bad.'

'Catch more flies with honey, huh?'

'Something like that.'

He went to the pole, hefted up the ladder, and returned it to the rear of the tumbledown shack that the poor guy called home, then returned, wiping his hands on the butt of his trousers.

'What do I owe you?'

'I make it forty-five bucks even.'

Tyler fished a fifty out of his wallet. 'He was a *rich* asshole.'

The attendant pushed the note into his pocket. 'Better to be poor and treat people good.'

'Amen.' Tyler retook the driver's seat.

'Says the guy not looking too poor to me.'

Tyler met the pointed look he was offered. 'Rich asshole, poor saint. Anyone say it was that black and white?'

The attendant shook his head. 'Shades of grey.'

The newly-appointed head of Pegasus tapped his forehead in a gentle salute and eased the Chevy away.

Having not entirely accepted Beckman's soothing words, Lolita spent most of the journey cradling the Luger in her lap. With a scarf around her head against the buffeting wind, she looked rather too much the Louise to his lamentable Thelma. Luckily, there were no steep drops in the neighbourhood.

Tyler must have made good time, as he'd reached the rendezvous first. If Beckman been conspiratorial—and he'd willed those nagging thoughts away—he would have wanted to be there first, to ensure the other party had arrived alone. Beckman was admittedly no master of espionage and surveillance, but he did own the DVD box set of *Mission: Impossible*.

As the next best safety measure, he ran the Miata around the far side of the abandoned gas station to check it on all sides. They seemed to be alone. Certainly, there was only one occupant of the Chevy.

He drew to a halt at what he deemed (in his great wisdom) to be a safe distance. Whilst he didn't take Tyler for an Ethan Hunt, he'd also never figured Mr Malvolio for a master puppeteer—and look how wrong he'd been there.

Tyler emerged from the car quickly, which the Sunrisers found encouraging. Nonetheless, Lolita curled her finger around the trigger.

Beckman hopped out and raised both arms aloft. He didn't hear Lolita curse under her breath, itself a futile gesture: if he were going to be shot, it wouldn't matter if he stood stock still, moonwalked, or practised semaphore—a defenceless man is still that.

Luckily for them both, Tyler mirrored the gesture.

Lolita didn't loosen her grip.

Beckman stopped six feet from his compatriot. 'So?'

Tyler shrugged, recognising this wasn't shaping to be a meeting laced with niceties. 'I want you to come work for me.'

He scoffed. 'As what? Boot polisher?'

'Head of Sales.'

'Where?'

Tyler's frowned. 'Pegasus.'

'You're staying?' he asked, incredulous.

'Someone's got to run the show.'

'Why—did Malvolio resign?' Beckman chuckled, half-hoping he'd be correct.

Perhaps the guy had finally seen the error of his ways. Retirement with fifty million in the bank was hardly a shabby way to go. Malvolio could get his own desert island—a real one, as opposed to the phoney ones he'd long-time promised the faithful subservient masses.

'Malvolio's dead.'

'What the…?'

Tyler regaled him. Beckman stood there with his mouth open, long enough in the balmy afternoon air that he might catch a whole swarm of flies. At the silence, Lolita took guard with the gun and stepped out of the car, fearing a downturn in events.

'He has no surviving relatives,' Tyler was saying. 'Company passes to the longest-serving employee.'

'Miss Broomhead,' he mused. 'She's not a relative?'

'I thought so, too. Niece, maybe. Sister.'

'It would explain actions, obedience—running in the family and such.'

'Maybe we'll find something.'

'Maybe *you'll* find something,' Beckman corrected.

'I'm thinking he saved her life.'

Beckman nodded, finding it a curio he could work with. 'Something weird. Rescued her from the bullrushes? Saved her from a house fire? Back aways, when his heart worked emotionally, as well as physically.'

'Or she's just loyal to the point of blindness.'

'"Was",' he corrected pedantically.

'We all have our motives, okay?'

'You want to move this little pitch along, Tyler?'

'We had a… discussion, Amaryllis and I, and I take over midnight tonight.'

'Why?'

He pondered the revelation of Miss Broomhead's first name and how its beauty counterpointed pretty much everything else that had gone on in that office block over the last twelve years.

'Because it's a job, one I'm damn fine at.' Tyler hit a tone the confident side of boastful, which Beckman regarded as a character upswing.

'Says you.'

'I stayed at Pegasus for the big win. We all did. You did. This is a big win. Real, not Malvolio's mirage. A guy like me needs money. Goals. So, I'll double the size of the company in three years. With your help.'

'And no false promises, I'm guessing.'

'It had a kinda warped logic, you gotta admit.'

'Warped, yeah. Logic?'

'Look at it like this, Beckman. Would you work hard for a promotion you never had a chance of getting?'

'Do I look that dumb?'

Tyler shrugged. 'So, there was his logic. If some guy reached Number One two, three years on the spin, the rest of the team would think he was uncatchable, so they wouldn't even try. Malvolio's sales force freewheels, the company stagnates.'

'But if you... *remove* the Number One, all the schmoes know they have a shot.'

'Even these two schmoes.' Tyler pointed at each of them in turn.

Beckman shook his head slowly, still coming to terms with it. 'It's not just warped. It's pretzel by Escher.'

'But we're out from under it. New broom. New order. All the perks, none of the bullets.' Tyler gave an encouraging nod.

Was it that easy? The pebble smoothed, the slot machine no longer rigged?

More than that—is Tyler a decent, trustworthy guy? A potential boss?

He came back to reality. Flashed a weak smile. 'Thanks, but no thanks.'

'Pays half a million a year.'

Beckman swallowed hard. He looked around. Lolita stood nearby, gun low but ready. She shook her head.

'Thanks, but no thanks,' he replied.

'With a golden howdy.'

Beckman shook his head.

'Of a million,' Tyler added.

Beckman bit his lip.

'And as much or little travel as you want.'

'Why?'

'Because you did right by me,' Tyler explained.

'I do right by everyone.'

'And I don't have to prove anything anymore. No ladder to climb.'

'Nor me. I'm done.'

Tyler sighed. 'I want you because you're good… and a good guy. And Pegasus is going to be a good guys only club.'

'I don't know.'

'Top of the tree, Beckman. Twelve years in the making, and no phoney prizes. Just the job you love, the money you deserve.'

Beckman turned towards Lolita. The gun was at her side, shoulders sagging. She was all out of fight.

Tyler spread his hands wide, welcoming, querying.

'So, Beckman? What do you say?'

CHAPTER 50

'Suitably businesslike?' Lolita asked.

Yes, it was a swing dress, but in smart navy, and the accoutrements were restrained.

He finished his breakfast coffee and walked over. 'Sure. The question is whether I need to pat you down for concealed weapons.'

'That's rich, coming from you.'

'You're up one-zero when it comes to windshields, in case you forget,' Beckman said. She acceded with a waggle of the head.

'This is a hell of a play, you know that?' he continued, more sombrely.

'It would be if there was a downside.'

'I thought there was no downside to being Number One,' he reminded her.

She straightened his collar. 'If Malvolio can listen to reason and make the right decision, anyone can.'

'For all the good it did him.'

She shrugged. 'Karma.'

'I guess.'

'You had me worried last night. With Tyler.'

'If Malvolio can make the right decision, anyone can.'

She smiled. 'I hope I'm worth it.'

'You have no idea.'

'Just one more good decision to nail.'

He held up the envelope. 'Two.'

'We did this. It's your money. Your rocks. Your mom.'

'I just don't want to come off wrong. One seems cheap.'

'Only *we* know that,' she pointed out.

'Two feels showy.'

'Beckman, I'm hardly the person to ask about family. Okay?'

He briefly ruminated, dropped three stones into the padded envelope, and sealed it good and tight.

'So, I'm all set.'

'Me too. We'll scooch by the postbox on the way,' she affirmed.

'You're sure he'll be in the office on a holiday?'

'He's a workaholic, remember.' She popped him a kiss. 'Let's get this done.'

Jack Milan turned over the final page, scanned its contents, and looked over at his visitors. He was a short man, and Beckman reckoned his office chair was jacked all the way up.

'Theory and practice are two different things, Lolita.'

Not "darling" or "sweetheart". But at least not "Miss Milan".

'So are bankruptcy and success. Jack.'

Touché, honey.

'Is this a "take it or leave it"?'

'You're the businessman, Jack. Remember, I'm only a woman.' She gave him a snide look.

'I won't say your plan doesn't stack up.' He thumbed the handful of pages on his desk.

She shook her head. 'Except it's not about the plan. It's whether you want to be an ass about this. Scuttle the ship to prevent a mutiny.'

He sat up straight. 'I don't appreciate being called an ass.'

'I don't appreciate being treated like one.'

Beckman had nothing to add. He was content to wait in the corner with a towel and sponge in case things took a wrong turn. As it transpired, Jack Milan was the one doubled over, the canvas swirling before his eyes.

Then he veritably stood ramrod straight and put his dukes up.

'Say I thank you kindly for this sterling idea, and have you escorted out of the building?'

Beckman prayed for the bell to clang for the end of the round.

'Then I take this,' she laid a finger on the open briefcase on the desk, 'And I go to Walter Whack. And I say his company will crash to be worth exactly forty-five million tomorrow when I tell the papers how EVI was using industrial espionage to steal a march on the competition. And because he's not an ass, he'll take the briefcase. And I'll take his office and this business plan, I'll make EVI my own, and I'll double their turnover in a year.'

'You and whose army?' Jack scoffed.

'First, I'll have a distinguished sales manager.'

Beckman smiled—she had this covered. Then he saw her looking at him. Then he realised what she meant and that he was supposed to be on the same page, so he nodded vigorously.

Mental note: Ask her later if she's gone crazy. I mean, Number One at Pegasus, yes, but this?

'With a stellar track record and an award to his name,' she continued.

'You know EVI just lost Wanda, thanks to you. Good credit control is vital,' Jack suggested.

'We have someone in mind. New in town. Excellent at obtaining money under duress.'

Beckman's gaze went to the wealth-laden case.

Definitely ask her later if she's gone crazy.

'Go on,' Jack said.

'And we'll invest, and the marketing will be shit-hot, and we'll wipe the floor with you, and you'll beg to sell the company to me for half this.'

'This kind of petty revenge is beyond you. I raised you better than that.'

'You didn't raise me at all, Jack. You were never there. You were here. You belittled me and abandoned me. And I'm prepared to pay you forty-five million dollars despite it. It's not revenge—it's business. I would have thought you, more than anyone, would see that. Simple choice—you swallow your pride and let me have the business the easy way, or I'll buy out the competition and then wipe you off the face of the Earth. I'd prefer the easy way—we might stay on speaking terms, or better. Plus, you'll get a pile of dollars to wallow in.'

'You really think we can work together?'

'Hell, no. You're retiring, Jack. You're retiring tomorrow with good grace and five percent share.'

'Five percent?' he spluttered.

'If you let me and EVI grind you into dust instead, you'll beg for *zero point five* percent. Take what's here now. I don't want to be a bitch. But I will if I have to.'

Jack exhaled a veritable tornado. 'Five percent,' he mumbled.

'You're missing the golden goose. What if the newspaper found out about EVI's espionage later, anyway? You know, through an anonymous source. And they lost customers, then lost market share and suddenly became open to a rescue bid? And I—we—were in a position to crush *them* into dust?'

'You'd do that?'

'Wouldn't you?'

A grudging smile emerged. He looked at the haul of money and diamonds, gazed around the office, then looked at Beckman.

'What about you, Spiers? Want to jump on the steamroller, too? Ask for my blessing or some other shit?'

Beckman's eyes met Lolita's. 'Let's not get ahead of ourselves, Jack.'

Lolita smiled, yet with a glint of something else.

He thought he recognised it, so continued, 'But, as we're here. You know. Just to save future time. Wouldn't want to interrupt your retirement if, *when*, the day comes that I put a ring on your daughter's finger.'

Lolita broke off her gaze and looked across the desk.

'So, Dad? What do you say?'

The sky above was deepening to navy, and distant smatters of firework pops and sparkles lit the air. In front of them on the lawn, the small fire crackled.

'That was a great parade. And I thought you couldn't see any more lights in this place.'

'Oh, believe me, Fourth of July is big in our little town.'

'Sunrise doing "normal"? Never thought I'd see the day.'

'I never thought you'd see the light,' she countered.

'I'm not blind, you might know.'

'But you still believe this is all a dream—right?'

'Can you blame me?'

'At first, yeah. Call it... acclimatisation. But you're smart.' She squeezed his hand. 'Stop wondering and just *be*.'

'It's not the worst reality, I gotta admit.'

'And Jack selling up wasn't exactly on the list of things I expected to happen this year.' She pulled him closer. 'For which I have you to thank.'

'I can't take credit for everything. Amazing where a flat tire can take you.'

'And leave you,' she added.

He smiled. 'Yeah.'

'Well?' She gazed down and to her left.

He picked up the object and tossed it onto the burning logs. Flames began to lick the fabric of his roller case. He slid an arm around her waist. The close-fitting sheath dress was much easier to encircle than the attire he'd become used to. He drank her in. Almost wanted to pinch himself. Again.

She didn't look like a million dollars. She didn't even look forty-five million. She looked priceless, and she had made his life just that.

His other hand, in a pocket, tickled against something. He drew out the small, slightly crumpled card. It had a familiar logo and nine haphazard stamps.

He sighed, but it was a happy sigh.

Maybe the best things in life aren't free.

He tossed the card on the fire. No need for it where he was going.

Absolutely nowhere.

THE END

Beckman and Lolita return in

"Go Away Zone"

The Sunrise Trilogy – book 2

A small town.
A happy couple.
An accountant with a grudge.
A corporate dealmaker on the prowl.
An unexplored portal to nobody-knows-where.

If Beckman Spiers thought life and love had been all figured out when he arrived in Sunrise, met Lolita Milan, and changed his career, he's about to find out things aren't that easy.

This quirky town has a secret, and Lolita's ex-fiancé has a scheme that threatens to scupper Beckman's new job, destroy Lolita's business ambitions, and drive a wedge between them.

The only way out may be to gamble everything—even their own lives.

The sequel to "Tow Away Zone" is a dramatic comedy caper fuelled by coffee, friendships, and switchbacks aplenty.

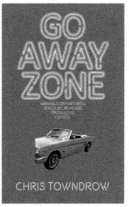

About The Author

Chris Towndrow has been a writer since 1991. He began writing science fiction, inspired by Isaac Asimov, Iain M Banks, and numerous film and TV canons.

After a few years spent creating screenplays, in 2004 he moved into playwriting and has had several productions professionally performed.

His first published novel was 2012's space opera "Sacred Ground". He then focussed on "hard" sci-fi adventures, and the Enna Dacourt pentalogy was completed in 2023.

He has always drawn inspiration from the big screen, and 2019's quirky romantic comedy "Tow Away Zone" owes much to the Coen Brothers' work. This book spawned two sequels in what became the "Sunrise trilogy".

His first historical fiction novel, "Signs Of Life", was published by Valericain Press in 2023.

Chris now returns to his passion for writing accessible humour and will largely focus on romantic comedy novels. Three of these are in development.

Chris lives on the outskirts of London with his family and works as a video editor and producer. He is a member of the UK Society of Authors.

Visit his website at: christowndrow.co.uk
X: twitter.com/TowndrowBooks
Instagram: instagram.com/towndrowbooks

If you have enjoyed this book, please do leave an online review. An indie author's ability to generate valuable sales is enhanced by the reviews of kind readers.

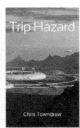

Near future sci-fi adventure

Post-apocalyptic   Space opera   Historical romance

Quirky romantic comedy / cosy mystery   Absurd humour

Printed in Great Britain
by Amazon

34445301R00162